PRAISE FOR W...

"A gripping, epic novel . . . a remarkable achievement."
—Paul Brinkley-Rogers, Pulitzer Prize–winning journalist and veteran
war correspondent; author of *Please Enjoy Your Happiness*

"A stunning, gorgeous novel. Zhang Ling's *Where Waters Meet* is haunting
and heartbreaking as it navigates mother-daughter relationships in the
face of war and famine. I simply couldn't put it down."
—Devi S. Laskar, author of *The Atlas of Reds and Blues* and *Circa*

"*Where Waters Meet* brings us back to the turbulent decades in
China where people fought one war after another, suffered famine,
and endured political persecutions. However, instead of focusing on
misery, Zhang Ling introduces us to those who defy their fates. They
are brave enough to try sneaking across the border, determined enough
to adopt a foreign tongue, and kind enough to care for their families no
matter what. A true masterpiece filled with idiosyncratic yet admirable
characters, suspenseful mystery, historical complexity, and ironic
humor."
—Jianan Qian, O. Henry Prize winner and staff writer at *The Millions*

PRAISE FOR *A SINGLE SWALLOW*

"[A] unique premise of ghostly rendezvous among soldiers, combined
with first loves for all three men . . . Clever use of newspaper accounts,
military reports, and letters to loved ones advance the plot and
complement the dialogue effectively and interestingly . . . superb . . .
highly recommended."
—Historical Novel Society

PRAISE FOR ZHANG LING

"I am in awe of Zhang Ling's literary talent. Truly extraordinary. In her stories, readers have the chance to explore and gain a great understanding of not only the Chinese mind-set but also the heart and soul."

—Anchee Min, bestselling author of *Red Azalea*

"Few writers could bring a story about China and other nations together as seamlessly as Zhang Ling. I would suggest it is her merit as an author, and it is the value of her novels."

—Mo Yan, winner of the Nobel Prize in Literature

AFTERSHOCK

OTHER TITLES BY ZHANG LING

Where Waters Meet

A Single Swallow

AFTERSHOCK

A Novel

ZHANG LING

Translated by Shelly Bryant

AMAZON **CROSSING**

Previously published as *Aftershock* by East China Normal University Press in China in 2009. Translated from Mandarin by Shelly Bryant. First published in English by Amazon Crossing in 2024.

Published by Amazon Crossing, Seattle

www.apub.com

ISBN-13: 9781662510373 (hardcover)
ISBN-13: 9781662509025 (paperback)
ISBN-13: 9781662509032 (digital)

Cover design by David Drummond
Cover image: © Black Creator 24, © Hibrida / Shutterstock; © CSA Images / Getty

Printed in the United States of America

First edition

To 1976, the most eventful year in my memory

FOREWORD

In 1976, the sky over China collapsed. That year, three great figures in Chinese politics, Mao Zedong, Zhu De, and Zhou Enlai, all died within a few months of each other. It had long been said that the sun never falls, but it had fallen indeed, leaving the world in chaos.

At 3:42 a.m. on July 28, 1976, when the people of Tangshan had endured an insufferable, sultry summer night, dawn began to break. Just 150 kilometers from Beijing, in Hebei Province, an earthquake shook Tangshan as its inhabitants slept. It had been lurking for a long time, but it still managed to swoop in on an unsuspecting city. The quake was officially declared a 7.9 magnitude on the Richter scale, but this record was later revised to an 8.1 by international experts. Several aftershocks followed the initial quake, leveling the densely populated city. According to the most conservative official statistics, 242,000 people were killed and 164,000 seriously injured, while 4,204 children were orphaned overnight. It was the highest death toll from a natural disaster in the entire record of twentieth-century earthquakes.

Thirty years later, the scars left on the landscape by this tragic event had been erased, and a brand-new Tangshan had replaced the old one on the map. The children who survived the '76 earthquake had grown up and were inching toward middle age. When they mingled with the crowds on the street, going about their busy lives, it was impossible to discern anything unusual about them. Only they themselves knew that when it was quiet at night, the aftershocks of the earthquake continued to touch the most vulnerable spaces inside them, radiating tremors that no one else could detect.

January 6, 2006
St. Michael's Hospital, Toronto

When Dr. Wilson walked into the office, he saw his assistant's eyebrows twitch.

"The emergency department transferred the patient here. She's been waiting for a while." Casey wrinkled her nose and indicated Consultation Room 1.

Dr. Wilson had been licensed to practice medicine for nearly two decades, but long before there was a psychiatrist named Henry Wilson in these parts, there was a medical assistant named Casey Smith. Casey had been working in the hospital for thirty-three years, and she had seen countless people. These people were like handfuls of fine sand, scraping Casey's nerves day after day, year after year. In the end, she had not only lost her sensitivity but also seemed to have lost all her emotions. It was extremely rare to see a look of surprise or sorrow on her face.

Dr. Wilson could tell that she had encountered a tough case this time. "The author of *Dream of Shenzhou* is here. She was just nominated for a Governor General's Literary Award. There was an hour-long interview with her on CBC's *National* last Saturday," she said.

Dr. Wilson grunted as he went to retrieve the medical records from the pocket on the door. He glanced at the name on the edge. *Shirley Xiaodeng Wang.*

"If the ambulance had arrived ten minutes later, she wouldn't have survived." Casey drew a finger across her wrist and whispered, "Suicide."

Dr. Wilson opened the medical records and glanced at the ER referral report.

Gender: Female

Date of Birth: April 29, 1969

Occupation: Freelance writer

Marital status: Married

Pregnancy history: Three pregnancies, one birth (has a thirteen-year-old daughter)

Surgical history: Appendectomy (1995), abortion (1999, 2001)

Overview of condition: Severe anxiety and insomnia accompanied by headache for unknown reasons, long-term use of sleep aids and painkillers, movement of right arm slow, X-rays reveal no skeletal abnormalities, attempted suicide by cutting right wrist with razor blade two days ago, called 911 for help afterward, police investigation records revealed that this is the third time patient has called for help after attempting suicide, previous two times were three years ago and sixteen months ago, both times patient overdosed on sleeping pills, no record of criminal or violent tendencies

Referral opinions: Transferred to the Department of Psychotherapy for comprehensive psychological assessment and treatment

Attachments: Police and ambulance on-scene reports, patient's daily medicines, patient's drug allergies

Dr. Wilson pushed the door open and walked in. He saw a woman in a white patient gown with blue stripes. She was curled up on the sofa, her legs pulled to her chest and her hands wrapped around both knees with her chin wedged between them. Hearing the door, she looked up, and Dr. Wilson saw two eyes like black pits on her face—large, dry, bottomless pits. They stared at one another for a moment, and the doctor was drawn involuntarily to the edge of those black pits. A chill crept over him, beginning from the tips of his toes and working its way up. He felt his legs tremble slightly, as if he were about to tumble into the abyss of eternal doom.

The woman's lips moved, and a faint sound escaped from between them. It would not be quite accurate to say that Dr. Wilson heard the words. Rather, he felt a slight tremor on his eardrums and, after a moment, those tremors began to take on the vaguely recognizable shape of words.

He suddenly realized what she had said. *Save me.*

Her words were like a slender iron awl, piercing a thin gap in the surface of the doctor's mind. Inspiration gurgled out through the gap unexpectedly.

"Please lie down, Shirley."

With a rustling sound, the blue stripes running along the length of the woman's body gradually smoothed out, becoming straight lines. The woman's hands were folded across her lower abdomen, and her sleeves were turned up, revealing layers of gauze wrapped around her right wrist. Several suspicious dark spots were evident on the gauze.

"Close your eyes."

The black pits on the woman's face disappeared, and silence fell over the room.

"Shirley, how long have you been in Canada?"

"Ten years. Please call me Xiaodeng. That's my real name."

"A Chinese name?"

"Yes. It means a little lamp to light the night."

"Xiaodeng, how much do you know about the Western theory of psychotherapy?"

"Freud. Childhood. Sex."

The woman's English was generally smooth. Though the difficult pronunciations were just a little off, it was easy enough to understand.

"That's just one part of it. What do you think of it?"

"It's bullshit."

Dr. Wilson couldn't help but smile.

"When was the last time you had sex?" he asked tentatively.

The woman's response came slowly, as if she were performing some difficult mental calculations.

"Two years and eight months ago."

"And when was the last time you cried?"

This time the woman's response was quick, with almost no hesitation or pause. "I've never shed a tear. Not since I was seven."

Dr. Wilson nodded slightly. "Xiaodeng, please keep your eyes closed. Take five deep breaths, very deep, so deep that the muscles in your abdomen are scrunched together. Slow down the rhythm of your breathing. Very, very slow. Relax completely, every muscle, every nerve. Now, tell me what you see."

They stopped talking. There was only the sound of the woman breathing, the breaths at first deep, then becoming increasingly ragged. Her breath rustled like a little snake sweeping through blades of grass, dense grass alongside a lengthy road, the snake slithering for a long time before finally stopping.

"A window, Dr. Wilson. I see a window."

"Try it. Open the window. What do you see?"

"Another window. One after another."

"Push it again. Go all the way to the end. What do you see?"

"The last window. I can't open it. No matter what I do, I just can't." She sighed.

"Take five more deep breaths. Relax. Now, push again. Push until you get it open, and tell me what you see."

There were more sounds of breathing, heavy and slow. She breathed with difficulty, like a pack animal climbing a slope.

"I . . . really . . . can't." She finally gave up and slumped into the sofa like a lump of soft dough.

"Then tell me about your childhood." Dr. Wilson covered her with a thin blanket.

She lay silently for a long time, the corners of her mouth twitching gently, as if she were in pain, a pain almost too heavy for the nerves and muscles to carry.

"If you don't feel strong enough to talk, we can always schedule another session." Dr. Wilson stood up, ready to end the conversation, even though it hadn't gotten very far.

"It's not that I'm not strong enough. It's just that I didn't have a childhood to talk about." The woman reached out from beneath the blanket and pulled at Dr. Wilson's sleeve.

"What about your mother? Everyone has a mother, right?" He sat down again.

When the woman opened her eyes, confusion was evident in them. An earthworm burrowed back and forth between the corners of her eyes and brows. Her forehead bulged and deflated, now bright, now dark.

Dr. Wilson knew her mind was traveling.

"Let me . . . think about it," the woman mumbled.

Dr. Wilson tore a sheet from his prescription pad and scribbled two lines of orders, one for Casey and one for himself. Casey's read,

Stop pain and sleep meds ASAP. Try placebo. One course of treatment. To himself, he wrote, *Encourage tears.*

April 1968
Fengrun County, Tangshan, Hebei Province, China

Seventeen-year-old Li Yuanni leaned on her walking stick as she sang beneath the locust tree in her yard. The song had an interesting title: "The Laundry Song." It was about a group of young Tibetan women washing clothes for the PLA soldiers stationed in their village. A loud gesture of praise and gratitude for the good deeds the soldiers had done for the locals, with the edge of propaganda smoothed over by the beauty of nature weaved into the lyrics in the form of snow-capped mountains, warm sunshine, and the glistening Brahmaputra River. Yuanni loved the song.

The tree had lived for many years. It had seen the stable boy of Emperor Kangxi watering the horses in this yard, and it had heard the young, reckless Boxers drinking and plotting a rebellion on the street corner. It had witnessed the dirty underbellies of Japanese planes as they hovered overhead, dropping their black waste over the land. The tree had seen all the ups and downs for countless years, witnessing both the thrill and the desolation of dynastic change. As the tree grew old, the stories it held multiplied, and so did its branches and vines, creating a dark patch of shade under the shining white sun. This was the season when birds practically tore their throats out in this canopy, each vying to sing louder than its companions—but now, there was only silence in the tree because the birds were entranced by Yuanni's voice.

Yuanni's voice was not a voice at all; it was a stream of qi. When the qi was generated just below the navel, it was gentle and unobtrusive, but as it climbed up through the organs, it picked up all sorts of emotions. By the time it made its way out over the tongue, it had become a pointed iron nail that pierced the eardrum, drilling one hole after another.

People from the county seat had heard Tseten Dolma's powerful singing on the radio, and they had seen the Red Guards from the provincial capital singing and dancing on the stage of the county's Revolutionary Committee. But all those voices were passed through the loudspeaker, filtered by the wires and iron box, creating an inexplicable feeling of estrangement. Yuanni's singing was completely unadorned, and though it was rough, it had a sort of naked intimacy. The people of the county seat had never seen anything of the world. They thought this was the sound of nature.

A crowd gathered outside the courtyard.

"Stop singing. Are you trying to attract the wolves?" Her mother came out of the house and held out a hot towel so Yuanni could clean her face.

Yuanni flicked her mother's hand away and hobbled to the courtyard gate. "What are you looking at?" She stood on the steps, spitting the words at the crowd. The words smashed a hole in the ground, stirring up a thin plume of dust. In fact, the words had an intended tail, an even more snappy "Fuck off"—it was on the verge of slipping from her tongue, but she bit it off. She knew the song she had just sung should never be allowed to develop a relationship with this phrase. She had witnessed with her own eyes the catastrophe that could be caused by such a careless mistake. Young and ignorant as she might be, she knew there was a limit.

Everyone was taken aback. What startled them was not the words she spoke, but her face.

The residents in the county were undergoing an unprecedented aesthetic crisis at the time. Ancient beauties like Imperial Consort Yang Yuhuan and Empress Zhao Feiyan had been knocked down and trampled in the dust, and later beauties like Ke Xiang and the Flower Girl, popular characters in modern revolutionary dramas, were still in the slow process of being conceived. It was in this unprecedented aesthetic break that Yuanni's face appeared. Without any furtive glances or whispers, in unison, those gathered outside the door let out an exclamation. Before the long exclamation could pull itself to its full length, it was cut off by the courtyard gate. Yuanni slammed the door with her cane. Those outside the door stood at a loss, digesting the shock and confusion, before finally dispersing in twos and threes.

"Too bad she's lame," someone lamented.

"She has such a beautiful face. Why doesn't she smile?" another said with a sigh.

"Ni, I know you are upset," Yuanni's mother said, "but no matter what, you're still better off than those youngsters sent to the border areas. Haven't you read the letter from your brother? Could you bear that kind of hardship?"

Her mother walked over and helped her back into the yard as she went on about Yuanni's second brother, who, at the beginning of the year, had been sent to Inner Mongolia as a part of the urban youth relocation movement.

"Anyway, you will still have your job in the state-run work unit."

Again, her mother offered her the towel to wipe her face. It was cold now, sticky and oily on the skin. It felt like there were hundreds of ants crawling on her calf beneath the plaster, but she couldn't scratch it. It was so itchy that she had goose bumps all over, and she wanted to grind her teeth to bits. Unbearably irritated, she turned her head, shaking the towel away.

"What a sour face. You didn't even have a smile for your seventh brother the day he left." Her mother sighed and put the towel away, then went back into the house.

Ah! Her seventh brother.

There were seven children in the Li family. Yuanni was the sixth, and the seventh was a boy, just a year younger than her. She was only a few months old, still in her mother's arms, still breastfeeding, when the next pregnancy came about. Yuanni held her mother's nipple in her mouth as she caressed the swelling belly and the soft lump curled up in it. Her brother felt it and stretched out his leg to kick Yuanni's palm gently. Before she could speak, she was already talking to her seventh brother through her mother's skin. Of all her siblings, she was closest to her younger brother.

It was often said that by the time parents came to their youngest child, they had no more vigor and energy to pass on, but in the Li family, the seventh child was the tallest and strongest. When he was sixteen, he was already six foot three. He played basketball in school, and he could grab a rebound just by raising a hand and jumping lightly. Because of his athleticism, he was selected as a sports soldier.

Yuanni had received the good news that her younger brother had joined the army two weeks earlier—the best future a young man could hope for in those days. She had been in the rehearsal room of the Provincial Song and Dance Troupe at the time, practicing the *Laundry Dance* to be performed on August 1, Army Day.

When she was in fifth grade, she had been selected by the song and dance troupe and sent to the provincial capital to become a dancer. At school, whether the performance was for Labor Day, Children's Day, National Day, or New Year's Day, the teachers had always asked her to come onstage and sing, dance, or recite a poem. Yuanni had always been just one among a crowd, never outstanding or dazzling. But that year, people from the song and dance troupe had come to the school and watched all the children in the propaganda team. None of the better dancers in school were chosen, but, as fate would have it, Yuanni was selected. Yuanni did not know until after she joined the song and dance troupe that she had been selected because her physique suited it, and because of her impeccable family background.

Of all those in the song and dance troupe, it was Yuanni who was most willing to endure hardship. When others got up at five thirty to practice, she had already been at the rehearsal hall for half an hour.

When the teacher asked them to stretch their legs for an hour before breakfast, she always spent a half hour longer than the rest. The others would go shopping in groups to buy snacks after dinner, but she stayed in the dormitory every day, listening to the radio to practice her Mandarin, repeating phrases over and over to erase her local accent. But just as it had been at school, she was always one among the crowd, always present, but never outstanding.

Left to boil for a few years, some of those who had joined the troupe with Yuanni bubbled to the top, a layer of oil on the surface of the pot, and they were made lead dancers. Others sank to the bottom and were finally poured out, sent away to a certain work unit in the Culture and Health System, where they became ordinary workers. Yuanni remained somewhere between the two—midpot, as it were—struggling and suffering. She didn't dare slack off for a single day, because she knew she was an arrow that had been shot out. She never thought about retreating, not even for a moment. She could only close her eyes and forge ahead.

Finally, one day, her opportunity came. It so happened that the alternate lead dancer of the *Laundry Dance* was spotted by a senior officer in the army during a performance, and she was whisked away to Tianjin with the army. The suddenly available role of alternate lead dancer fell unexpectedly to Yuanni. Of course, "unexpectedly" was the general opinion among the troupe members concerning this swift change of fate; Yuanni alone knew that she had put every ounce of strength she had into winning this opportunity. However, she had not anticipated that opportunity would come to her as a waxed thread, and if her hand was not firm enough to catch hold, it would slip from her grasp. In the end, she just couldn't catch the thread.

That day, she was in the orchestral rehearsal with all the performers of Group B. It was just an ordinary rehearsal, aiming only to achieve a matching of dance steps to the rhythm of the music. No one expected the dancers to display their full talent in such a rehearsal.

But that day, Yuanni surprised everyone.

That day, it seemed she had received an omen in the dark, knowing that this would be the last dance of her life.

That day, her heart was a bubbling spring, and warm fluid gurgled down to her fingertips, her toes, every inch of her body. Both the dance steps and her vision were soaked in the fluid, suddenly becoming very fresh. The dance soul, dormant for so many years, suddenly woke just at the moment when it was about to sink forever, and burned madly. Half water and half fire, her limbs became blue spirits beneath the fervent attack.

That day, everyone both on- and offstage understood that it was Li Yuanni's solo dance; the rest were just background and foils. The director and conductor whispered to each other, "Crazy! She's gone mad."

At that precise moment, the old man on duty in the reception room rushed into the rehearsal hall and shouted, "Li Yuanni, telegram from home!"

Both of Yuanni's parents had only the barest education. They could hardly recognize even a few characters, and they seldom wrote Yuanni letters, let alone sent telegrams. When she heard the word *telegram*, her heart sank and her eyes darkened, and she fell midleap. She crashed to the ground and fell headlong off the stage.

It was a comminuted fracture of the right ankle.

"Recovery will take at least three months," the doctor said. "Even if it heals completely, you won't be able to dance anymore. The foot can't take the strain."

It was on the way to the hospital that Yuanni learned the content of the telegram: *Seventh brother joined army. Return quickly.*

Yuanni was sent home to recover from her injuries. She lay in bed for three days and three nights. Even when her younger brother left, she said nothing.

Her mother sat at the head of the bed, puffing away at an old pipe that was stained yellow.

"Heaven can only give us the good that is allotted to the Li family," she said. "If it goes to you, there's nothing to give your little brother. If it goes to your little brother, there's nothing left for you. You're a girl. You can always find a good family to marry into sometime down the road. He's a man; he can't rely on a woman. It was fate—you can do nothing about it."

It was only then that Yuanni sat up. She lay on her mother's lap and broke into tears.

Three months later, Yuanni's foot finally recovered. She retired from the song and dance troupe and went to work in the county seat.

July 1968
Fengrun County, Tangshan, Hebei

The state-run Xinhua Bookstore served mainly as decoration; it sold very few books. The items available there could be counted on one's fingers: *Selected Works of Mao Zedong*, *Quotations of Chairman Mao*, *Poems of Chairman Mao*, *A Portrait of Chairman Mao*, the *Collected Works of Lu Xun*, the *Handbook of Basic Industrial Knowledge*, the *Handbook of Basic Agricultural Knowledge*, and the *Handbook of Rural Medicine and Health Care*. There were only a handful of customers, leaving the staff to idle languidly all day.

When Yuanni retired from the stage, she was assigned a job in the bookstore in the Culture and Health System. She could have rested for a few more months, but she grew tired of staying home and wanted to go out to work. Since standing for long hours was still a challenge after her injury, it was agreed that she would spend the first six months at her new work unit mostly sitting and doing only light jobs. When she arrived at the bookstore, she realized that there hadn't been any need to discuss such arrangements, because everyone there sat from opening until closing.

Including Li Yuanni, there were seven people working in the bookstore: a manager, an accountant, a cashier, and four salesgirls. The manager was the only man. He did not smoke or drink, surviving instead on a cup of tea and a newspaper a day. The Xinhua Bookstore ordered more varieties of newspapers and magazines than anyone else in town, aside from the County Revolutionary Committee, but that amounted to no more than five or six kinds. The shop was dimly lit, and the manager leaned into the dirty newspaper on the counter, his eyebrows and nose knit into a tangled ball of yarn, as if he were eating the words. Even if he read the entire newspaper front to back several times, not skipping a single word, it would not take up a full day, so the shop was often filled with the fine buzz of his snoring, like that of the wings of flies and mosquitoes.

The salesgirls occasionally flipped through the manager's discarded newspapers, mostly to see the pictures of the theatrical costumes. They spent the rest of the time huddled together, chatting. They were all married women, and the topics discussed always swirled around the news of this family or that. By the time they had run their tongues over each husband, child, mother-in-law, and relative, it was time to call it a day.

Yuanni sat far away to one side, passing a hook back and forth through the man's snores and the women's gossip. She had learned to crochet during her three months of recuperation. There were few colors of yarn available in the town's department store, only white, black, and army green. No matter how she mixed and matched these colors, they always had a rustic look. But she didn't care. The back and forth of her needle and yarn was only to kill time. She was not sure how many bags she had made in recent months. Now, when almost all of her relatives on both sides of the family went to the market, they carried bags she had made.

The women's talk had turned to the bedroom, and their tone gradually turned mysterious. The laughter spread unscrupulously, poking holes in the thick, sultry heat, making it grow hotter. She couldn't help feeling that there were countless insects crawling over her, making her tingly and wet. It was sweat, of course, but not only sweat, and she knew it was because of the way the women were looking at her.

Performers from the song and dance troupe were a rare sight that they only saw once every few years. And even when they did catch a glimpse, it was from a distance, always looking up at them onstage, a distance, it seemed, as insurmountable as a mountain or a great river. Now she was here, sitting in front of them, but sadly, the proximity was wasted, because she never took the initiative to talk to them. Gradually, their fervent curiosity soured. Dancer? So? Didn't she still have to tear off the toilet paper and run to the toilet, just like everyone else? Didn't she burp or fart when she ate the wrong foods, just like them? She saw the shift from sweet to sour in their eyes, but she didn't care. Ever since she had seen the X-rays in the hospital, she knew that the fall had broken not only her ankle but also her heart. The bones in her foot would heal, but her heart would not. As soon as a person lost her heart, her skin became thicker, and she developed a kind of fearlessness that nothing could shake.

The sun was high, shining straight down and washing out all the color from the scene, leaving it like water. The trees, the road, and the pedestrians had become a shining white patch. The cicadas ripped their bellies, cutting through one's head like a saw, leaving bits of meat all over.

What voices they were! If the cicadas' vocal cords could have been removed and put into someone's throat, that person would have been a better soprano than Tseten Dolma, Yuanni thought.

Just then, there was a commotion on the street. It was a parade. There were only a few people in the procession, but a long tail streamed behind it, a crowd enjoying the fun. At the front of the line were several people wearing tall paper hats, with signs hung around their necks. One of those in a dunce cap was an older lady in her fifties or sixties, with scarlet rouge on her cheekbones and two cloth shoes hung around her neck. A sign dangled from her breast with the words *Prostitute: Liu Jinxiang* scrawled across it. Every few steps, she banged a gong and shouted, "I'm a worn-out shoe," essentially declaring that she was a slut. Her tone was earnest, almost on the verge of being serious.

The crowd that followed her was made up of people who wore straw hats and carried bundles on poles, pushed bicycles, or carried schoolbags. They were standing on tiptoes, mouths agape and eyes filled with inexperienced eagerness and curiosity. Naturally, all eyes were on the woman. Each time she shouted, the crowd responded with a burst of laughter, momentarily drowning out the shouting and gongs. They went on like this, as if they were happily rushing to a market fair to watch a Yangko dance or stilt walkers.

The Cultural Revolution was sweeping through the whole nation, and scenes like this were a common occurrence. However, Yuanni's town, small and relatively isolated, was not like the provincial capital, where such boisterous, sensational events were a part of daily life. Such a scene was a rarity for the people in this town.

The Cultural Revolution was staged more extravagantly in the provincial capital. There, army-green trucks, army-green bullhorns, and school kids in army-green clothes with dazzling red armbands on their sleeves filled the streets. They moved in unison, as orderly as a group dancing. When a slogan came out of their mouths, it was shouted as neatly as a poetry recitation. Even for those who were the object of the public denouncement, the words on their signs and dunce caps were written in a neat, square font.

The provincial capital. Oh God, the provincial capital.

Thinking of the provincial capital made Yuanni's insides ache. It wasn't a heart-piercing pain, but a dull, inexplicable ache. She was not afraid of sharp pain, which was like the quick stab of a knife, but she feared the dull ache. The dull ache was like traces of fat clogging her blood. Whether awake or asleep, breathing in or out, it was an unbearable feeling that would not go away.

At that precise moment, in the provincial capital, the song and dance troupe was probably just getting to the final stages of rehearsing the *Laundry Dance*. She didn't know who would play the role of Mei Duo, the little Tibetan girl who grabbed the clothes basket from the squad captain. After three months, she still remembered every step of the dance, every gesture, every expression, even every beat and pause in the music. She did not know how many times she had danced it start to finish in her sleep, never making the slightest error. She couldn't forget. She would never forget. That dance was her torch, her beacon. She had thought it would light and guide her way to a long career on the stage, until she was too old to dance anymore. Who knew that its light could be so unreliable? In the blink of an eye, it was extinguished forever, leaving her in the same darkness she'd always known. But this darkness was harder to bear than before, because now she had seen light.

She didn't need to tiptoe. She didn't even need to open her eyes wide. She could see the road ahead easily. The days in the county seat were like a narrow alley whose end could be seen at a glance. In two months, she would be eighteen. The age of eighteen was the season when the rice was blooming, but she had already predicted that it would end with no harvest. How hopeless were the rest of her days? Even if she bought all the yarn in the city and crocheted a bag for every person in the world, she would never get rid of this void in her life. The days were too long, too hopeless.

Watching her grow more haggard each day, her mother could not think of any tricks to make her happy. She discussed the matter with relatives on both sides of the family, asking for help finding a husband for her daughter. Her mother didn't actually want her to marry so early, but finding a suitable match for her was better than having her waste away at home. After getting married and having a baby or two, she would be too busy to brood. Even if her hopes were sky high, it would all fade away over time.

Her aunts and uncles set up several blind dates for her. Yuanni went on them, but she always just sat looking down, drinking tea or eating melon seeds, not saying a word. When she would get home, her mother would follow her around, asking about the date. She would grit her teeth and say, "If two narrow alleys are placed side by side, they still don't make a broad road." Her mother knew Yuanni would forever continue to look down on the people in the county seat, even if they beat her to death trying to change her mind.

Later, her second uncle mentioned another fellow, the nephew of his oldest brother's wife, a former soldier who now worked in the transportation sector in Tangshan City. His family had two tile-roofed houses. He had graduated from middle school, had seen much of life, and was eight years older than Yuanni. Her mother had run up against a wall with Yuanni, so Yuanni didn't dare to give an answer too casually. She looked at Yuanni now and saw her blink. She knew there was a crack in the wall. Yuanni had just one condition: she didn't want the two relatives who had introduced them to be there. She would meet him alone.

It was arranged that he would pick her up after work. The bookstore opened at eight in the morning and closed at eight in the evening, and the staff rotated shifts, two days on, one day off. That evening at eight on the dot, he was waiting for her at the door to the bookstore.

The man drove his work unit's vehicle, a big Jiefang truck. When he hopped out of the truck and faced Yuanni, he was stunned. She was shocked at the sight of him too, because she had never seen someone with such dark skin in the city—he seemed to have absorbed all the sun in the world. He was so dark she started to wonder whether she would be able to see him once the sun went down. So tanned, so strong, and almost handsome. He did not say why he was stunned, but Yuanni understood. Men were always stunned when they saw her. Since she came to work in the bookstore, the number of shoppers had increased, but they weren't there to buy things. They just flipped through the books and looked at her, all of them with the same look in their eyes.

That night, the man took Yuanni for a ride in his big truck, traversing the entire county and Tangshan City. He rolled down the window, and the wind blew her hair and slapped her face. It was very pleasant. He took her to the most exquisite restaurant in the city, where they served Jiangsu and Zhejiang cuisine. There was a dish called squirrel fish, so crispy that it melted as soon as it touched the tongue.

During the meal, the man handed Yuanni an envelope, saying that he had brought it back from a trip to Shanghai. Yuanni opened it. Inside were all sorts of plexiglass buttons in red, yellow, green, and blue. They lay in Yuanni's palm, shining in the glow of the lamp. She had never seen diamonds or jade, not even pearls, but had only heard of them. Those red, yellow, blue, and green buttons were the most dazzling jewels she had ever seen.

"Take those. You can change the buttons on all your clothes," the man said.

He did not talk much, but he was a heavy smoker. He smoked one cigarette after another, each following on the heels of the one before. He lit each cigarette from the last, saving on matches. He smoked Pegasus cigarettes, which were not as harsh and irritating to the throat as her father's Big Harvest brand.

The man drove her home, right to her door. When she got out of the truck, she said, "If you don't have other plans, let's make it official on National Day."

She stared at the toes of her shoes as she spoke, not looking at him.

What had made up her mind was not the crispy fish, or the exciting ride in the big truck, or the shiny plexiglass buttons. They all occupied a place in her mind, but even all together, they would not have been weighty enough to pry open Yuanni's heart or her mouth. What moved her heart was the man's words. He had said, "Our work unit's broadcasting studio needs an announcer. Since you're with a state-run enterprise, you can be transferred immediately."

July 25, 1976
Tangshan, Hebei

The Wan woman was quite annoying to the people on the street.

According to her household registration, her name was Li Yuanni, but to her neighbors, she was just "the Wan woman," because Wan was her husband's surname. The neighbors knew her husband as Wan; very few knew his full name, so he was mostly called "Comrade Wan." Or at least, that's what they called him to his face. They called him many other names behind his back.

Comrade Wan was a long-distance freight driver, mostly running the Beijing–Tianjin–Tangshan route, but occasionally making trips between Beijing, Shanghai, and Hangzhou as well. With his monthly salary plus various travel subsidies, he earned seventy to eighty yuan per month, a fair bit higher than the average salary of a technician who had graduated from college. He came home once every ten days or half a month, where he sat by the door, rolling up his pant legs and rubbing the dirt from his feet as he smoked wearily, like people from the countryside who raked the fields.

Comrade Wan's sturdy, rustic appearance was deceptive. He was the most worldly-wise person on the street. He traveled between big cities all year round, and the dust he picked up on the street corner of a big city was rendered fashionable by the time he brought it back to Tangshan. Though he was very strict with himself, he was extremely generous with his wife and children. Each time he came back from a trip, he brought gifts of all shapes and sizes. As a result, everything the Wan family ate, wore, or used made them somewhat out of sync with the people on the street.

While others in the neighborhood relied on a few poor meat coupons to get something special to eat—which meant they seldom ate meat—the pot on the Wan family's coal stove was always bubbling, the scent of meat wafting out onto the street. Even the dogs knew the Wans were lucky; they rushed and fought over the Wan family's garbage. And if dogs could sense it, people certainly could. Neighborhood kids followed the Wan children in the street, drooling over their treasures, asking brazenly for half a piece of their White Rabbit Toffee, a huge luxury. No parent put a stop to this behavior; it couldn't be stopped. The ones with toffee and the ones without toffee were simply not on the same level.

The Wan woman was despised not only because of her husband, but also because of herself. Her coquettishness had long been observed by the people on the street. She had married into the Wan family in the autumn, when the weather was not yet cold. Still, the bride wore a thick padded jacket, and all the elderly neighbors could tell her waist and the way she walked were a bit weird. The happy event was held in October, and the next April, two children were born to them. Though the girl was as strong as a calf, the Wan woman dared to coolly stand in front of them all and say with a straight face that the children had been premature.

The Wan woman, like any married woman on the street, was a wife and a mother, but she was not just any wife or any mother. Her hair was always pinned up in a plastic hairpin, sometimes scarlet red, sometimes bright yellow, and sometimes emerald green. The hairpin folded her hair into a crescent-shaped arc behind her ears, framing a face that had been smeared with vanishing cream, the dark hair shining against the fair skin—what a picture! A light-colored shirt collar often stuck out from the Wan woman's coat, sometimes pointed, sometimes round, and sometimes trimmed with fine lace.

The Wan woman's pockets often had longan-colored or brick-red plexiglass buttons. Dressed this way and with her hair combed this way, she walked with featherlight steps, like a ballerina, through the dusty, narrow street, feeling all the eyes run over her body. She didn't bat an eye herself. She was used to living in other people's gazes and on the tips of their tongues.

It was a Sunday, and very early in the morning, there was already something stirring in the Wan family's yard. It was the Wan woman singing. Honestly, her singing was not bad, but unfortunately it was always "The Laundry Song," and the ears of the neighbors had already grown calluses from listening to it over and over again. The Wan woman's singing was like hearing an old record with many scratches, going round and round. "The warm sun . . . Shining, shining."

The neighbors guessed that Comrade Wan had come home. The Wan woman only got up early when Comrade Wan was home. And sure enough, before the record had made a full round, there was a thunderous cough from inside the house. It went on for quite some time, the signs of an illness caused by Comrade Wan's years of smoking.

Comrade Wan spat out a thick mass of phlegm and shouted to his children, "Xiaodeng, Xiaoda, if you don't get up now, your mother and I are leaving without you."

The four Wans were going to Grandma's house. The Wan woman, Li Yuanni, had a younger brother who had been a soldier with the PLA Navy for several years. He was newly promoted, and he was going to be home for a few days' leave. Yuanni had set a time for all her siblings to gather at their mother's house for a family reunion.

Xiaodeng and Xiaoda did not move at all. It had been wickedly hot the night before, and the two children had spent half the night scratching their heat rashes. They were knocked out for the second half of the night and now remained in a deathlike slumber. Yuanni walked over and saw that Xiaodeng lay on her belly like a toad, arms and legs spread apart, with one leg furled across Xiaoda's waist. Xiaoda's head was against his knees, body curled up in a ball, like a fetus waiting in its mother's belly to be born.

"What a bully," Yuanni muttered, pushing Xiaodeng's leg away.

They were twins, seven years old. Xiaodeng was just fifteen minutes older than Xiaoda, but even if it were just one minute, she would still be the big sister. As soon as Xiaodeng came out of her mother's womb, her cries were earth shattering, making the whole delivery room tremble. The small hand grabbed the midwife's pinkie, and it didn't break the grip for a long time. She was a very strong girl. When Xiaoda was born, he didn't cry at all. The midwife held him upside down in her hands and slapped him fiercely several times before he finally made squeaking sounds, like a field mouse who had had its tail stepped on.

Cleaned and wrapped, they were placed in two small beds, one large baby and one small, one pink face and one sallow. No matter how she looked at them, they didn't look like twins. After two days, the pink one was pinker and the sallow one sallower. A week later, the sallow one was barely clinging to life. Wan was not at home; Yuanni's mother was at her daughter's house to help with the confinement. Seeing the child's look, she said she was afraid he wouldn't make it.

Yuanni closed her eyes. "Carry the little one over to see the bigger one then, Ma," she said. "Let them say goodbye. After all, they started the journey together."

Her mother did just that, placing Xiaoda next to Xiaodeng. No one would have guessed that Xiaodeng would suddenly reach out her hand and place it on Xiaoda's shoulder. Xiaoda was startled. His eyes snapped open, he gasped for breath, and his face flushed. Yuanni's mother kept stamping her bound feet, marveling nonstop, believing that Xiaodeng had lent vitality to Xiaoda, saving her little brother's life.

From then on, Xiaoda slept in Xiaodeng's bed, and he grew stronger, helped by her vitality. Xiaoda seemed to know that she had given him life, so he was always patient with her, even as a very small boy. It was more like he was her big brother.

This morning, despite her repeated attempts to shake them awake, Yuanni could not wake the two children. When she saw that they had each placed their schoolbags under their heads, she couldn't help but laugh. Their father had bought the schoolbags when he passed through Beijing on one of his trips. They were of the same style, green canvas bags printed with an image and the words *Tiananmen Square, Beijing.* The children had registered for primary school, and now all that was left was to wait for school to start in September. At dinner the night before, their father had taken out the schoolbags and the two children had not let go of them since. They had carried the bags all night until bedtime, and then had slept with them under their heads, afraid of losing them if they let go. Yuanni went to pull out the schoolbags, and both children woke at the same instant. They sat up swiftly, eyes opened wide.

Yuanni slapped them both on the head and said, "Hurry up. Breakfast is in your lunch box. You can eat on the go. The sun is awful. Let's go before it gets too hot."

Then she and Comrade Wan went to push the bicycles. The Wan family had two bicycles, his 28-inch Yongjiu and her 26-inch Phoenix. Though the bikes were old, Yuanni cleaned them every day with the old cotton cloth her husband had brought back, then applied a layer of oil. The four steel rims were shiny and full of vitality.

Though Yuanni's family lived not too far away, it still took an hour or two to cycle there. When they set out early in the morning, the sun was already shining so brightly it washed the road white. The heat steamed up off the road, and the leaves were motionless. The cicadas were crying at the top of their lungs, so noisy it made one's ears buzz.

Comrade Wan's bike was heavier, the basket in front packed with preserved fruit, tuckahoe cake, and hawthorn paste, all of which he had brought back from Beijing to express his respect for his mother-in-law. Xiaoda sat astride the back of the bike, carrying a mesh pouch in his hand. In the pouch were two packs of filter-tipped Pegasus cigarettes for Yuanni's father. Yuanni's bike was lighter, with only a water bottle hung from the crossbar and Xiaodeng seated at the back. Xiaodeng was more sensible, knowing girls shouldn't sit astride, so she sat with both legs on one side of the bicycle.

Comrade Wan wore a dark blue work cap, originally intended to provide shade, but ultimately ending up as a sweat rag. Sweat dripped from his brow the whole journey, blurring his sight. As he took off his hat and fanned himself with it, he asked Yuanni if she wanted to bring her little brother back to stay with them for a few days, since the children were closest to this uncle.

Yuanni said, "That's a good idea, but where will he sleep?"

"I have to set out for Tianjin tomorrow and then to Beijing on the way home. It will take a week to go there and back. Your brother can share the room with Xiaoda, and Xiaodeng can sleep with you. Wouldn't that be okay?"

Xiaoda gave a kick from the back of the bike and said, "It won't be okay with me."

Yuanni scolded, "What's wrong with it? Don't you always say you want your uncle to come teach you to shoot a gun?"

Xiaoda snorted and said, "But I want to sleep with Sis. You can sleep with Uncle."

When Comrade Wan heard that, he laughed and said, "Wow, Mama, will you listen to that? The children in other families fight all day long, but these two can't stand to be apart."

After riding for half an hour or so, they gradually left the city, and the road opened up, without any shelter from the sun. Xiaoda was thirsty. Yuanni handed the water bottle over to let him drink, then asked Xiaodeng if she would like some. Xiaodeng did not want a drink, but said she was hungry.

Yuanni said, "Yesterday's leftover steamed buns are in your lunch box. Take those out to eat."

Xiaodeng said, "Who wants steamed buns? I want tuckahoe cake."

"What a brat!" Yuanni scolded. "That's for your grandma. What makes you think it's for you?"

Xiaodeng's face darkened and she sniffed. "Then I'll starve to death," she wailed.

Comrade Wan couldn't bear to hear such a thing. "It's just tuckahoe cake. There are two big boxes," he said. "What will it hurt if there's one piece less?"

Yuanni shot daggers at him with her eyes. "She's your daughter, isn't she? You're spoiling her like she's your grandmother."

Both children giggled from the backs of their parents' bicycles.

They pulled over in a shady patch, and Yuanni carefully took two pieces of tuckahoe cake from the top of a box, one for each child. Xiaodeng tore off a small piece and chewed it slowly, the sweet taste flowing coolly over her tongue. She suddenly stopped. Before the sweetness had even faded, a panicked scream escaped from her throat.

She saw a series of black balls moving in a long line along the side of the road, oblivious to anyone around them. Each one gripped the tail of the one in front of it in its mouth. The line was so long she could not see where it began or ended as it snaked its way across the far reaches of the field. It took a while for her to realize that they were rats.

"Mama!"

Xiaodeng's voice grew hoarse and her limbs weak. She had always been a little daredevil: she could stomp a centipede to death with her foot or crush a caterpillar between her fingers. The only thing she was afraid of was rats. As soon as she saw a rat, she turned to a quivering puddle.

Yuanni covered Xiaodeng's eyes and said, "Don't look. I'll tell you when they're gone."

Comrade Wan shook his head while picking his teeth.

"It's broad daylight and every rat in the city has come out of its hole. Is it a parade? They aren't afraid of people, but people are scared of them. I don't know why, but strange things have been happening all the time these days. When old Wang from our work unit went out in his truck the day before yesterday, he saw water gurgling up from the well beside the road, shooting a foot or two into the air, like a fountain. I heard someone say a fortune teller told them this was going to be an ominous year."

"Pah!" Yuanni spat. "In this day and age, you still believe such things?"

"Are they gone?" Xiaodeng shouted impatiently, her face sweating from being covered with Yuanni's hands.

"It's over. It's finally over." Yuanni let go of Xiaodeng and found a towel to wipe away the sweat from her face. "Look at you, little scaredy cat. When you grow up and are a bride, who's going to be there to cover your eyes then?"

"Wherever Sis goes to be a bride, that's where I'll go to be a bride too," Xiaoda said.

Comrade Wan and Yuanni couldn't help but laugh.

July 28, 1976
Tangshan, Hebei

Parts of Wan Xiaodeng's memory of that night were extremely clear, so clear that she could recall every texture of every detail. Other parts were blurred, only a rough outline with smudged edges remaining. Years later, she wondered whether her memories of that night were just an illusion, developed from reading so many documentary accounts of the event. She even thought that perhaps there had been no such night in her life at all.

It had been hot. Summer nights were generally hot in Tangshan, but this particular night was outrageously so. The sky was like a large clay pot that had been baked all day, overturned and sitting atop the earth, blocking out even the slightest hint of a breeze. It was not just the people who were hot, but the dogs too. They barked from one end of the street to the other, filling the neighborhood with the sound of howling.

The Wan family had an electric fan that Comrade Wan had built himself using leftover materials from the factory, but the fan's motor had burned out after constant use. The Wan family, like all their neighbors, was left without a fan as they suffered through the raw heat that night.

Her mother, Li Yuanni, had a bed to herself. Her father was on the road, and the two children were crammed into the other bed with their uncle. They had slung their army-green bags over their shoulders when they went to bed. Xiaodeng heard her mother and her uncle toss and turn, their thin fans sounding like firecrackers as they slapped, stirring up a breeze and driving away mosquitoes all at once.

"Isn't the food in Shanghai different from ours?" her mother asked her uncle through the thin wall separating the rooms. Her uncle's troop was stationed in a suburb of Shanghai.

"Everything comes in small servings. I'm so afraid I'll finish it all in one bite that I don't even dare start. It's very refined, a mix of sweet and sour," her uncle answered.

Her mother tutted enviously. "No wonder those women in the South have such delicate skin. See how they eat, and how we eat. I heard that the weather in the South is good too. The summers and winters there are not as uncomfortable as ours, right?"

"It's a coastal climate with four distinct seasons. Their winter is warmer than ours, but it's still uncomfortable without heating. In summer, it's hot during the day, but cool at night, so at least you can sleep well."

Her mother sighed. "All my life, I've been a frog at the bottom of a well. I really want to see the big city one day."

Her uncle was silent for a while, then mumbled, "It's my fault. If it wasn't for that telegram, you would be living in the provincial capital—"

Her mother interrupted. "It's all up to fate. Who can fight against fate? If it were not that telegram, it would have been something else. God doesn't like me."

Her uncle slapped a mosquito on his arm, killing it. He wiped the blood from his palm onto the wall. "When Xiaoda grows up, I'll take him to Shanghai to study. That can count as fulfilling your dream too."

Xiaoda stomped his foot on the bed board excitedly and said, "Xiaodeng and me will go together."

There was a rustling sound from their mother's bed. She got up in the dark and took off her close-fitting undershirt. She had never slept topless, but the past few days had been so unbearably hot.

"Isn't this year wickedly hot? Look at the heat rashes on the kids. They've scratched so much they have little white spots all over. When their father comes back and sees it, he's going to be so upset."

Their uncle laughed and said, "He seems easily upset with everyone, but when he sees these two precious kids, his temper disappears."

Their mother laughed too. "You should see his parents. They have three sons, but only one grandson, Xiaoda. They wish they could put him in the palm of their hand and worship him like a bodhisattva."

Their uncle felt Xiaoda's leg. The boy was thin, but very strong. He didn't move. He was probably asleep.

"He's grown well. He's a good kid. I've never seen him throw a temper tantrum. But I think you two are fonder of Xiaodeng."

"A son forgets his mother as soon as he's married, but when a daughter grows up, she's her mother's warm jacket. I just wish she were more easygoing. She holds a grudge." Her mother yawned, a long, slow yawn. "Go to sleep. Those two rascals have been talking to you all night. You're tired."

He grunted in agreement. The sound of fanning slowed down, and it was soon replaced by fine snoring. Xiaodeng's eyelids drooped, but she felt that there were ten thousand bugs crawling over the wet, sticky mattress, biting her. She heard her mother get up in the dark, grope about, bump into something, and let out a pained yelp. Xiaodeng knew that her mother was going out to the courtyard to relieve herself. She usually used the chamber pot in the house, but with the awful heat these days, the smell would fill the whole house. When she finally stumbled her way into the courtyard, Xiaodeng vaguely heard her mumble to herself outside the window, "God, why is it so bright tonight?"

Suddenly, an earth-shattering sound cut off her mother's voice like a knife.

Xiaodeng's memory also cut off here, losing shape. All she could remember were faint pieces, like dust particles flickering at the beginning of an old film. Later, she would try and collect these dust particles to connect them into a whole picture, but it never worked. It remained a deep, impenetrable darkness. Not the kind of darkness that arrives when you turn off the light at night—no, that darkness could be torn with a slit in the curtains or a crack of light under the door. This shadow was a quilt with no seams, draped over her head, smelling like dirt, growing heavier and heavier, until it felt as if her forehead were squeezed flat and her eyes were about to pop out from her head.

She heard people scream. Someone shouted, "The Soviets have dropped an atomic bomb!" Her mother was moaning, a string on a Chinese violin that was about to break. She tried to move, but found that only three toes on her right foot were functioning. She wiggled them back and forth, left and right. She bumped into something soft, a body. For a moment, she thought it was her mother—but it couldn't be; her mother was moaning somewhere far away. It was Xiaoda. She wanted to shout, yell, cry for help, but she had no voice.

After a great noise from the shifting rubble, her mother's voice suddenly became clear. "I need to get dressed. This is humiliating."

"Saving lives is all that matters. You're still worried about such things?" That was her uncle's voice.

Her mother remembered, and she suddenly screamed, "Xiaodeng! Xiaoda!"

For as long as she lived, Xiaodeng would never forget her mother's cries that day.

In the darkness, Xiaoda suddenly started to slam himself violently against the solid walls around him. Xiaodeng couldn't see his movements, but she could feel that he was like a fish stuck in a quagmire, desperate to escape. She moved her right hand and found that it was a little freer, so she directed all her strength into that hand and pushed upward. Suddenly, she saw a thin line of the sky. It was tiny, like the eye of a needle. Looking out through the needle's eye, she saw a woman covered in blood. The woman was wearing only a pair of underpants, and there were two plaster-covered balls dangling from her chest.

"Mama! Mama!"

Xiaoda started shouting at the top of his lungs. Xiaodeng had lost her voice, so Xiaoda's was now their common voice. He shouted for a long time, until his voice gradually weakened too.

"It hurts, Xiaodeng." Xiaoda fell silent, as if he knew their situation was hopeless.

"Oh God! Xiao . . . Xiaoda is under here. Help! Someone help me!" their mother cried.

Their mother's voice was not at all like her usual voice. It was more like a current that had broken from her body and gone on its own way, sharply barging through the air and cutting through everything that blocked its path, smashing it all to pieces.

There was a burst of chaotic footsteps, and the sliver of sky disappeared from Xiaodeng's sight. It was probably someone lying on the ground, listening.

"Here. I'm here," Xiaoda said weakly.

Then there was their mother's roaring, gasping sound, like a wolf. Xiaodeng guessed that their mother was digging through the rubble.

"It's useless. The child is under a cement slab. You can only pry it with tools. You won't be able to dig them out with your hands." This was the voice of a strange man.

There was another burst of chaotic footsteps, and someone said, "I've got the tools. Get out of the way."

There was a jingling sound, then it stopped again. A voice stammered, "This slab was laid flat. If we pry up one end, it will slide all the way to the other."

The two children were stuck, one on each side of the slab.

There was a dead silence all around.

"Please, tell me which one to save." It was her uncle talking now.

Her mother banged her forehead on the ground. "Oh God! God!"

Following a brief struggle, her mother's voice fell. Xiaodeng heard her uncle snap at her mother. "If you don't tell me which one, they'll both be gone."

After a seemingly infinite silence, her mother spoke.

Her mother's voice was low. The people around her may have only guessed at what she said. But Xiaoda and Xiaodeng both heard the two syllables perfectly, and the slight pause in the middle.

Her mother's words were "Xiao . . . da."

Xiaoda's body suddenly tightened, becoming a rocky lump. Xiaodeng expected him to say something, but he said nothing. There was a noise like rolling thunder overhead, and Xiaodeng felt that someone had slammed a hammer into her head.

"My sister . . . Sis!"

That was the last thing Xiaodeng heard before she fell into a deep sleep.

It grew light. The sky was ugly, full of disjointed, cottony clouds. The earth still trembled intermittently, and the razed city had suddenly broadened, making the horizon visible at first glance. Without the familiar buildings, the boundary between sky and earth seemed to have changed drastically.

That day, they found a little girl lying face up beside a huge, half-fallen banyan tree. It was a corpse that had just been dug up, and it had not been moved yet. There was a good deal of blood on her forehead but almost no visible injury to other parts of the body. Her eyes, nose, and mouth were covered with mud. It seemed she had suffocated. The sky-blue shirt she wore had been torn to shreds. She was practically naked, but she still had a nearly perfect army-green bag with an image of Tiananmen Square on it slung across her shoulder.

"What a pretty little girl."

Someone sighed regretfully, but no one stopped. They had seen too many bodies like this along the way, and they would see still more as they continued. That day, their concern was only for the living. They had no time to look after the dead—not now, and not for quite some time.

Then came the rain, a rain that stirred up dust and stories, a rain that carried color and weight. The raindrops hit the little girl, and beautiful mud flowers opened one after another on her face. When the mud was washed away, a clean water droplet that had sat on the girl's eyelid for some time suddenly quivered and rolled down. She opened her eyes.

She sat up and stared blankly at the wilderness surrounding her, having completely lost her bearings. After a while, her eyes fell onto the bag she clung to, and the scattered memories gradually began to fall into place. She recalled something that seemed to have happened in the distant past. She stood up, swayed, and tore at the bag strap on her shoulder. It was a strong strap. She could not tear it off. She bent to bite it. Her teeth were as sharp as a little beast's, and the threads began to slip between them, groaning miserably. Finally the cloth broke. She rolled the bag into a ball, then flung it away ruthlessly. It spiraled through the air and got entangled in the branches of the half-fallen banyan tree, where it hung alone and helpless.

She only had one shoe left. Using her clad foot, she searched for the road, which was really no road at all anymore. She walked along it for a while, then stopped and looked back at the path she had traveled. She saw the bag she had tossed, like an old sparrow hawk shot by a hunter, one dirty wing drooping from the branches of the tree.

Wan Xiaodeng did not know at the time that this would be her last memory of her childhood.

December 24, 2005
Toronto

The doorbell rang, startling Wang Xiaodeng.

Thank goodness! She's finally back, Xiaodeng thought.

Xiaodeng covered her chest to ease her racing heartbeat and ran downstairs, but her husband, Yang Yang, had already rushed ahead of her to open the door. A row of women stood there, dressed in long corset dresses and red capes, each holding a sheet of music. It was the Salvation Army's Christmas carolers.

The lead woman struck her violin lightly, and a burst of music flowed out like water.

> Emmanuel, we beseech you, come
> Redeem the captive Israel
> Fallen in a foreign land, lonely and sad
> Longing for the Son of God to come

It was not her. Xiaodeng stopped in her tracks, closed her eyes, covered her ears, and sat in the darkness in the corner of the staircase, utterly disappointed. She knew that the Christmas tree on the windowsill was shining, gold and silver, and the snow on the road had been painted in a burst of color by all the lights on the street. She knew that rounds of laughter and good cheer were whipping in the wind at that moment, and she heard the bells jingling at the wrists of the women as they sang. She knew that this would be the one sleepless night of the whole year, but all those colors and sounds seemed to have nothing to do with her. She couldn't stand the gaiety today.

Rejoice! Rejoice
O people of Israel
Emmanuel has come!

Xiaodeng's head began to hurt again.

Her headaches had a long history. X-rays, EEGs, CT scans, MRIs. She had submitted to every examination modern science could offer, but they found nothing out of the ordinary. Over the years, she had tried Chinese medicine, Western medicine, acupuncture, massage, and all sorts of pain relief methods. She had even approached Native American healers to try to find a remedy, but nothing had proved effective. Once, she had participated in a pain management experiment organized by a renowned medical school, and an expert in the field asked each of the patients in turn to describe their pain. The descriptions varied. Some said it was like being pierced with needles or bitten by huge bugs, others, being hit with nails or slashed with a knife, and still others, being strangled with a rope. The list went on.

When it was Xiaodeng's turn, she thought for a long time before saying that it was like the heavy blow of a hammer—a big hammer with a long handle and a square head, the kind used by a construction worker or a blacksmith. It didn't smash her directly; it was more like it came through several layers of quilts. The area of impact was not small, and the pain was not sharp, but a diffused, dull, aching pain that had a massive echo. It was as if her head were a flimsy, poorly inflated ball, and it took a while to bounce back into shape after the hammer fell. Her pain had two layers: first when the hammer fell, and second when it bounced back, doubling it.

After listening to her description, the expert was silent for a while before asking, "Are you a novelist?"

Her headaches often came without warning and with almost no transition. One minute, she was a person with completely normal sensations, and the next, she was curled up in a pain so intense that it nearly paralyzed her. As a result, she was not up to any jobs that required regular contact with people, so over and over, she had lost prospects that sounded very promising, jobs such as teaching or being a librarian or court translator.

It was not only career opportunities that were lost to her; eventually, she could not even drive. Sometimes, she felt as if her writing career was a direct result of her headaches. While others' thought processes were peaceful and continuous, hers was chopped into incoherent fragments by bouts of pain. She lost peace, but she found impulsion. She lacked the tenacity needed for continuity, but she had gained an abrupt, unpredictable explosive power. While others grew drowsy with the inertia of daily life, she could only pick up fragments of clear thought in a sober moment, working frantically in the gaps between headaches. She had only two states of existence: pain and no pain. Pain was the end of painlessness, and painlessness was the beginning of pain. Such beginnings and endings were like rings of high-quality iron, linked one to another, locking her life in shackles. The little bit of feeling squeezed out of these iron rings was like powerful water rushing through a small faucet, giving it unexpected sharpness and strength. She did not know what to do with this momentum but be a writer.

Even with her ears covered, Xiaodeng could hear the chaos of voices downstairs, the loud exchanges of "Merry Christmas" as Yang Yang said goodbye to the carolers. Xiaodeng guessed that he was fumbling around in his pocket to find appropriate change. Every year since Yang Yang and Xiaodeng had moved here six years earlier, these women had gone through the street singing on Christmas Eve to raise funds for the Salvation Army.

But Christmas this year was different from previous years: it was their first year without Susie.

Susie was their daughter. She had left home the day before.

It was not the first time Susie had run away. She had been running away since she was nine years old. But it had always been some sort of childish prank, like walking halfway and turning back, or getting to the park, sitting in the shade doing nothing for a while, and then turning around and going home.

Susie left for a variety of reasons. Sometimes it was because she had dyed a strand of her hair purple, or because she wore a top that showed her belly button, or because she had brought home a less than stellar report card. She had a bad temper, and anything Xiaodeng said could set her off if she didn't like what or how it had been said. But her temper was like a thunderstorm on a hot day, coming and going in a wink. In all of Xiaodeng's memory, Susie had not been a vindictive child.

But this time, it was different; Susie had not come home that night. Xiaodeng called all of her classmates and friends, but no one knew where Susie was. Of course, she had called the police too. But there were too many such cases during the holidays, and the police responded casually that if there was no news within forty-eight hours, she should call again, and then they hung up on her.

"How could I have thought it's Susie? She has keys. She never rings the doorbell when she comes home," Xiaodeng muttered to herself.

She hardly noticed when Yang Yang came and sat beside her on the stairs.

In fact, when she saw Susie the previous afternoon, she had known then it was the real deal. Xiaodeng had been looking at Susie's computer, checking her daughter's online chat records, page after page. Susie was not at home; she had gone out ice-skating with her friends. As Xiaodeng read the chats, she became absorbed and forgot about the time. Then she felt the heat on her back. When she looked over her shoulder, it was Susie. She had not even heard her daughter come in the door. Susie's eyes didn't move, boring into Xiaodeng. After going through several tentative transformations, Xiaodeng's expression finally settled into something between sarcasm and inquisitiveness.

"Who's Robert? You've never talked so much to your own mother," Xiaodeng said coldly.

Susie's face changed all at once, the blood flowing out like the tide, leaving only a jagged paleness. She turned and left without a word. Tap, tap, tap, tap, every inch of the floor that she touched smoldered.

Go! Go after her now! Bring her back!

Xiaodeng's brain cried out to her body, but it failed to command her tongue or her feet. She slumped back in the chair, like a deboned fish, feeble and limp, unable to move, as she sat listening to Susie's footsteps thump down the stairs and through the hallway, finally disappearing somewhere outside the door.

Susie had not come back since.

"Xiaodeng, maybe you shouldn't keep her on such a tight leash," Yang Yang said hesitantly to his wife, still sitting on the staircase.

"You mean I keep you on a tight leash too, don't you?" Xiaodeng opened her eyes and looked straight at Yang Yang. Unable to bear up under such a look, he lowered his head.

"It's better to let her make a mistake under your nose, where you can see her, than for you not to be able to see her at all. She's just thirteen. Don't forget what we were like when we were thirteen."

This poked a sore spot for Xiaodeng, and she jumped up like a spring. Her eyes seemed ready to burst out of their sockets.

"You didn't know me when I was thirteen. You'd better shut up about things you don't understand."

Xiaodeng was very near him, and specks of spittle flew onto the tip of Yang Yang's nose.

Yang Yang leaned back and said defensively, his voice low, "I just meant, give her some space. If you hold the leash too tight, it will break."

Xiaodeng laughed coldly. "If you have something to say, just spit it out. Don't use your daughter as an excuse. You want me to leave you alone so you can have a bit of privacy with that woman, don't you?"

"Please don't drag others into this. You yourself are a shadow, so you only look for shadows in others."

Yang Yang turned and slowly walked downstairs. The way he walked was very strange that day, both legs of his trousers dragging the floor, as if his feet had been cut off.

"Everyone is a shadow. Only she is sunshine. What a pity."

Yang Yang walked to the door, turned around once more, and said, "Xiaodeng, since you're so strong, why don't you keep everyone in the world on your leash?"

The door closed with a bang, making the windowpanes hum. Xiaodeng wanted to grab something and smash it against the wall, but she felt all around her and found nothing she could grab. She dug her fingers into the palm of her hand, her nails piercing flesh. She shivered violently.

You can't count on anything, not a damn thing in this world, Xiaodeng thought bitterly.

She knew that she would be spending this Christmas alone.

December 25, 2005
Toronto

The sound of the loudspeaker woke Yang Yang suddenly. He looked at the electronic display board in the subway car. It was 1:28 in the morning, which meant that the subway train had already brought him across the boundary between yesterday and today.

He was the only passenger in the long car. He didn't know how many rounds the train had driven along the same route, but he remembered that he had fallen asleep the moment he leaned back in the seat. His sleep was unbroken, without any joints or patches, a perfect stretch from start to finish. He wiped a trace of saliva from the corner of his mouth and took a long breath. He had not had such a relaxed sleep in a long, long time.

All these years, he had been tense, like a string stretched taut. Xiaodeng held one end of the string, and Susie, the other. Day after day, year after year, the two of them had developed a tacit understanding in this tug-of-war: when one of them held tight, the other would release a little. Like the mainspring of an old clock, he was constantly wound by the two of them—sometimes his wife and sometimes his daughter, but rarely both at the same time.

But just two days before, that tacit understanding was broken, after so many years. Both women had pulled the string with all their might at the same time.

Before leaving home, he had said to Xiaodeng, "They snapped." He meant his nerves, and he knew she understood what he meant.

Xiaodeng was curled up at the turn of the stairs. She looked up at him, and he saw an unfamiliar look in her eyes, like an injured dog looking at passersby, weak, desolate, helpless, and with a faint hint of a plea.

In that instant, he almost decided to turn around, give her a hug, and tell her, *Deng, you're sick. Let's get better together.*

But before he could say anything, she cut him off.

"Mine snapped long ago."

What she said was not all that cold, but the tone in which she said it was pure ice. Those words, wrapped in that tone, were like a hard bullet, instantly blowing away whatever little hope he had still held. How naïve, and how wishful he was. Even if another ten thousand years passed, there would be no feeling such as pity in Wang Xiaodeng—for anybody else, or for herself.

Resolute, he walked out of the house.

Ah! Susie! Where was Susie, his only daughter, at that moment? He had looked for her all day, going to every place he could think of in search of her. He didn't find her—not even the slightest trace of her, as if she had never lived in this world at all. His Susie had suddenly turned into water, leaving no trace behind once she had flowed past.

When a person ran into some minor trouble, they might cry out a little. This was a sort of anger that still held some hope. But when a person encountered real disaster—the sky falling or the earth collapsing—they would most likely be silent, sunk in a helpless numbness. When he reached forty, he finally came to understand that despair could also calm people. When a person realized that no matter what he did, he could not change the status quo, he would hand over the fate that he had held so tightly to God. By that point, he could finally unload his burdens. This must be the state of mind one would experience at death. Perhaps death was, then, the ultimate release.

He had not felt like driving tonight. Driving required the difficult work of finding his way. Tonight, he did not want to be bothered with that. He preferred to be like driftwood at sea, letting the wind and waves push him to whatever land they pleased. It was better to float along, far away, never landing.

He was so tired. He got onto the subway as soon as he left the house. But this was the last train, and he had no choice but to get off.

He glanced at the sign on the platform: *Greenwood Station*. His heart skipped a beat. It was a small station. He had just hopped onto the train without knowing or asking where it was going. Who knew it would end up leading him to Xiangqian's home?

It must be God's will. God's will.

When he got out of the station, he saw the dark night sky. The snow had stopped, the stars looked at him coldly, and there were a couple of mindless dog barks from somewhere far down the street. He had never met the city head-on at this time. Over the years, his feet and his car tires had covered parts of the city more times than he could count, but he never had to put his heart into it. He was busy. He spent every day thinking about how to pull checks from the pockets of difficult parents, and how to convert these checks into Susie's education fund, or his and Xiaodeng's retirement fund, or new shingles on the roof, or new hardwood floors in the living room.

He was too busy, leaving no time for the city and no time for himself.

But now, the opportunity suddenly presented itself. The night pushed the troubles of the day away, emptying his mind unexpectedly and allowing him to finally take a careful look at the city that had momentarily lowered its guard.

It was supposed to be a night of festivities. This was a night when a birth was rapturously celebrated, a night for hope to spring, wounds to heal, comfort to be granted, and wars to come to an end. But he couldn't bring himself to celebrate.

The Christmas lights had now been extinguished, and the lights behind the windows of every house had long since dimmed, leaving only a few yellowish streetlamps, faintly illuminating a city crumpled with fatigue, the kind only sleep could reveal. The most festive night of the year had come to an end, emptying the city and emptying his heart. The city was so old, drained, and wrinkled. Yang Yang suddenly felt that he and the city shared a mutual empathy.

The cold gradually bit through his coat and leather boots, reaching deeper into his skin. His breath grew heavy with moisture that formed a thick frost at his nostrils. He began to tremble. At first, his limbs quivered uncontrollably, then he heard his teeth fighting each other. The wind seemed to grow a long tongue of iron thorns, rushing at him with a whimper, licking him until he had no skin left. He knew that if he continued to walk in this twenty-below temperature, he would become a modern version of the little match girl.

He finally took out his phone and dialed a number. His hands were stiff, and it took several tries before he got through. The voice that answered was unusually calm but alert, without the least trace of surprise, as if it had been waiting a lifetime for this call.

"Where are you?" Xiangqian asked.

"At the door. Yours," he said.

A light snapped on upstairs, tearing a hole with fuzzy edges in the darkness. A silhouette appeared in the hole, sharp and exaggerated like in a shadow play.

She didn't speak. It was not an empty silence, but it was formless. The silence was asking a soundless question. This had always been how Xiangqian presented her questions.

"Is Wenwen asleep?" He could only deter her questions with questions of his own.

Wenwen was Xiangqian's eleven-year-old daughter.

"Who but me would still be awake at this hour?"

"Me," he said.

She smiled softly. Through the phone, he felt her smile brush his ear like a breeze. It hurt a bit as it thawed his eardrum.

The door opened. Xiangqian covered herself in her thick nightgown and stood in the doorway to meet him.

Not wanting to wake Wenwen, she did not turn on the ceiling lights on the stairs. He lost his bearing in the dark for a moment and nearly stumbled. She held out a hand and led him to the main floor. Her hands were huge, firm and rough, and he could feel the dry, flaky skin rubbing against his palm. Such hands did not seem to belong to a painter, but to a mason who worked in the scorching sun and wind all year round.

She lit a Christmas candle and sat down facing him on the living room rug. He did not want to sit on the sofa, and neither did she. The sofa had an aloofness, an alienating feel that was not suited to this night. The orange candlelight sprinkled a layer of bronze across her face, making her momentarily seem like an old portrait that had been in an antique store for years.

"It's late. Why aren't you asleep?" he asked.

"Thinking. Of you," she said, looking at him as she enunciated each word.

Xiangqian and his wife, Xiaodeng, really were the two most distant points on a straight line. He couldn't help but sigh. One of them always expressed weakness with the strongest voice, and the other always conveyed strength with the weakest voice.

42

"Susie. She left home." He lowered his head, unable to sustain her straight, heavy gaze.

"Oh." She raised her eyebrows slightly. He knew this was the ultimate expression of surprise from her. She seldom made noisy displays. "When day breaks, we'll go to David Liu. Remember? He's the student who won first prize in the community painting contest. His father is the chief of police or something. He'll help."

She spoke quietly, as if she were speaking of an innocuous little incident. She always took the shortest time to find the clearest direction through the most chaotic situation. In her hands, there seemed to be no crisis that could not be settled.

Yang Yang's heart melted all at once. He wanted to stand up, walk over, put his arms around her, and lay his heavy head on her broad shoulders. But no—he would have preferred her to stand up, hold him in her arms, surrounding him with her firm, welcoming breasts and belly, letting him enjoy a serenity away from this chaotic world, like a fetus in the womb, even just for one night.

But he did not stand up. And neither did she.

The wick of the candle popped, making a soft crackling noise. The candlelight began to flicker, casting a thin shadow on her face.

"Do you know a good doctor? I mean, a good psychiatrist?"

He chewed on this sentence all the way from his mind to his mouth, and when he spat it out, it had already lost its shape.

"For Susie?" she asked.

"No. For her mother."

Xiangqian's eyebrows twitched again. They both knew, without exchanging a word, that a rule had been shattered. A boundary, based on a tacit understanding developed between them over the years, had been crossed.

They had first met while setting up crafts stalls at Eaton Centre. Since then, they had talked about almost everything, from history, philosophy, literature, and art to driver's license tests, business

43

opportunities, and cheap secondhand goods. Only two things were off-limits: her husband in China and his wife here. Whenever the conversation drew near this reef, there was always a breeze or a cluster of waves that gently pushed it to a safe distance, intentionally or otherwise.

But now, they had finally struck the reef.

"Does it work? Those witch doctors?" she finally asked after a moment's hesitation.

"There's no choice. She really can't go on like this. She's going to destroy Susie."

"And you," she said.

He had nothing to say to that.

The wick grew longer, the flame sputtering and sending a wisp of smoke drifting around the room, like a ghost that refused to go away.

"Can you talk about it with her mother? I mean, your mother-in-law? Sometimes a knot you can't untie, her mother can."

"She doesn't have a mother. Both her real mother and her adoptive mother are gone."

She paused, then asked, "Her father? Can you talk to him?"

"She's not in contact with her adoptive father. We can't go near this topic, not even a word, or she immediately tenses up and turns hostile."

She paused, then asked, "Yang Yang, how well do you know her?"

He was stunned. It was the first time anyone had asked him such a question.

He had known Xiaodeng for almost twenty years and had spent almost half his life with her. In the earliest days, he was in the foreground and she was his background. She looked at him with admiration, willingly serving as his foil. But those days soon passed, and he receded from the foreground to become her background. Over the past ten years, his life had revolved around her. She was the coordinate, and he the arc that circled the coordinate. He thought he had seen the coordinate in every light and shadow, from every angle, and knew its every detail. But he forgot that before she met him, they each had their

44

own worlds. She knew his past well, but he knew almost nothing about hers. Did he really know her?

He searched his soul but he could not find a single word to answer. The silence was like a mountain, lying between them, pressing his bones and muscles until they rattled.

Finally, he could not bear the weight any longer. He stood up and said, "Give me a lift home, please."

She went into her bedroom, silent, changed clothes, and came back with her car keys. She didn't ask him to stay and she didn't ask him why he was leaving, just as she had not asked why he came.

Winter nights in the north were long and the sky was still dark, showing no hint of dawn. The tires ran across the icy snow with a loud screech, shredding the tranquility of a city deep in sleep. Drowsiness struck him without warning again, and he started to feel the weight of his eyelids.

"I'm sorry," he said, a half-minded apology for not staying.

"It's fine," she said quietly, glancing at him. "You know what they say: 'Be ready to assemble at the first call, be ready to fight upon arrival, and be ready to withdraw the minute the mission is accomplished.' That's me. I know my role."

He didn't speak, just punched the seat. The punch was so hard it startled her, but she just laughed out loud. "What's wrong? Can't take a joke? Have you thought about how you'll explain yourself when you get home, spending the whole night out?"

Once the taboo topic had been broached, the road to conversation was all clear. No probing, no circumlocution, no circumvention. It was a direct, naked head-on collision.

"Who said I was out all night? It's still dark. The night isn't over yet," he said.

"There are still four hours before dawn. But how do you explain the four hours before that?" she pressed.

He pondered for a while, then said, "I'll take the Fifth."

They laughed in unison. There was no Fifth Amendment in Canada.

After getting out of the car, Yang Yang walked to the doorway. He stumbled over something soft and almost fell. He grabbed the door handle to steady himself. The thing rustled and slowly grew taller. It was a person. In the dim light of the streetlamp, Yang Yang looked at the unkempt face.

"My God! Susie! It's you," he cried.

Susie's frozen lips quivered for a long time before she finally uttered a sound. "I don't want . . . to go home . . . but I've . . . got nowhere else to go."

Something pierced Yang Yang's heart like a dagger, and he twitched in pain. He knew he couldn't pull it out. That would only make it hurt more.

He hugged Susie tightly. "Baby, I know."

He turned his face away so that Susie would not see his tears.

July 30, 1976
Dalian Port Hospital

The OR doctors and nurses had practically been living in the hospital in recent days. A steady stream of earthquake casualties had been transferred from Tangshan and Tianjin. Every bed in the surgical ward was full, and many temporary beds had been added in the corridor. Everyone from the chief doctor to the newest nurse wore a confused expression. Although Prepare for War and Famine was a slogan any of them could blurt out even in deep sleep, it was only when they were called to put it into practice that they realized emergency skills couldn't be built in a day.

"Awake! Awake!"

Unprompted, a young nurse who had just been put on shifts without supervision ran out of the ward and rushed into the duty room.

The three nurses on duty raised their heads and in one voice said, "Oh!" There was a hint of uncontrolled surprise in their voices. They did not need to ask. They all knew that the one who was awake was Wan Xiaoda in bed 11.

"Awake" and "dead" had been the most frequently addressed topics between them in recent days. These words were as common as *eat* or *sleep*, and no one was surprised to hear either one. The mysteries of life and death that took a lifetime to unravel in normal times were revealed in a single prod when there was a natural disaster.

This was nothing new. It took only one earthquake to push people from sensitive and fragile to numb and heartless. Before that event, they did not know their hearts could develop such rough, hard calluses. Yet, even now, there were a few tender spots even the calluses couldn't reach. Those patches of flesh were the deepest, innermost parts of the heart, and if they were inadvertently touched, the pain slammed straight through.

Wan Xiaoda had inadvertently touched such a spot.

When he arrived at the hospital, bandages covered the entire right half of his body, and they could not see the severity of his injuries. Throughout the tossing and turning along the journey, he had been in a deep, coma-like sleep. When the nurses lifted him from the ambulance, they all noticed his appearance. His skin was so fair and clear that not a single pore was noticeable. *Exquisite* was not even the word. His eyelashes were like fine-toothed combs. There were two shallow swirls at the corners of his mouth, as if he were forever smiling. His hair was slightly curly, and it piled into small circles on his sweaty forehead. In their extremely limited aesthetic vocabulary, of course, there were no such words as *Michelangelo* or *David*. They were just surprised that such a handsome girl could live in Tangshan—they all mistook him for a girl at first.

And then he opened his eyes briefly before falling back to sleep. It was the glimpse of his eyes that really surprised them. His eyes gave them the real view of his face. The light that shone in them was the kind that had known pain. A light that was broken, but more powerful than ever. They were not only surprised; they were amazed.

When they later removed the bandages, they found that his right arm had been pulverized from the shoulder down, leaving the bones of the elbow exposed. He had not been given any painkillers, as there were none to give amid the chaos, but he didn't cry at all. The nurses were the ones who cried. Even before the surgeon arrived, they knew that amputation would be the only option. They had seen beauty and they had seen defects, but placing such defects on such beauty was a cruelty they could not stand.

When they pushed him into the operating room, Xiaoda suddenly woke up, looking dazed and disoriented. The nurse stroked his sweaty hair and said, "Be good. Just sleep a little longer, and then you'll feel better when you wake up."

Xiaoda moved his mouth like a fish out of water and said something vaguely. The nurse leaned very close, but she could not hear it clearly. He seemed to be calling his mother and sister. The nurse quietly asked the others beside her how many members in his family had survived, but nobody knew. This was one of the most common questions the nurses asked when receiving the wounded, but when they asked after Xiaoda, it was different. They were asking how many had lived, instead of how many had died.

Xiaoda continued to have a high fever for two days after the amputation, during which he did not wake up. The doctors used various antibiotics, and ice was placed around the bed to bring down his body temperature, but it was no use. When the doctor came into the ward in the morning, he didn't say a word, and his face was dark with gloom. The nurses knew he feared there was no hope for the child.

To everyone's surprise, at noon that day, without any warning, Xiaoda woke up.

When he woke, Xiaoda saw sunlight blasting the room with white light, with countless gold and silver dust particles floating in the air. The room was full of people in white coats. They rushed in and out like the wind, but their voices were as thin as a mosquito's buzz. On the bed beside him, a lean old man was hitting the bed boards, shouting, "God! Oh God!" Xiaoda felt a little itch, like a thin line of ants winding along the palm of his hand and crawling all the way to his shoulder.

He couldn't help but scream.

Two white coats fell like clouds in front of the bed, and an expression of joyful surprise burst out on both faces, old and young.

"Son, you're awake. Does it hurt?"

"Itchy. My hand," Xiaoda said weakly.

The young nurse sat down, put his hand on her lap, and scratched it gently. Xiaoda felt that her thigh was like a pile of new cotton, and when his hand dropped, it was into endless softness.

Xiaoda held back for a while, but finally said timidly, "Miss, it's the . . . the other hand."

He did not understand why this simple request made the nurse burst into tears.

The older nurse sighed and told the younger nurse, "Go ahead. Wheel his mother in."

Xiaoda's mother, Li Yuanni, had been brought in with Xiaoda, though the staff didn't know at the time that they belonged together. She was now in the women's ward next door. Her leg had been injured. When the earthquake started, she had run out of the yard in time and suffered only minor injuries. She had later climbed into the remaining half of the house to find a mat. The mat had been dragged out of the house, but there was an aftershock, and a piece of concrete fell, breaking her thigh.

When the younger nurse ran into the ward, she found Yuanni lying straight in the hospital bed, white sheets pulled all the way up to her nose, leaving only her eyes exposed. But they were closed tightly, making it hard to tell if she was asleep or awake. The light flickered on her hair.

When the young nurse approached, she heard a faint rustling sound, like a well-fed silkworm crawling over a mulberry leaf or a sprout breaking through the soil after an early morning rain. She stood for a moment, then it dawned on her. What was growing was gray hair. The twenty-five-year-old woman's hair had turned gray overnight. The nurse called twice before Li Yuanni opened her eyes. At one glance, she noticed that the two eyes were like black holes, or rather, two bottomless, dead wells.

"Comrade Li, your son is awake, and his fever has subsided," the nurse said.

A breath of wind passed, stirring up a tiny ripple. The well was not completely dry.

The nurse pushed Yuanni to the ward next door. As soon as they met, one voice called, "Xiaoda," and the other, "Ma!" Both voices were a little hoarse.

After a long while, Xiaoda said, "Ma, my right arm is gone."

The dimples on both sides of his mouth leaped as he spoke, and a faint smile appeared on his face. At that moment, the nurse realized that every muscle in the boy's face was tied to those two dimples. If the muscles moved, the dimples moved. Aside from when he was completely still, he always seemed to be smiling.

The young nurse was on the verge of tears again. The old nurse gave her a stern look, then squatted and took Xiaoda's left hand. "Child, there are many people in the world who work with their left hands. When you go to school after you get out of the hospital, you can learn from scratch. You can start out writing with your left hand."

"Your father has always been left-handed. You can do it too," Yuanni said to her son.

She did not know that her husband was no longer alive. Comrade Wan had been staying overnight in a guesthouse when the earthquake came. The entire first floor had collapsed, and neither he nor the two people in the room with him had survived. It would take a few days for the bad news to reach the ears of his wife and son.

"Ma, you . . . lost . . . Xiaodeng."

Xiaoda looked straight at Yuanni as he carefully articulated each word. The words were like a needle puncturing an airbag that had just begun to inflate. Yuanni's whole body went soft.

"Your sister . . . I didn't even get to cover her." She burst into tears.

The older nurse sighed and said to the younger nurse, "Her daughter was already dead when they dug her out. She wanted to find a mat to cover the body, but when she crawled out of the house with the mat, it had already been carried away. She had no idea where it was taken."

Early Autumn 1976
A Military Station in Tangshan, Hebei

It was an unusually gloomy night. The sky was hanging so low that it seemed it could be poked through with a hand. The clouds were like old cotton balls soaked in water. Any random gust of wind could whip up a few drops of dirty rain.

There was rustling in the shack, sounds of paper, scissors, and fingers colliding. Several soldiers were teaching children how to make paper flowers. Some with sharp petals, others round. Of course, everything was white.

The instructions were relatively simple: *First, cut papers into small squares, then stack five squares together, fold them into a long strip, and tie it with a string in the middle. Then, cut both ends of the paper into round or sharp corners and separate them, layer by layer.*

The adults avoided each other's eyes. At a moment like this, any inadvertent eye contact could trigger an unintentional sigh. And even the most casual sigh could trigger an earth-shattering cry.

The children had been crying all day. The person they all thought would never die had died. The sun that never set had fallen forever.

When the earth shattered during the quake, even in the panic, there was a feeling that at least the sky was still there to shelter them overhead. The sky covered the earth, and no matter how broken it was, the earth was still the earth. But when the sky also fell, the earth was truly without hope. In the brief period of just over a month, the children had experienced the collapse of both the earth and the sky. They did not cry for their parents, because the adults had told them over and over that only soft bones shed tears. But now the adults themselves were crying, so naturally, it was impossible to persuade the children not to cry. The children's lives were like a song that had had an out-of-tune start. It was hard to tell if the right tune could ever be sung in the future. The adults didn't know, but they could not bear to make the children cry anymore, so they tried hard to hold back their own tears.

"Why are you using this hand, child?"

A soldier saw one child in the corner wielding the scissors with her left hand. The child lowered her head and kept her eyes close to the paper. Her bangs fell over her forehead, fluttering with each breath. The child held the scissors in an unfamiliar way, and the edges of the paper came out jagged and crooked. The soldier took the scissors from her left hand and put them into her right. He said, "Change it now, or it will become too hard to break the habit."

The child tried using her right hand to cut the paper. After a few cuts, the scissors clacked and fell to the ground.

"My arm is broken," the child said.

The soldier was taken aback. These children were orphans who had not yet been resettled. They had been taken in here for the time being, and they had all undergone physical examinations. The soldier had picked up a little medical knowledge over the last two months of rescue work. He straightened the child's arm now, swung it back and forth, left and right. The arm was firm and strong. His tone became more serious as he said, "Your arm is fine. From today, you're not allowed to use your left hand anymore."

The child picked up the scissors and went on cutting with her left hand. Not looking up at the soldier, she said softly, "You're not an X-ray. How do you know my arm's not broken?"

The children around her giggled, a sprout of joy instantly springing from the tearful ruins.

"Sir, she's crazy," a boy whispered into the soldier's ear.

The girl threw down the scissors, and they landed with a clang. She leaped up and flew out of the room. The soldier couldn't refrain from saying to the soldier beside him, "This child is so strange. So many people cried today, but she didn't."

The other soldier said, "Not only today. I've never seen her cry. The people at the medical station said she suffered a concussion and can't remember anything before the earthquake."

The first soldier said, "I heard from the political supervisor that a couple is coming to adopt a child. I think we'll give them that child. She can't remember the past, so it'll be easier for them to cultivate a relationship."

Among the soldiers, *that child* had become a sort of nickname for the girl. She had no name. Or, to be more precise, she could not remember her name, so everyone used the general name *that child* for the time being.

She had been discovered by one of the soldiers three days after the earthquake. She was curled up in a small ball, sleeping like a mouse under the seat of a military vehicle. No one knew where she had come from or how long she had been hiding under the seat. She was covered with a plastic sheet full of holes, and her hair was so matted that it looked like a bunch of twisted, muddy worms. There was a wound on one side of her forehead, not deep, but covering a large area. When the soldier took her out of the vehicle, hot urine leaked out all over his body. She was disoriented.

The soldier fed her half a can of fruit, and she sobered up a little. When he asked her name, she said nothing. He asked her parents' names. She still said nothing. When he asked her where she lived, she still said nothing, but she suddenly reached out with her left hand and clutched the right, shouting over and over, "My arm is broken!" She trembled in pain with each word, a trickle of sweat running down her muddy forehead. The soldier rushed her to the first aid station, but after a full checkup, the doctor found no broken bones.

"Amnesia combined with delusional victimization, a common disorder after a catastrophe," an experienced doctor said.

The doctor cleaned and bandaged the wound on her head and sent her to the quarters for foster children. A month later, because she could still not recall her own name or her family and no relatives showed up to claim her, she was assigned to a group of children waiting to be adopted or to be sent to the Yuhong School for Orphans.

That child was generally easygoing. She spoke very little and never acted up with the adults. The only thing was that when she looked at someone, her eyes were always fixed, as if she wanted to bore two holes through them. No one could stand such a gaze. Her silence was like a ribbon of police tape, the kind the children coming out of the quake had often seen around the piles of rubble. The tape itself held no deterring power. The true power lay in what it represented. As a result, though that child had no friends among the other children, she had no obvious enemies either, and no one dared to provoke her.

A few days later, a middle-aged couple came to see the child. The supervisor called her out and said that Uncle Wang and Aunt Dong wanted to talk to her. Both the man and the woman had a stooped appearance, as if still in shock from the quake. They wore factory uniforms of the same style and color. The garments had apparently come from a disaster relief warehouse, and the woman wore wide-rimmed glasses with one broken temple.

When the couple saw the girl, they were flustered. The man coughed, and the woman wiped her nose on her sleeve. Both ran their eyes over her, head to toe, several times. Their eyes couldn't speak yet somehow managed to say a lot. Their expressions were like silk cotton dipped in warm water, wiping the heavy layer of dirt from her. She felt refreshed and comfortable under their gaze.

After a long pause, the woman called tremblingly, "Baby." There were tears in her eyes.

When the man and woman left, the supervisor said to that child, "Uncle Wang and Aunt Dong have no children. They would like to take you to their house. Would you like to go?"

She actually couldn't remember what the couple looked like. All she could recall was a black mole in a vague shape on the woman's chin. It had bounced up and down as the woman's expression changed, making the face lively and endearing.

The girl nodded.

The next day, the child moved into the shack belonging to the Wang family and became their adopted daughter. The woman took her hand and asked, "You really don't remember your mother?"

That child looked steadily at the woman and said, "You're my mother."

The woman cried again, this time with joy.

The girl stood before the couple, motionless as she stared at the toes of her shoes. She let the woman cry, but she herself did not shed a tear. When the woman had finally finished blubbering, the girl raised her head and asked softly, "How long?"

The woman didn't understand. "How long for what?"

The girl's eyes moved from the woman's face to the man's, then back again. After a long while, she said carefully, "You two are taking me in. For how long?"

The man and woman both caught her meaning at the same time. They hugged her tightly, sobbing.

"For a lifetime. We'll be with you for our whole lives."

As they went through the adoption procedures, the Wang family discussed the girl's name in the most democratic way, including her as an equal partner in the talks. The options were Wang Xiaojue, Wang Xiaoling, Wang Xiaowei, Wang Xiaoyan, and Wang Xiaoya, each denoting a different positive quality. The woman was a schoolteacher, and the names she came up with were all gentle, elegant ones, combining a woman's greatest wish and a mother's highest hope. The child listened blankly, neither agreeing nor disagreeing. She thought for a while and then said, "Is Xiao . . . Xiaodeng okay?"

The woman asked, "Which character for 'Deng'? The one meaning climber?"

The child was momentarily stunned: this woman whom she had only met twice in her entire life had immediately guessed her birth name. Then she shook her head emphatically. "No! Not climber. Light—a little lamp."

The woman exclaimed, "A little lamp! Yes, that's it. You're the little lamp of our family."

And so the daughter was registered in the Wang family's household registration as Wang Xiaodeng.

February 17, 1977 (Chinese New Year's Eve)
A Simple Residential Area in Tangshan, Hebei

The lid of the pot over the open fire throbbed. There was not much in the pot, but it was at a loud boil—half-filled with cabbage and tofu soup. After ladling the soup and taking her seat, Dong Xinqin loosened the collar of her padded jacket and called, "It's time to eat!"

It was only when the cooking fire was lit that there was some meager heat in the room. Dong Xinqin had been fussing over this meal for some time, hoarding food for it starting months earlier, like a little mouse stocking her home. There were braised duck eggs, thin rice noodles stewed with mushrooms, fried bamboo shoots with golden needle mushrooms, and wood ear mushrooms with garlic moss—all plain dishes, but when laid out together, at least sufficient to fill half the table.

The most treasured dish was in the earthenware cooking pot, still covered, placed at the center of the table. When the lid was removed, a scent strong enough to knock a person from their seat burst out. In the middle of the earthenware pot was a pork knuckle as big as a man's palm, a Spring Festival gift from the workplace to ring in the New Year. Dong Xinqin had spent the whole afternoon—and several charcoal briquettes—cooking the knuckle. Once the knuckle was finally stewed to a pulp, the soy sauce seeped into the meat, turning the outer layer shiny red, like a layer of wax.

Xinqin ripped open the knuckle with her chopsticks, picked up a large piece, and placed it in Xiaodeng's bowl. She then picked up a slightly smaller piece and placed it in her husband Wang Deqing's bowl. Finally, she picked up a piece of bone and began gnawing on that herself. Oily juice dripped down her fingers. Reluctant to waste it, she licked each finger in turn.

Deqing picked up the meat in his bowl and tossed it into Xiaodeng's. "Pa likes to eat cabbage and tofu," he said.

Xinqin glanced at her husband, but said nothing.

On this evening, all the neighbors were having more or less the same meal, but it did not taste quite the same as the one in the Wang household. A disaster had ripped a bloody tear through those families, leaving a gaping hole in their family photos. As the neighbors ate this meal together, they were thinking of those who were now gone. At the Wang table, there was no decrease in the number of people, but an increase. The Wangs' family photo was just right—perfect. But the blessed addition in their perfect family portrait was actually another family's missing treasure. The thought startled Xinqin, making her feel a little guilty. But the secret joy in her heart was unimpeded and unstoppable, and it was more than she could stand. Looking at Xiaodeng's oily lips, Xinqin felt herself bursting with happiness. She couldn't hold it in. It bubbled over from her, dripping onto the table and streaming onto the ground.

"Will Miss Sun still teach Chinese next term?" Xinqin asked Xiaodeng.

Miss Sun was a new teacher at the school. She had come in after the previous teacher, the older Mrs. Sun, had been killed in the earthquake, and she was promptly put in charge of the first grade. It was a makeshift school, just a couple of wooden shacks. It had only been a few months since the earthquake, and everything was still a work in progress, but at least the children had gone back to school.

Xiaodeng nodded.

"Is she a good teacher?"

"She's fine," said Xiaodeng.

"I noticed she stutters a little."

"Yes, a little."

Xinqin stared at Xiaodeng, her eyes wide, like two open barrels eager to catch every word that dropped from the girl. But Xiaodeng's mouth was like a river with a tall dam, beyond which no one could glimpse the water.

Xinqin turned her eyes to her husband.

"Deqing, Miss Sun said that Xiaodeng is very talented and might become a writer one day."

"A writer? You mean you still don't understand how the world works? Misfortune comes from the pen. It's safer to rely on numbers, like me. Be an accountant when you grow up, Deng. What do you think?"

Deqing nudged Xiaodeng for a response. The girl's head moved slightly, but he couldn't tell whether she was nodding or shaking it.

"The little mouse sees no farther than his nose." Xinqin gave her husband a sideways glance. "Now that there's a different set of people in power, policies are sure to change drastically. And being a writer isn't something just anyone can do. It takes talent. Miss Sun said our little Deng has literary talent, and we should cultivate it."

Deqing snorted and said, "This Miss Sun has only been teaching Deng for a few days, right? Our daughter doesn't even know enough characters to fill up half a page. Who can say whether she could be a writer?"

"She's wise beyond her years. Miss Sun told me she gave the children a picture in class and asked them to tell a story from it. The others talk about how the child in the picture is helping the old man push the trolley and how grateful the old man is. But our Deng starts out with 'In the morning, the reddish-orange sun rose in the east.' Miss Sun was shocked. She said that at this age, very few children will know to first describe the scene. No one taught her to do that."

Deqing asked, "Deng, did the picture have color? How did you come up with 'reddish-orange'?"

Xiaodeng said, "Don't you remember all the colors in your mind? If you just close your eyes, all the colors come out."

Xinqin grabbed her husband's sleeve. "That's called imagination. Don't you see?"

Deqing laughed and said, "I don't get it, but as long as Deng gets it, that's fine."

Xinqin shook her head and said, "Forget it. I don't want to talk to you about it. It's like playing a symphony for a cow."

Before she finished speaking, they heard a loud bang outside the house. After a brief silence, someone shouted, "Earthquake!" The voice, bent by fear, was like an iron hook that poked into everyone's heart. After the catastrophe, the survivors' hearts were too frail to take such stabs. They scattered at once. In an instant, the streets were filled with the sound of footsteps.

Deqing slammed down his chopsticks, grabbed Xiaodeng with one hand and Xinqin with the other, and flew out of the house. They ran too fast, and Xiaodeng stumbled in the doorway. With a yelp, she dropped to the floor like a sack of rice. Deqing couldn't move her. He called his wife over, and with one of them holding her feet and the other holding her hands, they finally dragged her into the street.

In the open space between the makeshift houses, a group of people had gathered, forming a dark mass. Frightened dogs burrowed through the crowd, a tentative, quivering whimper in the air soon snowballing into a sustained storm of ear-piercing barks. The night wind bit through the heat left from the stoves, and everyone put their hands into the sleeves of their padded jackets, jumping up and down to keep warm.

One old man could not stand any longer. He shouted, "Oh my God," and slumped to the ground. "Never mind if the earthquake kills me. At least then I won't have to worry about it every day. I'm tired of living. I can't go on like this!" The cry was like an infectious disease spreading through the crowd. It wasn't long before the crowd was filled with the sounds of people blowing their noses.

A man suddenly called out, "Which of you little fucks set off a firecracker? Can't we even enjoy a New Year's Eve meal in peace? Next person I catch doing that is going to jail. It's counterrevolutionary!"

The crowd slowly dispersed.

When they returned to the house, they found that Xiaodeng had a bump the size of an apricot on her forehead. Xinqin put a hot towel over it. She could not help but sigh and say, "When will people stop crying wolf?"

Deqing put the now-cold food into the pot and reheated it. He shook his head and sighed. "Next time we hear someone cry wolf, we won't leave our little nest. If it really is an earthquake, the sky will fall and the earth will collapse whether we're in the house or outside. Isn't it the same? And it will be fine, as long as we all die together, won't it?"

Xinqin snorted and said, "What a thing to say on New Year's Eve."

The three of them sat down to eat again, but they had lost their enthusiasm. After hastily finishing their meal, when the dishes had been cleared from the table, Xinqin poured a pot of hot water and told Xiaodeng to take off her shoes and wash her feet.

Xiaodeng wore the cotton-padded shoes she had brought back from the military garrison. They were brand new, and only two sizes too big. She wore two pairs of thick socks, and a piece of cloth was tucked into the front to make the shoes fit. She sat on the stool and tried in vain to remove her socks. Bands of dense frostbite had formed on her toes and ankles, and when the room had warmed up a little, the frostbitten skin had developed blisters, which broke with one tap, forming scabs and sticking to the socks. When she finally got the socks off, they were stained with blood.

Xinqin pulled Xiaodeng's feet into her lap and started to clean the blood off with iodine. Xiaodeng frowned and hissed, pushing Xinqin to the verge of tears.

"I don't know when the residential block will be built. The walls of this house are like paper. Never mind us adults, but how can the children survive the winter like this?"

Deqing lit a cigarette and squatted on the ground, smoking it slowly. The smoke slithered in the air like a snake, slinking upward before it hit the ceiling and died.

"Mama," he said, "why don't I agree to the transfer to Shijiazhuang? At least there are normal heating facilities there. Our Deng can go to school there; they have better teachers. My director asked me what I thought about the idea, but I didn't say anything; I was afraid you wouldn't be able to find a suitable work unit."

Xinqin looked at Xiaodeng. The girl did not say anything, but she felt the feet twitch a little as she held them.

"There is a shortage of English teachers everywhere. If we go, we'll find a way. There will always be a place for me," Xinqin said.

The fire gradually dimmed, but it was not yet time to add a new briquette when Xiaodeng woke up. She was covered with the thickest quilt in the house, and her own padded jacket and trousers were piled on top of the quilt. Still, she was so small; she was no match for the long winter nights in Tangshan. The cold was like a thin, little worm, but it had thousands of mouths, biting all over her body, face, hands, feet, and even ears and eyes. She could feel the pain, but couldn't see it or catch it. She was just cold.

She didn't dare turn over. She had been lying in this position for a long while, and the bed was finally moved by her dogged patience, grudgingly yielding a shred of warmth that she did not want to lose.

But the pillow was a little too high, and her neck was a bit stiff. She knew it was because of the two—oh, no, *three*—things pressed beneath her pillow. They had been placed there by Dong Xinqin before she had gone to bed.

"When you get up tomorrow, put these on," she told Xiaodeng.

It was a purplish-red padded jacket and a pair of black corduroy trousers, all brand new. Xinqin had used all the fabric coupons she had at home for this outfit. In the pocket of the corduroy trousers, there was a small envelope made of red paper, which contained lucky money. Xiaodeng secretly squeezed the envelope. It was a folded note, maybe one yuan, maybe two, or maybe five. The answer would not be revealed until dawn.

Suddenly, she heard a rustling in the corner of the room. Night turned her into a hound, with ears so sharp and alert that every little sound became thunder. At first, she thought it was a mouse, and every hair on her body stood on end. She had carried her fear of mice with her from her mother's womb. Someone told her that when her mother was pregnant, she had watched a puppet show in which two mice fought, and the baby had been frightened by it.

How come she suddenly thought of *her*? Xiaodeng shook her head involuntarily, trying to shake off the memory. Some memories deserved to be buried.

She listened carefully and realized that the sound came from the space behind the curtain, from her adoptive parents' bed. They only had one room, so they all slept and ate in one place. At night, a curtain was drawn down the middle of the room to separate her bed from theirs.

Whoo whoo. Her adoptive mother was panting. Xiaodeng had never heard this sort of panting, as if the weight of a mountain were pressed against her body. The squeak of the bed was unruly. Her adoptive mother was turning over, as if trying to shake off a weight.

"It's been a long day. Rest," she heard her mother say. The voice seemed pressed as well. It was very low, very flat—so flat it almost held a faint trace of resentment.

A reluctant sigh came from the darkness. It came from a man.

"It's New Year's Eve, and you still won't give it. You always say you're tired."

After a moment's silence, the bed started to make noise again. This time it was not unruly, but it had a distinct rhythm to it: squeak, squeak, squeak. Xiaodeng's ears suddenly grew eyes, and she could picture her mother's body being rolled over and over and squeezed into a pancake, or rather, a puddle of paste. She could hear a broken moan.

Xiaodeng curled her fists tightly. She felt a sharp pain, her fingernails digging into the palms.

After a long while, the bed finally quieted down, and there were two currents of breath in the air, one thick and one thin. Gradually, the thin one was completely covered by the thick one, which turned into a snore as loud as rolling thunder, shaking the house with its unintended power.

"Deqing! Deqing!" She heard her mother push her father.

"Huh?" The snoring paused momentarily, and the man responded in half sleep.

"Why do you think . . . she's never close to us?"

"Um . . ." The man was drifting away, too drowsy to talk. The snoring started again, as loud as ever.

"Hopefully it will all be fine, after some more time. Some people just need more time to warm up."

The woman got out of bed, muttering to herself and fumbling as she poked in the stove. There was a sound of the iron tongs slamming together—the woman adding a briquette to the fire.

The fire hissed, and there was soon a hint of warmth in the room. Xiaodeng finally turned over and started a new round of negotiations with the bed. Her body warmed and loosened a little. Gradually, the bed changed its size and shape, becoming a mat—a shiny bamboo mat stained with sweat from different people.

She noticed an extra person on the end of the bed at some point. She kicked him, and he kicked her, each gently testing the other. But with just a light touch, she knew: she knew the foot. She raised her body to look at the face, but the wall of darkness in the room was too thick for her eyes to penetrate.

She stretched out her foot, and he stretched out his. Their feet met midair, sole to sole. There was a tight seam binding every inch, toe to heel. The foot was exactly like hers, a mirror image. Her foot pushed gently, and he pushed back, and they continued to spar in midair for a while. Later, when she was tired, he was tired too. In unison, they both put their feet down, still keeping their soles together.

With a sudden bang, the roof was lifted, and she saw the sky. She had never seen such brightness, like ten thousand suns and moons put together. Before she could even blink, the sky cracked like a porcelain bowl that had fallen to the ground. Through the crack in the sky, she saw another layer of sky, still bright. This sky didn't hold up either. It also cracked like a porcelain bowl. The sky cracked layer by layer, and the earth receded from the sky. She panicked, searching all over the bed for the foot. But it was gone, and her body floated in the air like a kite. She stretched out her hand, trying to grab something, anything, but up, down, left, right—there was nothing she could hold on to.

"Xiao . . . Xiaoda!"

Xiaodeng sat up. Her heart raced like a galloping horse.

Xinqin pulled on a padded jacket and ran over. She hugged Xiaodeng tightly.

"Deng, what are you dreaming about? Good heavens, look at the cold sweat!"

She took off her padded jacket and wrapped Xiaodeng in a tight embrace. As soon as Xiaodeng's face touched the chest, she knew it was not her own mother's breast. It had never been filled with milk. It was like two balls of unleavened dough, flat, dry, and unyielding. Xiaodeng's head rested on the bony chest, and her whole body trembled uncontrollably.

"My head . . . My head hurts," she murmured.

February 14, 2006
Toronto, St. Michael's Hospital

When Wang Xiaodeng walked into Dr. Wilson's clinic, the secretary, Casey, was engrossed in reading a women's home lifestyle magazine. Casey was so intrigued by a recipe for strawberry cake that she didn't even hear the sound of the office door. After a while, she noticed from the corner of her eye the faint sweep of a blur of red clouds. When she raised her eyes, she saw Xiaodeng.

Xiaodeng wore a black woolen coat with a pink scarf around her neck; a portion of a long, bright pink dress was visible below her coat.

The edge of the dress quivered with each step, recalling a cluster of brilliant peach blossoms.

"Buddha Must Be Packaged in Gold." Casey suddenly recalled the title of a chapter in Xiaodeng's book *Dream of Shenzhou*.

"The bus was late . . . The roads are slippery . . . There's a traffic jam . . ." Xiaodeng's voice was weak, and Casey had to stretch her ears to catch these few words.

"Dr. Wilson has to go to Montreal for a meeting. You have forty-five minutes left before he leaves for his five-thirty flight."

Xiaodeng pushed open the door to the consultation room, and at first glance, she spotted a bouquet of roses on Dr. Wilson's desk. The roses were white and their petals tightly wrapped. They looked like they were still a long way from blooming. They had apparently just been delivered—the plastic wrapper had not even been removed yet. There were layers of transparent plastic, dotted with pink stars.

"Birthday?" Xiaodeng asked.

"Didn't you get flowers? Everyone in the city should have some today."

It was only then that Xiaodeng remembered it was Valentine's Day. She smiled faintly and said, "Dr. Wilson, I must be the only exception in the whole city, then. If I weren't, would I travel across the city to see you?"

Dr. Wilson laughed. "Just call me Henry. Actually, though, you don't need to wait for someone to give you flowers. It would be as nice if you gave them to someone else."

"What about you, Henry? Are these flowers your gift for someone, or did someone give them to you?"

Strong woman—at least, her tongue is, Dr. Wilson thought.

"How did you sleep last week?"

Xiaodeng sat down, took a stack of papers from her purse, and handed it to Dr. Wilson. "This is what you asked me to record."

February 7—Slept for 2 hours and 45 minutes, 30 minutes
during the day, and two or three segments at
night, between 2:00 and 6:00, lots of dreams

February 8—Slept for 3 hours, after 1:00 at night, intermittent and lots of dreams

February 9—Slept for 3 hours, one hour during the day
and two at night, between 4:00 and 6:00, fully
asleep, some dreams

February 10—Slept 3 hours, at night, after 1:00, in two or
three segments, some dreams, but not many

February 11—Slept 5 hours!!! One hour during the day and
from about 11:00 to 3:00 at night, uninter-
rupted, some dreams, earliest and best sleep
since taking the new medicine

February 12—Slept 4 hours, all at night, after 12:30, some
interruptions, few dreams

February 13—Slept 5 hours again, all at night, some interruptions, lots of dreams

Placebo starting to take effect, Dr. Wilson wrote in his notebook.
"Tell me about your dreams. What were they about?"

"I can't remember exactly. It seems there are still those windows,
one after the other, so many. In fact, it's not exactly a dream. Sometimes
I can see it when I just close my eyes."

"What color are the windows?"

"All gray and covered with dirt, a dust like lint."

"The last window, did you push it open?"

"I can't. I can't open it." Small beads of sweat appeared on her forehead.

"Think. Why can't you open it? Is it too heavy? Is there not enough time?"

Xiaodeng thought for a few moments, then said hesitantly, "It seems to be rusted."

Dr. Wilson tapped the table in excitement. "Great! That's great, Xiaodeng. When you next see these windows, I want you to remove the rust. Remind yourself over and over to do so, every time."

Xiaodeng nodded. Dr. Wilson looked at the chart to revisit their last conversation, and then asked, "Have you cried?"

Xiaodeng shook her head sheepishly, her expression that of a child who had done something wrong.

"I tried, though. I really tried. I thought I would cry today, but I didn't."

"What happened today?"

Xiaodeng did not say anything, but she pulled at the tassel of her scarf over and over until her hand was full of pink thread ends.

"Henry, is there a disease that blocks the tear ducts? I very much want to cry, but I can't squeeze out the tears. It's like a water pipe, a pipe blocked at the faucet."

"Are you sure the blockage is at the faucet, not at the source? Emotions go way back and gather as we grow. If we find a way to open that last window, it might open the way for tears to come."

"I'm still so far away." Xiaodeng sighed faintly. "Today, I . . . moved out. We just finished signing the separation papers at the lawyer's office."

"Why did you choose to do it on Valentine's Day?"

"We didn't remember that today was Valentine's Day. We haven't celebrated this day in years."

"Separating on Valentine's Day. Ironic." Dr. Wilson tapped the desk lightly with his pen. "What about your daughter?"

"She'll live with him for the time being. We'll talk about it again when I'm better."

"Was it you or him who suggested separating?"

"I brought it up, because I knew his heart was no longer here. He has a colleague who's always admired him."

"And him? Does he like her too?"

"I don't know. He never mentioned her before."

"Then how do you know his heart is with her?"

"Because silence is itself an answer."

"So you want to get ahead of him, end it before he can. That makes you feel in control. You've always been the one in control, haven't you?"

Xiaodeng was taken aback.

"Henry, there's nothing in this world that you can hold on to forever. You may think you have something, but it slips through your fingers before it even grows warm in your hand."

"But why must you hold on to it? Perhaps holding on isn't the wisest thing to do."

"No matter what you do, it's no use. There's nothing in this world you can keep."

"Maybe not romance. But what about friendship? Or family?"

"No, Henry, none of it. Not even friendship or family."

"Then why did you dress so beautifully today? To go to the lawyer's office? Or is it that, subconsciously, you still want to hold on to him?"

Xiaodeng was taken aback once again. She paused for a long moment before she finally stammered, "I just wanted him to . . . to remember me looking my best."

"Well, Xiaodeng, can we pursue this topic today? Let's talk about your marriage."

Late Summer 1988 to Autumn 1989
Shanghai, Fudan University

When Susie was still at the age where she always wanted to cling to her mother, following her everywhere, Xiaodeng talked about what had happened on August 29, 1988. Xiaodeng told her about her experience that day many times, and each time she shared, there were little changes to the details. The memories were like a piece of worm-riddled wood, the years brushing over them, filling the holes with plaster and paint. Over time, it had gradually become unclear what was wood and what was filling. Fortunately, Susie didn't care about the details. She just asked over and over, "Ma, if you hadn't met Pa that day, who would have been my parents?"

Xiaodeng had no answer to this philosophical question. All she knew was that day was picked by a divine hand; it made Susie's birth possible and set the trajectory of Xiaodeng's life, even if she didn't know it at the time.

In the summer of 1988, she passed the college entrance exam, earning the second highest score on the foreign language test in all of Hebei. She left home for Shanghai on August 29.

Before that trip, she had always believed she was quite familiar with Shanghai. Her mother, Dong Xinqin, had died of cancer six years earlier. Xinqin had studied in Shanghai for six months. For a long time after she came back, all she could talk about was Shanghai: Shanghai food, Shanghai fashion, Shanghai's garden residences, Shanghai men, and Shanghai women. The vague outline of Shanghai left in Xiaodeng's imagination was trimmed and corrected by Xinqin's repeated narrations, gradually becoming clearer and more accurate. But six years later, when Xiaodeng got on the southbound train and actually headed for Shanghai, she was suddenly aware that all of her knowledge about Shanghai was picked up from her adoptive mother. None of it was actually her own.

The train gradually moved deeper into the South, and the color of the soil and vegetation grew richer and there was an unfamiliar accent in the calls from the snack vendors at each stop. Xiaodeng's once very clear image of Shanghai collapsed brick by brick, becoming more blurred, less complete. When she disembarked from the train with her big suitcase and set foot on an asphalt road softened by the sun, she finally realized that she knew absolutely nothing about this city.

On that strange street, surrounded by strange people speaking a strange dialect, she soon got lost and was like an insect that had fallen into a spider's web, foolishly searching for a way out. After the seemingly endless process of finding her bus and then changing buses along the way, when she finally found Fudan University, it was nearly evening. The exhaustion from the journey had diluted her excitement as she stood face to face with this renowned institution. She desperately needed a toilet, having held it through most of her journey across the city. When she put down her luggage in front of the reception desk for freshmen in the Department of Foreign Languages and Literature, her face had turned red with the effort. Squeezing her knees together, she asked brazenly, "A restroom, the nearest?"

The staff member who received her had had a long day and looked tired. His green T-shirt with the words *Fudan University* was covered with patches of sweat, as if he were wearing a map. He didn't answer her, just checked her documents and admission notice and asked her to fill in a form. He then said to the person beside him, "Dayang, take her to building 9, room 106."

Dayang picked up her luggage and led her down a path. The man was extremely tall and strong, and her large suitcase rested on his shoulder as lightly as a straw basket. When the man had taken just a few steps, he was already far ahead of her, and she could barely see his head as she trotted along behind. His head floated above the noisy crowd, a strand of upturned hair bouncing in sync with his steps. His shirt was dirty, covered with dust and streaks of mud, probably from carrying luggage. Xiaodeng guessed he was a worker at the school.

The man walked for a while, then suddenly stopped and stood the suitcase on the ground, sat on top of it, and waited for Xiaodeng. She caught up with him, but he continued to sit, pointing with his chin toward a small building beside him. "Third door on the left, any floor."

Not quite understanding, Xiaodeng hesitated. He said, "The restroom. Hurry up."

Xiaodeng quickly ran to the toilet, squatted, and released the longest, most satisfying stream of urine in her entire life. She felt the heat of the day rush out with the stream, making her whole body suddenly feel cool. When she returned to the path, there was a lightness in her steps as if she had acquired wings, despite a slight lingering discomfort from her overstretched bladder. It was only then that she began to pay attention to the scenery around her. She saw a green lawn in front of her and a marble statue at the center of the lawn. When they were halfway down the path they had started on, they circled behind the statue. Even though she couldn't see the face, she knew it was Chairman Mao. The lawn, the statue's hand raised high above its head, and the clouds above it mingling with the twilight were all familiar to her.

She had kept a set of pictures of the Fudan campus since she started middle school. Over the years, she had savored and caressed the scenery in those pictures countless times, to the point that, even with her eyes closed, she could recreate every edge and corner, every hue of the scene. Now that she actually stood in the scene herself, she felt that the statue, the lawn, and the clouds were all smaller than she had imagined. On that late summer evening, as the Jiangnan breeze caressed her cheek with an unfamiliar tenderness, Xiaodeng suddenly understood the concept of aesthetic distance.

She began to notice the crowds coming and going on campus. Those who rode bicycles were returning students, while those who walked with their luggage were new students who had come to report.

Of course, most of the new students did not carry their own luggage. The adults behind them, backs hunched under their loads, were most likely parents who had come to escort them. Xiaodeng's own father had repeatedly offered to accompany her to Shanghai, and he had even bought a train ticket, but she had firmly refused.

"Is my suitcase heavy? I brought a lot of dictionaries with me." Xiaodeng felt a little uneasy when she saw the beads of sweat dangling from the man's eyebrows.

"Look at you. Anything would be heavy for someone like you." The fellow had to lean over to talk to her. She had been tall in elementary school and had always had to sit in the back. By middle school, her growth had slowed, and she was moved to the third row. In high school, she had just about stopped growing. In recent years, her clothes had always worn out, instead of her outgrowing them.

"You're from Shijiazhuang," the man said. "Why didn't you go to Peking University? It's nearer. Even Nankai is closer than Shanghai."

"My mother liked Shanghai. My uncle from when I was young was a soldier stationed in Shanghai, and when he came home, he always said Shanghai was good too. I've always wanted to come to Shanghai."

"What do you mean by 'my uncle from when I was young'? Isn't he still your uncle?"

The man was just making an offhand joke, but Xiaodeng's face tightened. It was then that he started to suspect, though vaguely, that this woman might be temperamental.

After a long moment, Xiaodeng exhaled heavily and said, "Actually, I just want to get away from home."

The man laughed. "That's a given. At your age, who doesn't?"

They soon arrived at the dorm. It was still hot, and they glimpsed a few thinly clad girls walking around in the corridor, making it improper for Dayang to enter the building. He put Xiaodeng's luggage down at the entrance. "Try to find a lower bunk near a window, if they aren't all taken," he instructed.

Xiaodeng hurried in, forgetting to thank Dayang. She turned back and ran out again. He was still waiting at the entrance. He took a stack of meal vouchers from his pocket and told her to put her luggage away and hurry to the cafeteria before it closed, which it soon would.

Xiaodeng said, "How will I pay you back?"

Dayang wrote his name and building and room numbers on the back of a voucher and left. It was only then that Xiaodeng realized that Dayang was a nickname. His real name was Yang Yang.

Xiaodeng entered the dorm and found that she was assigned to a room with eight bunks. Three of the four beds by the window had been claimed, leaving only one upper bunk vacant. She pulled out a stool, stepped on it, and lifted her luggage to the empty upper bunk, then climbed after it and sat down. The room was very quiet. The girls who had reported before her must have gone to the cafeteria to eat.

Xiaodeng's nerves had been tight all day, but she finally relaxed now. Kicking off her shoes with a thud, she splayed her toes like flowers blossoming in the thickening twilight.

"Finally," Xiaodeng muttered to herself, "a new start."

After dinner that evening, Xiaodeng took her newly purchased meal vouchers and went to look for Yang Yang at the address he had given her. The building in which he lived was deep inside the campus, and he stayed on the fourth floor. The door was unlocked. Xiaodeng pushed it open. A man stood up and said, "What's the rush?"

It took her a moment to recognize Yang Yang. He had showered and washed his hair, and he now wore a red T-shirt and blue jeans. His partially wet hair was fluffy. He looked clean and tidy now, young, and even a little handsome, surprising Xiaodeng.

"Your . . . place is spacious." Xiaodeng noticed that there were only two beds in the room, and they were not bunks.

"Graduate students have bigger rooms," Yang Yang said. "And the ones in the Chinese department have to take turns rooming with the foreign students—cultural immersion, supposedly—so our rooms are even more spacious."

Xiaodeng was taken aback again, the surprise written all over her innocent face. "You're . . . a graduate student?"

Yang Yang laughed. "Did you think I was a porter? A teacher from your department just roped me in to help for a while."

Xiaodeng's face grew warm. In the half light, her cheeks were like two pieces of rice paper, ready to break with a single gentle tap, her blush flowing across them like a disorderly ink pattern soaking in. In a daze, Yang Yang looked at her, thinking, *Another year in Shanghai and her skin will thicken up.*

The pair sat across from each other, saying nothing. The door was open, and people kept coming in and out, looking for Yang Yang. Restless, Xiaodeng stood and picked up a book from Yang Yang's bookshelf. It was *Stones of the Wall,* a book that had stirred up heated discussion nationwide a few years earlier.

"I've been looking for this book for a long time, but I can't find it anywhere. They say it's banned. If you'll loan it to me, I'll return it soon," Xiaodeng muttered.

Even though she had no experience with love at all, she knew that borrowing a book was probably the only way to be sure she would see Yang Yang again.

Yang Yang walked her to the door to the corridor. With a casual wave, he said, "Okay, girl, work hard, and don't play too much." Then, he went back to his room.

The summer heat that had oppressed her all day had dissipated, and the early night breeze brought the first trace of autumn coolness. The streetlights pulled Xiaodeng's figure, making it extremely thin and long among the shadows cast on the path. She clasped her arms, as if cold, and stepped on her own shadow with each stride as she walked through the still unfamiliar campus. The word *girl* lay nicely in her heart, with a slight warmth. *Yang Yang. Yang Yang. Yang Yang.* She said his name silently all the way back. She felt that she had located a coordinate in this huge, strange city, and she at least had a bearing.

Xiaodeng later learned that Yang Yang was a writer of some renown. As an undergraduate, he had published several stories in the best literary journal in the country. Yang Yang didn't mention it himself, and she didn't ask him about it. She just borrowed his stories through various channels and read them in bed at night, by flashlight, after the lights were out. She read his stories over and over, and with each reading, she felt herself draw a step closer to him. Yang Yang was a second-year graduate student during that turbulent period, and she was only in her first year of undergraduate studies. The distance between them was not simply about the difference between their levels of studies, but of experience, exposure, and things of that sort. But she believed she would eventually catch up with him.

Xiaodeng went to his dorm from time to time to visit him. He was usually happy when he saw her, and he let her keep using the excuse of borrowing and returning books, even when it had been stretched to the extreme. He never used her name when talking to her, calling her things like "girly girl" instead as they made small talk. At first, she liked it, but she eventually grew tired of it, feeling that she had no chance if he always treated her like a child. *Yang Yang, one of these days, I'm going to make you look at me through different eyes,* she thought as she clenched her fist.

One night, Yang Yang appeared at her dorm, looking for her. All of her roommates were studying in one of the classrooms, and Xiaodeng had the room to herself. She had changed into a casual set of clothes—practically pajamas—pulled her hair back, and put on slippers. She was not prepared to see Yang Yang. Her face flushed. It was the first time he had been to her dorm.

Yang Yang picked up a notebook from the table and flipped through it randomly. He said, "I have a friend from my hometown who lives upstairs from you. I thought I'd stop by here on my way to see her, just to make sure you're studying hard, girl."

Xiaodeng was about to snatch the notebook from him, but it was too late. He raised it and asked casually, "What kind of account is this? You note each *fen* in such detail."

Xiaodeng lowered her head, and her face turned a darker shade of crimson. After a moment, she said, "It's the money my father sends me. I'm going to pay him back every fen one day."

Yang Yang couldn't help but laugh. "It's your pa, not some stranger. You still have to be so careful?"

Xiaodeng raised her head, the color gradually fading from her face. Her eyes were fixed, looking right through Yang Yang and through the wall before landing on some unknown spot.

"He's not my father. My father died a long time ago. Have you heard of the Tangshan earthquake?"

Yang Yang was shocked. "What about your ma?"

Xiaodeng paused for a while before answering. "All dead. My whole family. I'm an orphan. I was seven years old. Ruins—have you ever seen such ruins? All the landmarks were gone, and people just crawled on top of them, like ants crawling in a large open space. I fell on top of someone and couldn't move my legs. At one point, I thought a rope had caught me, but when I looked, it was the guts spilling out of someone's belly. I pulled them off, then crawled on. I didn't care where I crawled to—anywhere was fine, as long as I crawled away."

Yang Yang felt like a rough wooden stick was slowly being driven through his heart. A dull pain rose with his breath and jammed in his throat. He coughed a few times, but he could neither swallow nor spit out the pain. His voice went hoarse.

He walked over and pulled Xiaodeng into his arms and held her tightly. He stroked her messy hair again and again.

"Xiaodeng, I always thought you were a fledgling that had never flown through the forest," he said, voice quivering. It was the first time since they met that he had called her anything but "girl."

"Not every bird needs to fly to understand the forest."

It was many years later before Yang Yang really understood what Xiaodeng meant. For now, he was only moved by her literary talent.

October 1, 1992
Shanghai

Yang Yang and Xiaodeng rode their bicycles, squeezing and weaving through the bustling crowd, wearing terry cloth sweatshirts, jeans, and sneakers and carrying travel bags on their backs. Mingling with the chaotic colors and sounds of the street, they looked like two young people taking advantage of the National Day holiday to relax. No one would have guessed that they were getting married that day.

Yang Yang had stayed on to teach at the university after completing his graduate studies, while Xiaodeng worked as an editor and English translator in a publishing house since finishing her undergraduate degree. Xiaodeng had started preparing for their wedding, not wasting a single day after her studies were done. Actually, the word *preparing* was an exaggeration, because they did not do much beyond carrying their two quilts and putting them onto one bed. Yang Yang had just been assigned a new, smaller dorm room at the school, and Xiaodeng's things had been moved there little by little.

Yang Yang had only seen this sort of simple wedding, which was almost like playing house, in books and movies from the 1950s. It had not been his intention. His plans had included a trip to their hometowns to visit her father and his parents, and a small banquet when they came back, to which they would invite a few close friends and classmates. He had been working for more than two years and had a small nest egg to pay for such a trip. He even gave the money to Xiaodeng for safekeeping, but once the money was put into her hands, it gradually disappeared. One day, he stumbled across a notice of remittance to Shijiazhuang in her wallet, and he understood where the money had gone.

He didn't hide his displeasure well. "You could have taken your time to repay him. Why do you want to take away from your own wedding?"

"I didn't want to wait a single day. I want to settle accounts with him as quickly as possible. I don't want to owe him anything."

"You can pay the money you owe, but what about the love he's due? He's your father. He raised you after all."

"I'm only indebted to my mother. She raised me."

"What are you talking about? Without your father, your mother couldn't have raised you all on her own, even if she wanted to. You didn't even let him know you're getting married. That's a bit heartless."

Xiaodeng's face flushed dark with rage. She stared at him, saying with a sneer, "It's the money, isn't it? I'll pay you back in the future. Or you can change your mind, if you don't want to get married."

He could not say anything else by this time. When she saw that he had backed off, she also backed down. After a moment she stammered a half apology and suggested they go see his parents on New Year's Day.

With that, the hurdle was passed.

As they rode their bikes that day, Yang Yang, on a whim, suddenly put his feet to the ground and said, "Deng, let's go to Wang Kai to have photos taken. It will be a memento." Wang Kai was the best-known, most expensive portrait studio in Shanghai.

Xiaodeng looked at herself and said, "Like this?"

Yang Yang said, "Yes, like this. Let's do it now when we are still pure, clean streams. Tomorrow, we will have already passed into the sea."

Xiaodeng pouted. "Don't be silly. A stream? The sea? You're barely even a mud puddle."

So they changed course, worming their way through the holiday crowds to Wang Kai's photo studio.

When they entered the studio, the photographer asked what the photo was for. Graduation? Work ID?

Yang Yang looked at Xiaodeng and said, "It's a fool taking a wife."

The photographer snorted and swallowed his surprise. He had never seen a bride and groom dressed so casually. The couple were contorted into various poses by the photographer until they displayed a reasonable proximation of love and harmony. The light flashed, and their smiles were instantly frozen forever. Many years later, on various occasions, when Yang Yang and Xiaodeng came across this photo of them grinning broadly, they always agreed that it was the simplest, happiest day in their lives.

After they had taken the photo, they rode back to the dorm, stinking of sweat. Since most of the people had left for the holiday, the building was empty. Their footsteps echoed in the corridor. Pushing open the door to the room, they saw autumn sunlight illuminating the unadorned walls, mottled with the bloody imprints of squashed mosquitoes.

Xiaodeng squatted, fumbled through her old luggage, and finally found a red scarf at the bottom of it. She taped the gauzy fabric to the window. "A sign of the fool's marriage, and no other fools are allowed to enter without authorization," she said.

Yang Yang felt hot and ready. He went to undress Xiaodeng. He was already very familiar with the body under the clothing; he just hadn't taken the crucial step yet—Xiaodeng wouldn't allow it. Her body was like a garden, a complex structure with many scenes. He had already walked through nearly all the pavilions, streams, and groves in it. There was only one last door, which Xiaodeng guarded firmly, denying him entrance time and again. Holding out for so long had made him fervently curious, and his patience was wearing thin. He began to push ahead with an eagerness and force that surprised him. In his urgency, he heard Xiaodeng sigh softly in his ear, "Yang Yang, actually, I am no longer a white sheet of paper. It's been a long time since I was."

Yang Yang paused for a moment, trying to take in what she had just said. But the long pent-up desire had by now become a torrent that no flimsy gate of reason could ever stop. Her words relaxed him, unbridling his energy.

Just then, he heard a deep cry escape from Xiaodeng, as if she had been knocked with a shovel. Startled, he pulled away and immediately noticed the blood. It twisted over the sheet like an earthworm, a scarlet line across the white surface.

He quickly crawled out of bed, grabbed his clothes, and wiped Xiaodeng's body. There was a lot of blood, and it took a while for it to finally dry. He threw the soiled clothes aside and held her in his arms. "Does it hurt? Are you okay?" he asked incoherently. "Deng, you're still a . . . blank page . . ." But before he could finish, tears came to his eyes.

Xiaodeng's lips moved a few times, but there was no sound. The sunlight outside seeped through the scarf she had taped to the window, suddenly growing heavy and covering the whole room with floating scarlet dust.

What Xiaodeng did not say then was *Yang Yang, your eyes are too clean. You can't see the marks on the page.*

That day, she thought of someone: Wang Deqing.

Winter 1982
Shijiazhuang, Hebei

Before winter, the life of middle school English teacher Dong Xinqin was in a state popularly known as "prospering," in the lingo of the day. She had been rated as an excellent teacher that year, and the class she led had achieved the highest college entrance rate for the second consecutive year. Her husband, Wang Deqing, had just been promoted to director of the factory's financial department. Their adopted daughter,

Wang Xiaodeng, won first place in the city's junior high school English composition contest. More importantly, the whole family had just moved out of an old, dilapidated building into a new house with a living room and two bedrooms.

Wang Deqing and his family had been transferred to Shijiazhuang by his work unit five years earlier. Five years was not a long time, but it was just enough to wipe the uncouth, timid expression of an outsider from their faces, so that they had begun to feel a solid foundation beneath their feet when they walked in the street.

Xinqin turned forty-eight that year, meaning it was the year of her sign in the Chinese zodiac, a potentially perilous year according to popular belief. At the beginning of the year, Deqing had half jokingly said he would buy his wife a red belt to ward off evil spirits. But she was basking in good fortune at the time, and typical of anyone who is riding on the crest of success, she was oblivious to the shadows lurking behind her. So she responded scornfully to her husband's suggestion: "I don't believe in evil spirits."

But that winter, everything changed. It began with a bout of coughing. The "bout" was both singular and plural. It was usually made up of several "small bouts" strung together to become a "big bout." The chronic cough started in summer, then continued into early autumn, late autumn, and the beginning of the following winter. By early winter, Xinqin could not stand it anymore, so she took time off to go to the hospital.

The morning she went to the hospital was no different from any other morning. She and Xiaodeng woke up to the morning news on the radio at almost the same instant. Since moving to Shijiazhuang, she shared a bed with Xiaodeng, leaving Deqing to sleep alone in the other bed. In the kitchen, breakfast was almost ready. Deqing's work unit was in the suburbs, and he had to travel more than two hours by bus each way. He usually stayed in the factory, only returning home on his day off each Wednesday. On the days he was home, he always got up early to cook, so that his wife and daughter could sleep for an extra fifteen minutes.

Xinqin had been preparing lessons until late the previous night, and she woke up feeling a little dizzy. Xiaodeng had gone to bed at the usual time, but she had not slept well, being constantly disturbed by the racket of Xinqin's coughing. So even when mother and daughter were both awake, they continued to lie in bed, one at each end, covering their mouths as they yawned.

"Xiaodeng, you kicked all night and kept shouting, 'Xiaoda.' Why do you always call Xiaoda? Who is that?" Xinqin asked.

Xiaodeng hesitated, then after a long while, she sat up limply and said, "Ma, you must still be drowsy. I don't know anyone named Xiaoda."

It was cold. The heat was thin, and the windows were thick with frost. Xiaodeng leaped to the floor and scurried around like a mouse, looking for her slippers. The cotton underclothes she had bought the previous year seemed a little tight. Two small pouches bulged from her chest. When Deqing had finished warming the milk, he came in to urge her to hurry. With half of his body leaning on the doorframe, he suddenly stopped and stood stock still.

"Xin . . . Xinqin, our Xiaodeng has grown up," he muttered.

"She's still thinner than most of her classmates. A slip of a girl, and she gets headaches all the time." Xinqin pinched Xiaodeng's shoulder and sighed.

Xiaodeng felt their eyes crawling all over her body, so she quickly searched for a sweater to put on. She pulled her head through and straightened the sweater, dusting off the eyes that clung to her half-formed chest. Turning her head, she suddenly noticed the blood on her mother's face.

"Ma, what's wrong with you?" Xiaodeng asked, pointing at Xinqin's chin.

Xinqin wiped it with the back of her hand and said, "I don't know what's going on with this mole. It's been bleeding a lot recently. I've taken the day off today. Your pa is free, so he can come with me to see a doctor and get some ointment for it."

After they had cleaned up, the three of them sat down for a breakfast of milk and steamed buns with pork-and-vegetable filling. Xiaodeng forced herself to drink a little milk from the cup, then set it down and went to get her schoolbag. Xinqin chased after her and made her finish the rest, and the three of them prepared to set off in two separate directions, Xiaodeng to school and they to the hospital.

Xinqin was wearing a gray cotton-padded jacket with blue floral print and a black woolen scarf around her neck. The jacket was very new, and its thick, fluffy padding created clusters of deep wrinkles around the shoulders, cuffs, and elbows. The wind was strong, and as soon as she stepped outside, the scarf flew out like a harrier with broken wings. After washing her face that morning, Xinqin had applied some antiwrinkle cream, and its jasmine scent was blown far, far away by the wind. Sleet began to fall, hitting the ground with a sizzle like sand rolling over in an iron pot while frying peanuts and chestnuts during Chinese New Year. These colors, smells, and sounds were forming what would become Xiaodeng's final impression of her mother in good health.

When they reached the intersection, Xinqin ran over and put a one-yuan note in Xiaodeng's hand. Xiaodeng felt that her mother walked a little strangely that day, one foot higher than the other, as if there were a stone in her shoe.

"If I'm not back on time, buy yourself a bowl of noodles at lunchtime—beef noodles."

When she said it, neither of them realized that it was a prophecy. After Xinqin left the house that morning, she never came back. She stayed in the hospital from then on.

Lung. Liver. Cancer cells had already swarmed both sites. But neither was the place where the cancer had started. It had been growing in the black mole on her chin for many years. A malignant melanoma, the doctor told them, and it was at an advanced stage and had already metastasized. She died just a month after the diagnosis.

Xinqin died on the twenty-fifth night of the twelfth lunar month. In the end, she did not survive the year of her zodiac sign.

Xinqin's death came at a time when the overwhelming concern about the income and health of teachers and middle-aged intellectuals was a hot topic, so it was considered a significant event. Prominent figures from all levels came to the memorial service, and newspapers and radio and television stations swarmed the place. There was earth-rending mourning from students, parents, colleagues, leaders, and everyone else.

Xiaodeng did not cry. Her eyes were like two icy caves, the cold air flowing out and condensing into frost on her face. Amid the mourning music, Xinqin's urn was placed in Xiaodeng's hands. Xiaodeng's lips moved as she said something in a soft voice. No one heard what she said, except Deqing, who stood right next to her. He heard it clearly.

Xiaodeng said, "Ma, you lied to me."

Of course, it was only Deqing who could understand what she meant. When they had brought Xiaodeng home, she had asked twice, "For how long?" The question had brought both of her parents to tears. Xinqin had held Xiaodeng and reassured her over and over, "For a lifetime. We'll be with you for our whole lives."

When they returned home from the funeral, Deqing fell ill. He alternated between high fever and chills. When Xiaodeng prepared his medicine and gave it to him, she suddenly asked, "What about you? Will you go too? To be with her?"

Xiaodeng's face seemed to have become sharp and angular overnight. The sharpness was a shell that enveloped all emotions except fear. Fear permeated every crevice. Deqing hugged her and stroked her hair, which was as coarse as a horse's mane, and he couldn't help bursting into tears.

"Deng, Pa won't leave you. Never. There's only the two of us left in this world, father and daughter."

He stroked her forehead, her eyebrows, her nose, and her lips, and his breathing grew heavier, like a small engine whirring across Xiaodeng's neck. His trembling hands reached into her collar, and they lingered on the two little bulges there. His fingers rubbed the half-hard, half-soft spots for a while before continuing downstream until they reached between her legs. His fingertips were like ants, crawling all over her body, leaving behind a trail of damp, tingling warmth. Xiaodeng started to perspire.

Push him away, push him away, Xiaodeng told herself over and over, but she was paralyzed by a sensation that she had never experienced before. She couldn't move. Her mind and her body wrestled violently, with neither emerging as a winner, and she just started shivering.

"Don't be afraid, Deng. Pa won't hurt you. I just want to get a good look at you."

Deqing took off Xiaodeng's clothes and drew his face near. Her naked body glistened like a fish, shedding a bluish-white light on the twisted features of Deqing's face. Suddenly she felt that something had come in—a finger. Once inside, it grew into a ball of leavened dough, swelling and filling the space inside her, generating a faint pain.

Xiaodeng suddenly straightened her legs fiercely. Her pa was kicked unawares to the ground. He got up, his voice shattering as he stammered, "Pa . . . Pa is just lonely. Your ma . . . for a long . . . long time . . . there was no . . ."

The next week, when Deqing came home on his day off, Xiaodeng was not there. A note was left in the house: *I'm going to stay at my classmate's house. Don't come looking for me.*

The note was not addressed to anyone, and there was no signature. It was stuck to the bedroom door with a sharp paring knife.

Xiaodeng was thirteen years old then.

Summer 1980
Tangshan, Hebei

All the staff in the cafeteria wore the same uniform: an earthy blue apron with earthy blue oversleeves and an earthy blue cap. Li Yuanni always managed to come up with some small trick to poke a hole in this ironclad uniformity, and she did it without leaving a trace.

Yuanni's trick was simple: a small white velvet flower. Flowers were so common, and any mourning woman could have such a flower—even though it had been four years since Comrade Wan's passing. In the center of the flower, Yuanni had pinned a small yellow plexiglass button, and the bright yellow made the white flower simultaneously vivid and ambiguous. This type of flower aptly identified Yuanni: a young woman who had lost her husband, still mourning, but whose heart had not yet turned to stone.

In the earthquake four years earlier, countless widows had suddenly appeared on the streets of Tangshan. They walked on the streets and blended indiscriminately into the gray streetscape. But the little white flower with its desirous yellow stamen sitting on Yuanni's hat made her easily stand out in the crowd.

She had shouted herself hoarse as she tried to dig her children free in the aftermath of the earthquake, permanently damaging her vocal cords. She drank countless decoctions afterward, but could not recover. As a result, she could no longer work as a radio announcer and was instead transferred to the canteen. The canteen staff had to work shifts, alternating every week. When she worked the early shift, she had to get up at four in the morning. Though it was difficult, she was at least able to come back after work and prepare dinner for Xiaoda. When she worked the late shift, she had to prepare his dinner early in the morning for him to warm up on his own when he came home from school. This was fine in the winter, but in the summer it was too hot, and the food was sometimes spoiled by the time Xiaoda got home. Yuanni had to draw a pot of well water and rest the dishes in the water to keep cool, but in recent days, it had been extremely hot and the basin of water had become lukewarm by afternoon. Her usual method being unworkable, Yuanni had to leave five fen each day for him to buy a steamed bun to tide him over until she got home at nine and cooked for him.

It was Yuanni's turn to work the night shift, selling the staple dishes at the first window. Her mind was not on what she was doing, but on thoughts of Xiaoda. School was out for summer vacation, and he was supposed to be tutoring with Mr. Qin. Before the start of summer vacation, Xiaoda's head teacher had visited Yuanni at home and told her Xiaoda had failed two subjects the past semester and only barely managed to pass after taking the makeup tests twice. The teacher said that during the summer vacation, Xiaoda really needed his parents' help on his homework, or else in the new semester, when the lessons became more difficult, he would not be able to catch up. Yuanni racked her brain, and she finally decided to ask Mr. Qin, a technician from her work unit, to come to her house twice a week after work to tutor Xiaoda. When Comrade Wan had been alive, he had occasionally brought items in short supply back from Beijing or Shanghai for Mr. Qin's family, and the two households were rather friendly. Yuanni only had to say the word, and Mr. Qin happily agreed. He had already tutored Xiaoda twice. Today was the third time.

Yuanni watched the hands crawl across the wall clock like ants. When they finally crawled to eight thirty, she closed the window with a snap and started clearing pots and spoons from the table. She remembered to go to the kitchen and buy a few catties of pork head meat, which was several *mao* cheaper after work. She needed to keep half for herself and give the other half to Mr. Qin as a way of showing gratitude, she silently reminded herself.

When Yuanni got off the bus, it was already dark. The sun had set long before, but the heat had not dissipated at all. The night was thick and gloomy, leaving no cracks for the wind to pass. Her clothes were soaked with sweat, sticking to her skin like nylon, and she could feel the weight of her injured leg. The package of cold meat in her arms had grown warm as she held it.

The residential area had been built after the earthquake. Though the houses were still simple, they were much sturdier than the previous shack-like homes. Swarms of people were forced out to the streets by the heat, sitting like locusts under the streetlamps, and the smoke from the mosquito coils stung the eyes. The men sat in circles, shirtless, playing poker and chess, and the sound of palm fans filled the air from one end of the street to the other.

From the midst of the poker players, someone who knew Yuanni shouted from a distance, "Hey, Xiaoda's ma, better hurry home. His grandmother's there."

Yuanni was taken aback. Her husband's hometown was in Xuzhou. A few days earlier, Xiaoda's aunt had sent a letter inviting Xiaoda to stay in Xuzhou for a while during the summer vacation. The grandparents missed their grandson. To Yuanni's surprise, before she even had time to reply, the grandmother had shown up at her home.

She trotted the rest of the way home. At the door, she bumped into Mr. Qin on his way out. She stopped and said, "Why don't you stay for a late-night snack before you go?"

Mr. Qin shook his head and said, "Hurry and go in. Xiaoda burned his hand."

Yuanni panicked. Forgetting all about niceties, she was about to rush into the house when Mr. Qin grabbed her cuff and said, "The old lady dotes on her grandson. She's losing her temper. Brace yourself."

Yuanni nodded. Suddenly remembering the package of meat in her arms, she removed the portion she had separated out and stuffed it into Mr. Qin's hands. "Eat it when you get home. It won't keep until tomorrow."

Mr. Qin wouldn't accept it, and they pushed it back and forth. Yuanni's expression changed, and she said, "If you don't want it, I'll throw it to the dogs."

Mr. Qin accepted it then, and they went their separate ways.

Yuanni took out her key and opened the door. With one glance, she saw a thin, shriveled old woman in the house, holding a bowl in her hand, from which she was feeding Xiaoda mung bean porridge. Hearing a sound at the door, the old woman turned and her eyes swept over Yuanni. It was a sharp look, raising goose bumps all over Yuanni. She knew it was because of her attire. She was wearing a new polyester blouse with a light yellow base beneath a pea-green floral pattern. The waist was a little tight and the collar a little low. When she looked down or leaned over, you could see the white singlet inside. It was not something made at the tailor's shop. She had designed it herself based on one she saw in a movie magazine.

Yuanni straightened her blouse and said, "Ma, why didn't you tell me you were coming?"

The old woman snorted and said, "You were too busy to respond to the letter. Why would I trouble you to pick me up at the station?"

Yuanni didn't say anything. She just went to check on Xiaoda's injury. In the hot weather, he had stripped to just his briefs and tossed his prosthesis on the bed. At eleven, Xiaoda was going through a huge growth spurt. He was tall, dark, and slim, no longer Michelangelo's David. The stump of his severed arm swayed back and forth with the movements of his body, and the dark scar where it had healed looked like a circle of dung beetles. There was a row of bean-like blisters on his surviving arm, glowing pink as they soaked in thick safflower oil.

Yuanni gasped. "Da, how did this happen?"

"I was hungry, so I went to make a bowl of instant noodles. The handle on the kettle was oily. I didn't get a good hold of it, and it slipped."

The old woman slammed the bowl on the table with a thud, and the mung bean porridge splashed out, a green trickle slinking across the tablecloth.

"He eats irregularly. Look at this sack of bones." The old woman took out a handkerchief and wiped her eyes. Tears and snot left a few dark spots on the front of her blue shirt.

Yuanni took out a cloth, wiped the mung bean porridge from the table, picked up the bowl, and started feeding Xiaoda.

Xiaoda turned his head and said, "I can do it myself, Ma. I can still bend this arm. You should try the porridge. It's made from the new rice Nainai brought from Xuzhou."

Yuanni went and scooped out two bowls of porridge, one for her mother-in-law and one for herself. She had rushed home as soon as she got off work, and she had not yet had time to eat. Her brain might not have registered her hunger, but her stomach had. The first sip of porridge ignited a shameless rumble. She opened the package of pork head meat and put some in both her son's and her mother-in-law's bowls. The meat was still shiny and had a fresh pink glow, but she had lost her appetite.

"Ma, I have no choice. I have to work to support Xiaoda," she said.

"There's only one seedling left in the Wan family. Is this the way you're going to raise him?"

Yuanni felt a flush of anger rising inside her, blocking her throat. She knew that the rage was just waiting for her orders so it would know which direction to fly. If to the eyes, it would be a pool of frustrated tears; if to the tongue, words as sharp as a blade. She didn't want to cry, and she didn't want to say such words. She could only hold back the anger with all her might. She was very stubborn, and so was her anger. She battled until a bulge appeared on her forehead.

"Ma," she said finally. "Xiaoda is my only seedling too." Though she tried to keep the anger from her voice, it squeezed through. The blade may have been blunted in the process, but it still gave an edge to her words.

"You're a woman. It's different. You can marry again and have other children. But my son, my son has no other hope." The old woman blew her nose again.

Yuanni noticed that the porridge on her spoon had grown a little salty. The tears of frustration had found their way out after all.

"Ma, even if I have ten more children, I'll never get back my warm jacket, my little Xiaodeng."

The old woman sighed, and after a long pause, she said, "I'm not trying to be mean to you. I'm just asking you to remember how well your husband treated you, and how well he treated your family."

Yuanni got up and poured the unfinished porridge back into the pot. "Ma, you've been on the road all day. You should go to bed early."

That night, her mother-in-law shared a bed with Xiaoda, and Yuanni slept alone. When she had lain down, she heard her mother-in-law fanning Xiaoda. Yuanni had been working hard all day, and she fell asleep as soon as her head hit the pillow. When she woke later that night, she saw a little red light flickering in the corner of the room. It was her mother-in-law, smoking. The old woman was very addicted to smoking, but she couldn't afford store-bought cigarettes, so she only smoked low-quality shredded tobacco that she rolled herself. It was very strong, and the smoke scraped the throat like a knife.

"Yuanni, I won't stop you from marrying again, but you can't take Xiaoda away," her mother-in-law said after an earthshaking bout of coughing.

"Ma, I don't want to marry anyone," Yuanni said as she groped her way to the bathroom.

When she returned, the red light was still flickering.

"You're not even thirty yet. How could you not marry?" asked her mother-in-law.

Yuanni lay down again, but said nothing. She knew that her mother-in-law was waiting for a particular answer. This particular answer was too heavy, and she could only bear the weight of it by putting the rest of her life on the table. She was just twenty-nine. A twenty-nine-year-old woman was like a pool of water. Though the first crop of lotus had bloomed there and borne the first seeds, she still had good times left, many more lotus flowers to bloom, and much more fruit to bear. She really could not say those resolute words, and even if she said them, she wouldn't have really meant them. So her only choice was silence.

Her mother-in-law could wait no longer. She broke the silence by asking, "Who is that man who was tutoring Xiaoda?"

The house filled with the sound of her smacking. She was very loud when she smoked.

"Your son's colleague."

"He wears glasses. It makes him look respectable. Educated guys are popular again now. I think he's very patient with Xiaoda."

The red dot flickered for a while before finally disappearing, and the darkness in the room was now seamless. There was a rustling sound, her mother-in-law grinding the cigarette butt with the sole of her slipper.

Good thing it's not a wooden floor, Yuanni thought.

"Ma, he's very patient with his wife too."

Hearing that the man was married, her mother-in-law was taken aback. "That man has a wife?"

"She was crushed in the earthquake, paralyzed."

Her mother-in-law lay down, and neither of them said anything. Just as Yuanni dozed off, her mother-in-law woke her again.

"Ni, I heard that in Tangshan, there are many lonely people like him who can't get married, so they just stay togeth—"

"Ma! Do you want the child to hear?" Yuanni cut her mother-in-law off in a low, muffled voice and pulled the quilt over her head.

The next day when she got home after work, Xiaoda told her that his grandmother was gone, and she had left an envelope for Yuanni. When Yuanni opened the envelope, she saw two hundred yuan inside.

The heat continued, and Xiaoda's wound became infected and full of pus. They applied countless medicated patches to little avail. After more than a month of unrest, the wound finally closed, leaving a snaking red scar on his arm.

"Ma, I've already lost one arm. If I lose this arm too, I couldn't even pretend to beg for food," he said.

The child's innocent joke left Yuanni stunned for a long time.

The following day, Yuanni was working the night shift, but before four in the afternoon, she returned home with half a roasted chicken, a live fish, two pieces of fresh lotus root, and a tenderloin, all carried in her mesh bag. They were items she would never buy on a normal day.

"Ma, how did you get off work so early today?"

Yuanni smiled and said, "I don't have to work anymore. I can stay home with you from now on. I'll cook delicious food for you every day and watch you grow up and get married."

Yuanni had just quit her job.

Xiaoda was shocked. "Ma, what will we eat if you don't work?"

"We'll eat exactly what we've always eaten. Nainai left some money for us, and I'm going to borrow some more from your other grand-mother. I'm going to open a tailor shop here at home. Just trust your ma. I can do it."

The news was too heavy and too cruel, and eleven-year-old Xiaoda couldn't get it straight for some time. He stared blankly at Yuanni as she broke open the fish's belly and sent its scales flying like a thin golden rain in the sunlight.

"Ma, if it was my sister who lived, you wouldn't have to work so hard," Xiaoda muttered.

Yuanni turned and stroked Xiaoda's hair with her arm. "You're the only seedling of the Wan family. If you'll stay safe, I'll be fine."

Xiaoda pushed her arm away and looked at her steadily. "If I wasn't the only seedling of the Wan family, who would you have saved that day?"

Xiaoda's gaze was so straight and so stern that Yuanni had to look away. She turned to cut the fish, but her hand was unsteady, and the knife trembled.

The room remained very still for a while. Yuanni went to the cupboard to get a plate for the fish. When she turned around, she saw tears on Xiaoda's face.

"Ma, that day, she heard everything. She was waiting for me to say something, but I didn't."

Yuanni tossed the plate aside and hugged Xiaoda.

"Son, there used to be four of us in our family. Now there's just the two of us left. We need to live for the two who are gone. Just try to make the family proud."

Xiaoda's head moved at her bosom. She knew this was his promise.

July 28, 1987
Tangshan, Hebei

Yuanni watched Xiaoda as he ate breakfast, put his schoolbag on his back, and went out. Xiaoda would be in the third year of high school the following semester, and he was preparing to take the college entrance exam. Although he took makeup lessons with Mr. Qin every summer, his grades never improved. This past summer, Yuanni had signed him up for a full-time crash course, four days a week. Since the summer vacation had been no different from a regular school year, Xiaoda was naturally dragging his feet. But he knew he could never best Yuanni, so he finally set off for school, albeit reluctantly.

After Xiaoda left, Yuanni sat down at the sewing machine and started singing. She sang "The Laundry Song," of course, her old go-to tune. Over the years, this song had slipped over her tongue countless times, turning her from a laundry girl who knew nothing of the world's affairs into a thick-skinned seamstress. It was still the same song, but the voice was different. Her voice now was like a brush pen, its bristles worn to baldness after years of use. She didn't care, though. She sang this song for herself. The mouth was willing, and the ear was willing too. That was something nobody could take from her, not even God.

Yuanni had been running her tailor shop for seven years. Seven years earlier, she had quit her job and bought a sewing machine with the five hundred yuan gathered from her parents and in-laws. She had gone to Shanghai and stayed with a friend of her brother for more than a month. She learned many unique tailoring skills there. When she returned, she opened a home-based tailor shop, calling it Shanghai Scissor King.

Yuanni's earliest customers were all acquaintances and friends. She made it a rule that anyone who came to the door for the first time would not be charged, but the next time they came, they had to bring a friend. This was her marketing strategy, but of course, the word *marketing* wasn't even in the popular parlance until several years later.

What really multiplied Yuanni's business was not this marketing approach, but her advertising. *Advertising* was a new buzzword around this time. Yuanni had heard of it before, and while she didn't really understand what the word meant, the only thing she didn't understand instinctively was the kind of lifeless advertising printed on paper. She had long known about live advertising, even without a teacher. She knew that words would not paint an accurate picture, but seeing was believing, so she put great effort into the style of the clothes she made. At that time, there were no fashion magazines, so Yuanni's patterns could only be drawn from film and television pictorials. Her eyes latched onto them, and they were firmly locked into her mind with just one glance; she would never forget something once she had seen it. First it was women's clothing, then men's, and finally, children's. The clothes she made were always just a little different from others seen on the street. It might be a collar or a strip of lace, or maybe a zipper or a button that was attached in an unexpected place.

These little differences quietly encouraged the aesthetic enthusiasm that was just awakening in the Chinese public. Her customers wore her clothes in the streets and alleys of Tangshan City, and they soon attracted attention. Her live advertisements kept bringing in new customers. To her surprise, business was booming in her little shop, and she could even buy things without thinking twice.

She was sewing a shirt made of ultra-fine polyester fabric she had asked her brother to send her from Shanghai. It had a light blue base interwoven with dark blue twisted pinstripes, just right for early autumn wear. It would be another year or two before such fabrics would become popular in Tangshan.

As she picked at the thread ends with a pair of thin tweezers, she found a patch of ash on the fabric. She picked with her nails and blew on it, but could not get rid of it. When she looked up, she realized that it was the shadow of a human figure.

It was Mr. Qin.

"Why didn't you go to work today?" Yuanni asked, surprised.

"I'm going to Taiyuan on business tomorrow. The leader gave me half a day off to pack my luggage."

"Why are you here then?"

"I wanted to see you," he said.

"All right, then sit. Take your time and observe."

She buried her head in the piece of clothing she was stitching. When she had finished one sleeve, she turned it over and showed it to Mr. Qin. "Does it look good?" she asked.

He nodded and said, "The things you select are all first class."

Yuanni raised a corner of her mouth and said, "Wait till I finish, then you can take it with you."

Mr. Qin quickly declined. "No, I can't. You've already given my wife so many clothes, but she's just lying in bed and doesn't go out. She never has a chance to wear them."

Yuanni couldn't help but chuckle. "Did I say this is for her? Can't you tell the difference between men's and women's clothing?"

Mr. Qin waved his hands like they were large fans. "How could I wear that? Don't you know I'm in my forties? How could I wear such a fancy shirt?"

Yuanni tossed the shirt away. Her face tightened, and she said, "Forget it then. How much have you seen in life? Go to Shanghai and Guangzhou and you'll see this color of fabric all over the street. Even old men in their fifties and sixties wear it!"

Mr. Qin laughed and said, "Fine, I'll wear it. I have to work hard to keep up with the trends."

Yuanni's face relaxed.

Mr. Qin took a box from his pocket and said, "I happen to have something for you too. My wife's younger sister got it on a business trip to Japan. I thought it was quite nice, so I brought it to you."

Yuanni opened the box and saw that it was a small white silk scarf. The silk was extremely fine, with a pink flower printed on it. Yuanni thought it was a peach blossom, but when she looked again, she realized that it was cherry. The flower was so vivid that it seemed to jump off the cloth. Yuanni had never seen such a delicate scarf before, so she couldn't help but look at her reflection in the mirror with the scarf around her neck, turning back and forth.

Suddenly, she seemed offended. She took off the scarf and tossed it on the table. "She bought it for her older sister, didn't she?"

Mr. Qin didn't say anything.

Yuanni sneered. "If you want to give me something next time, go buy it specially for me. Don't try to win me over with someone else's rejects."

Mr. Qin's face turned beet red, and he kept rubbing his hands like he was trying to remove a layer of skin. His lips trembled for a long moment, but all that came out of his mouth was a long string of "I . . . I . . . I . . ." A layer of sweat formed on his forehead.

Yuanni sighed, picked up the scarf, and put it in the drawer on the side of her sewing machine. "All right, all right, I know you're sincere. It's just . . ."

She cut herself off, then sat down again and continued sewing. Her mind was a mess, and the stitches were too. She had to pull out the row of stitches she had just made and redo it. She could no longer focus.

Mr. Qin didn't sit. With arms across his chest, he paced the room. Yuanni became dizzy watching him.

"If you've got something to say, say it. I know you've got something on your mind."

Mr. Qin started, "Yuanni, please don't be angry." But then he refused to go on.

Yuanni looked up at him, snorting. "Don't you know who I am? I've swallowed more gossip than rice in my life. Do you think there's any gossip I haven't heard before? If it bothers you, then don't come."

Mr. Qin hesitated, then said, "It's not that. It's . . . it's Xiaoda."

Yuanni was suddenly alert, and every part of her body was awakened. "Xiaoda? What happened to him? What trouble is he in this time?"

Mr. Qin shook his head and said, "You spent that money in vain. He hasn't been going to class at all."

Bang! It was as if the sun had fallen to the ground and shattered into thousands of pieces. The roof tilted slowly. The sky, the earth, and the house all turned dark, the kind of darkness that had no beginning or end, the kind that rendered one totally blind. She didn't know where she was; she was just falling, confused, falling continuously.

"Yuanni! Yuanni!"

Mr. Qin was alarmed by her expression. He quickly wrung out a cool, wet towel and started wiping her face.

"You've got to give him more leeway. He's just not suited for academics. Anyway, the academic path isn't the only way to get through this world."

Yuanni looked steadily at Mr. Qin but without really seeing him. Her eyes were blank. She didn't know what she was looking at.

"You . . . should go," she said feebly, after a long pause.

As soon as Xiaoda entered the house, he threw his schoolbag on the table and called, "Ma, what's for dinner? I'm so hungry I could faint."

There was no response from inside the house. Yuanni sat in a chair, staring out the window, a half-sewn men's shirt in her lap. The summer sun was very playful, refusing to return home at this late hour, and the clouds burned like a row of dense flames. The sun did not set, and the cicadas had to keep it company. They were tired of chirping but couldn't rest, and so continued to squeak noisily.

"Ma, what's wrong?"

Yuanni turned and smiled. "Da, what did you do in class today?"

Xiaoda lifted the hem of his shirt and wiped the sweat from his face. "Even if I tell you, you won't understand."

"How do you know I can't understand if you don't tell me?" Another smile.

Xiaoda wasn't sure where the smile was coming from. After a while, he settled on a safe answer. "It's the same old thing every day. Math, physics, chemistry."

Yuanni snorted and stood up. She walked over and fixed her eyes on her son.

"What's the surname of the tutor who teaches math? Is he any good?"

Xiaoda hesitated, avoiding Yuanni's eyes. "Mr. Chen. He's okay—"

Before he could finish, he was interrupted by a blast of wind. It came so fast he couldn't even blink before it knocked into him, sending him staggering. He used his one good hand to support himself on the wall, steadying himself. He felt a burn on his cheek. He wanted to wipe it off, but he couldn't. After a moment, he came to his senses and realized he'd been slapped.

"I was so blind, saving an ungrateful brat like you!" Yuanni shouted. The throat that had been torn shouting in the earthquake eleven years earlier was torn again. This time, the tear was complete, and she spat out the dregs.

Xiaoda felt a wet itch on the inside of his cheek. He licked the spot. It was salty—blood.

"If you regret it, you can take me back there and bury me again," Xiaoda said coldly, spitting out bloody phlegm.

Yuanni was taken aback. It wasn't what Xiaoda had said that shocked her, but the look in his eyes when he said it. Over the years, despite his lack of academic progress, Xiaoda had always been very docile. Now, Yuanni was looking into the eyes of a leopard. The big cat might have been caged for many years, and if it hadn't been for her slap, he might have remained caged for many more. But her slap had shattered the cage, and the leopard couldn't be stopped. It had not yet had time to adapt to its newly gained freedom. It stood close to her, so close they could hear each other's breathing and heartbeat. It stared at her; she stared at it. Both were afraid.

In the end, she blinked first.

"Wan, you inconsiderate pig! You left this home to me. Did you even bother to ask if I wanted it?"

Yuanni slammed her fist into the wall over and over again and burst into tears. She had cried before, but never like this. It was the cry of someone whose innards had been tied into a dead knot. It was the cry of someone trapped in a tunnel with both ends blocked, with no hope for escape even if they crawled a thousand miles. It was the cry of a blind person who could not find the way, or a deaf person who tried to hear. There was no pain in the cry, only despair. The cry ripped Xiaoda's heart to shreds.

"Ma, don't do this. We'll become a laughingstock if the neighbors hear."

Xiaoda came over and helped Yuanni to a stool.

"My son isn't afraid of being a laughingstock. Why should I be afraid?" Yuanni brushed his hand away.

Xiaoda stopped trying to comfort her. He just let her cry until the wail gradually wore itself out, finally becoming nothing more than a thin thread of ragged breath.

When Yuanni finally stopped crying, she stood up and wiped her face with a towel. She then went into the kitchen to wash the rice and start cooking.

Feeling a weight at her back, she knew Xiaoda was following her.

"Ma," he said hesitantly.

"I'm not your mother," Yuanni said coldly.

"Ma, it's not that I don't want to study. I just don't have the brains for school. I start snoring when I open a book, and that interrupts everyone else's studies."

The corner of Yuanni's mouth lifted involuntarily for a brief instant, but the smile withered before it could really bloom.

"Ma, I didn't go for tutoring, but I wasn't out having fun either. I went to Sanzi's house the last few days. We're talking about going to the South."

Sanzi was Xiaoda's classmate who lived in the same residential block.

"The South?" Yuanni's eyebrows twitched.

"Sanzi's uncle is in Guangzhou, and he said it's easy to make money there. He's only been there six months, and he's already saved up ten thousand yuan."

Xiaoda shot Yuanni a tentative look. Seeing that she didn't say anything, he gradually grew bolder.

"Ma, you know I won't be able to get into university. What kind of job can I find in Tangshan? Why don't you let me go to Guangdong and try my luck there? I might strike gold. You never know." He added, "Do you know what's going on in the tailor's market? Nowadays, everyone wears ready-made clothes. No one wants clothes you've made stitch by stitch. Pretty soon, you won't have any customers. Do you want us both stuck here, starving to death?"

After a long silence, Yuanni spat out a rock-hard response. "You can go when I'm dead."

The meal was meager, just a plate of scrambled eggs and tomatoes and a bowl of cold tofu with shallots. The food was sloppy, and so were the eaters. Both of them had a new wound in their hearts. The wounds were open and raw, and the scars had not yet formed. The slightest look—the slightest breath—made them hurt.

After dinner, Yuanni got up to clear the dishes. "Today is the anniversary of your father's and sister's deaths," she said. "I'll burn ghost money for them later."

March 12, 2006
Eaton Centre, Toronto

By the time Wang Xiaodeng put down the backpack she was carrying, bought a cup of coffee from the food court, and sat down, she was so hot she started to sweat. It wasn't because of the weather. Ontario's winter had to go through much coaxing before it would hand over the trees, sky, and streets to spring. Though it had stopped snowing, there was still an edge to the wind that hit those walking on the street with unexpected force, taking them by surprise. No amount of winter clothing could protect against such untempered pain.

And anyway, Xiaodeng didn't have to walk far; she walked up from the subway station, and the shopping mall was right there. What really made her sweat was the load in her backpack: a laptop, a bulky power cord, an English–Chinese dictionary, a Chinese–English dictionary, and a few bilingual reference books. These items pressed on her back like a load of bricks, making her feel like a camel climbing a mountain when she walked, but she seldom went out without them. What provided structure for her writing in English was her Chinese thinking. Thinking was the bones, and words were the skin, but there was a thick layer of flesh between skin and bones. Over the years, she had been working hard to bridge the gap between them, with the help of a few dictionaries and reference books she carried everywhere.

She used to write at home. There was a room on the second floor that served as her writing space. With the door closed, it was her solitary paradise. There were cracks around the doors and windows and in the walls, so there was always some noise, like soft-shelled insects crawling quietly along the cracks in the doors, windows, and walls and into the room. They scurried cautiously around her, trying to avoid notice—but Xiaodeng's eardrums were like magnets, able to catch even the faintest sound of dust settling in the room.

Each sound held its own meaning. The clacking sound, for example, was Susie's fingers on her computer keyboard. When that sound crawled across Xiaodeng's eardrums, she knew that her daughter was talking with classmates—mostly boys—about topics she would never raise in conversation with her mother. Since Xiaodeng had peeped at the record of those chats on the computer, Susie had set a difficult password, and a door to Susie's mind had been forever closed from then on.

The intermittent buzz was Yang Yang making a phone call in his room, with the door closed. It was carefully concealed, but the heater's duct was the longest, sharpest tongue in the house, and there was always a way to send those private words to Xiaodeng's ears, even though they had been chewed into indistinct morsels. Yang Yang was probably talking to Xiangqian about things he had not discussed with his wife in a very long time. They were the sorts of words that might have been exchanged many times during the day when they worked together in the art school. Some words were forever fresh to the ear even if repeated a thousand times; others, say, coming from a wife, would evoke a yawn on the first utterance.

The asthmatic hiss was the old heater in the basement dragging out its feeble existence. When Susie was home, she always turned the heater to twenty-four degrees Celsius. A heater this old could not climb such a steep slope, and it was always short of breath as a result. Each time it hissed, the needle on the gas meter quivered gleefully.

These sounds, full of meaning both explicit and implied, floated through the air like dust motes, filling every corner of Xiaodeng's study. When the pores of her mind became clogged with this dust, her breathing was not easy, so when Yang Yang and Susie were home, she could hardly write.

A month earlier, these sounds had disappeared. Xiaodeng had moved out of the house and into a small apartment in the city center. She had taken a fancy to this apartment—even though it was so small it didn't even have a separate living room—because of the subway station downstairs, and because when she looked out of the window, she could see the sun the moment she opened her eyes.

She soon discovered that there was a sound here too, a different sort of sound. When she moved here, she came to understand that silence was also a sound. It was the heaviest, most heart-wrenching noise in the world—like drums, gongs, and hammers pounding on her nerves endlessly. All other sounds would come to a weary end eventually; silence lurked beneath them all, never fading. Her only choice was to escape again, so she went to the mall to try her luck.

The noise at the mall was varied and strange, but Xiaodeng soon realized that this noise was different from all the other sounds because this noise had nothing to do with her. Here, the world bustled past her, but it was not the sort of sound that could hook her ears or mind. In this huge whirlpool of people, she felt an unprecedented serenity. She sat in the center of the whirlpool, turned on her computer, and wrote like a god.

When she had lost herself completely in her writing, someone suddenly flicked the cover of her computer with a finger and said, "Could I be so fortunate as to share a table with a famous writer?"

Xiaodeng raised her head and stared for a moment before registering that it was Dr. Wilson. He wore a green-and-white ski jacket and well-washed jeans, making him look much younger. He looked a little different from the doctor in a white coat in the hospital. Xiaodeng was caught off guard.

"Why are you here, Dr. Wilson?"

"I'd like to ask you the same question, if you agree to call me Henry."

"Okay, Henry. Now I finally understand why I have to spend so long in your waiting room. You're one of those doctors who always has to sneak out for coffee during the busiest hours."

Dr. Wilson pursed his lips and smiled. "May I remind you that today is Sunday?"

Xiaodeng glanced at the date displayed at the top of her computer screen. She patted her forehead and said, "Now you've finally discovered my problem. I have dementia."

Xiaodeng stacked up her books to make room for Dr. Wilson to put down his cup of coffee.

"Are you writing a new book? What's it about?" Dr. Wilson asked, flipping through one of her reference books.

"A woman whom everyone has presumed dead. She tries everything she can think of to prove to them she is alive."

"Oh! Sounds like a really gruesome spy novel."

Xiaodeng couldn't help but smile, but she lowered her head as she did. "Thank you for always trying to make me laugh, Henry."

"You have a lovely smile—it's like a rainbow."

"It's better not to be a rainbow. Such a fleeting thing! And you have to pay such a price for it: a heavy rain, and maybe even a mudslide."

Dr. Wilson laughed. Taking off his ski jacket, he sat down across from Xiaodeng.

"Well, today, let's talk about your writing. That's something we've never talked about before."

"But you're not wearing your white coat."

"Then I won't bill the OHIP today."

He started drinking his coffee. He had the lid open and the steam fogged his glasses. Through the fog, he saw Xiaodeng lower the laptop's cover, and her eyes grew hazy and distant.

"Actually, my husband is the real novelist. He published his first novel at just nineteen. He wrote it because he was madly in love with words. When the madness faded, he just decided to stop writing. He is master of his text; I'm not. I'm a slave to mine. I write to escape. There's something chasing me, biting at my heels. I can't turn back, and I can't stop. If I do, I'll die."

"That's the most bizarre motivation for writing I've ever heard. Can you tell me what is chasing you?"

Xiaodeng bit her lip, as if there were an intricate lock on it and her teeth were struggling to find the key and open the door.

"Despair. It's like a man who is buried under the ruins, and he sees a sliver of sky through a gap. The hope of survival is so close, he can almost touch it with a finger. The distance between his finger and the sky, that's life and death. Hope is so near, but he just can't catch it. What kind of despair is that?"

Dr. Wilson turned the coffee cup in his hand. "Thank you for sharing this metaphor with me," he said, after a lengthy pause. "Maybe that's the power of literature, a vision of a small piece of the sky, always there, even if out of reach."

"But I can't write about the sky. I can only write about the finger that can never reach the sky."

"Xiaodeng, does your husband know your writing as well as you know his?"

Xiaodeng flinched as if she'd been stung. This question was an old wound wrapped in a thick bandage, tucked out of sight in the most secret corner of her mind for many years. No one dared to touch it, not even her. But now, Dr. Wilson suddenly pulled it out into broad daylight, scraping off the thick scab and revealing the tender flesh underneath. Xiaodeng groaned.

"That's the real reason he wanted to leave me, I think. The other woman was just a cover. He couldn't accept that his wife of mediocre talent could write more compelling novels than him. He could bear any other injustice in life except that. He loves words too much. He can't stand for anyone to insult or neglect words. Who am I to claim a success that should be his? It's a cruelty he can't stand. That's why he never reads my books."

As she spoke, her expression displayed the weariness of someone who has just endured a severe pain. The topic had been a thorn in her flesh for many years. She knew it was there, but she never dared to touch it, let alone remove it, because she couldn't face the agony it would cause. But Dr. Wilson had pulled the thorn out now and, to her surprise, while the extraction was indeed painful, it was not as bad as she had expected. She suddenly felt a sort of resigned relief.

"Maybe," Dr. Wilson said. "What you're saying is only a possibility. But there's one thing I can never agree with your husband about."

"What's that?" she asked curiously.

"That you're of mediocre talent."

Xiaodeng couldn't help but smile.

"How is the separation? Are you okay with it?" Dr. Wilson stumbled over the word *separation*.

"I'm getting used to it. It's a life without time, without noise, and without restrictions," Xiaodeng said.

Dr. Wilson finished the last sip of coffee and glanced at his watch. "Xiaodeng, this is an operation on a habit that's been cultivated for years. The incision might take a long time to heal. But it *will* heal eventually, if you want it to."

Xiaodeng suddenly noticed an indentation on the ring finger of Dr. Wilson's left hand. It was the mark left by a wedding ring.

Summer 1996
Shanghai

Wang Xiaodeng got off work half an hour late after completing a draft that had an urgent deadline, and she anxiously rushed out on her bicycle to pick up her daughter. Though Susie's nursery school stipulated that they closed at six, the teacher's countenance generally darkened after five thirty.

As soon as Xiaodeng got married, she became pregnant, not wasting a single day, just as she had gotten married immediately upon her graduation from college. Yang Yang proudly told Xiaodeng, "The first seed I sowed in your field bore fruit."

Xiaodeng was not totally convinced. She told him that even the best seeds were useless if the soil was not fertile. The seed/soil debate had raged on, continuing even now, when their daughter Susie was three years old.

Yang Yang was now teaching at Fudan University while pursuing his PhD, and Xiaodeng was still working as a junior foreign language editor at the publishing house. Yang Yang had half-heartedly tried to persuade Xiaodeng to take the postgraduate entrance exam too. Xiaodeng replied, "Are you out of your mind? Doing an MA in English lit here? If I want to do it, it has to be somewhere overseas. What can you pick up here?" Then she added, "Don't you get enough Yangjingbang English from your Chinese professors?"—a jab at the pidgin English that had developed in Shanghai during its semicolonial era.

As soon as he heard this, Yang Yang became agitated. "I'm a Chinese major. What would I do if I went overseas with you? Even if I become a beggar and beg in impeccable Mandarin, the people won't understand me over there."

From then on, Yang Yang carefully avoided inciting career ambitions in Xiaodeng.

Xiaodeng hurried to the nursery school. It was five forty-five by the time she got there. To her surprise, both teachers greeted her from a distance, even before she had dismounted from her bike.

"Susie's ma! Say thank you to Susie's grandfather for us. Your father is very kind. He brought so many gifts from so far away."

Xiaodeng was momentarily stunned. "You're mistaken. Susie doesn't have a grandfather."

The two teachers glanced at each other, then one of them said, "We checked his ID. He's from Shijiazhuang. His name is Wang Deqing. He knew your name, and Susie's father's, and your address and workplace. There's no mistake."

Xiaodeng's head shattered into countless little pieces. It took a while for her to come back to her senses. She grabbed a teacher's sleeve tightly, as if wringing water from a cloth. "Did you say he took Susie?"

Startled by Xiaodeng's expression, the teacher stuttered, "He picked Susie up at three and said he would go to the park. I thought you knew."

Xiaodeng let go of the teacher's arm, jumped on her bike, and raced off. Immediately understanding the urgency, her bike sliced like a finely made blade through the traffic of that busy street. The street felt the pain, fighting back with a string of shouted obscenities, to which Xiaodeng turned a deaf ear. The ride that usually took twenty minutes needed just ten that day. When she reached the dorm, her arms and legs were sore, and she couldn't close the lock on her bike for some time because her hands were trembling.

When she reached their room, she saw that the door was ajar. She called out to Yang Yang, but there was no response. When she pushed the door open, she heard the sound of splashing water in the kitchen. Taking a few steps forward, she saw a large aluminum basin on the floor. Susie sat naked in the basin of water, singing and playing with her toes. A man had his back to Xiaodeng, and he was washing Susie's body with a towel.

Susie suddenly stopped singing and joyfully cried, "Ma!"

The man turned around and saw Xiaodeng. Their eyes met, and time froze.

"Yang Yang opened the door for me," the man hemmed and hawed. "He went to the cafeteria to pick up some food, and he asked me to give Susie her bath. She played all day and was very sweaty."

What happened next seemed to Susie to take place in slow motion, like in a children's cartoon. Her mother's eyes opened very wide, and Susie wasn't sure what she saw in them, maybe fire, maybe blood. Like a mother leopard, Xiaodeng pounced and snatched Susie from the water. Before she had come to a full stop, her leg was already in the air, kicking the man to the ground. The man was caught off guard, and he slid a long way, his back slamming hard into the doorframe. A vase fell with a loud bang, smashing into pieces.

Frightened, Susie burst into tears. Her cry was like a power drill set to the highest speed, screeching and spinning against Xiaodeng's temple. Xiaodeng didn't soothe her, or even speak. She quickly carried her daughter into the bedroom, snatched a thin blanket from the bed, and wrapped her child in it. Xiaodeng held Susie very tightly to her, as if she wanted to embed the child in her own flesh. Susie was still sweating from the hot bath, but she suddenly stopped crying, vaguely aware that something extraordinary had happened. Her mother had never held her like this before. Never.

There was a shuffling sound behind her, and Xiaodeng knew that Wang Deqing had followed her into the room. She heard her teeth rattle and she shivered like a leaf in the wind, so violently that she feared she would drop Susie to the ground at any moment.

"If you touch my daughter again, I'll kill you. You hear me?"

Xiaodeng heard her own voice, squeezed out through her teeth like an icicle hanging under the winter eaves, ready to stab with its cold rage.

It had been several years since they had seen each other. The man had hardly changed, aside from the graying hair. He was visibly shaken. Every part of his face, the cheekbones, jaw, brows, eyes, nose, and ears, was trembling, twisting his features into a farcical expression between grinning and weeping.

"Deng, Pa has done one wrong thing in his life. Does that one wrong thing erase all the thousands of good things?" the man asked.

Xiaodeng looked up and stared at the man, nailing him to the wall with a long, piercing look.

"That depends. What was the one wrong thing?" Xiaodeng said.

"I've been looking for you for years. I miss you. Even if you don't miss me, surely you miss your mother, right? All these years, you haven't been to tend her grave."

The man saw a slit in Xiaodeng's expression. It was very narrow, but he wanted to try to wriggle a toe into it.

"Pa is getting old—soon to retire. I don't want anything else, just to see my granddaughter from time to time."

The wet towel in the man's hand was still dripping. A dirty black worm crept across the floor where the drops fell.

The slit in Xiaodeng's expression slammed shut, squashing the man's toe flat.

"Don't even think about ever seeing Susie again."

She took an envelope from her pocket, the salary she had been paid earlier in the day. She fished out a few notes and tossed them at the man.

"That's enough for a hotel room and train ticket. Just go."

The man didn't move, but his eyes continued to rove, trying to catch her eyes but failing.

"Can I stand outside the nursery tomorrow, just to have one more look at her?" he asked, haggling humbly.

"You'd better leave before Yang Yang gets back. Don't make me kick you out in front of him."

Knowing he had hit a dead end, the man picked up his wrinkled old satchel and walked out. As he went through the door, he turned back and said, "Someone from the Tangshan Municipal Government came asking about earthquake orphans, some sort of a follow-up survey. They asked if you remembered the past. They will contact you."

Xiaodeng didn't say a word. She just stared at the toe of her shoe, as if a giant wasp rested there. After a while, she turned and went to the kitchen. Taking a jar of yogurt and two apples from the refrigerator, she stuffed them into the man's bag.

"Go. I don't want Yang Yang to talk to you."

"Deng." There were tears in his eyes.

He finally left. His legs dragged, as if unable to carry the weight of his body, and his knees bent like a bow.

When Yang Yang came back with boxes of food, he found Xiaodeng sitting in a chair, staring blankly with Susie in her arms. Susie had been changed into clean clothes, and her hair was still dripping wet. Xiaodeng's chin rested on Susie's head, sharp, as if trying to drill a hole in the skull.

"Where's your father?" Yang Yang asked.

Xiaodeng didn't move, and she didn't speak.

Susie broke free from Xiaodeng's embrace, jumped down, and ran to Yang Yang, eager to see the content of the boxes.

"Ma kicked Waigong out. She was angry at him," Susie said.

Yang Yang was shocked. "What happened, Xiaodeng? He came all this way to see you, and you didn't even let him stay for a meal?"

Xiaodeng still said nothing.

Yang Yang had bought a lot of cooked food. He spread it out, covering the table with dishes of all sizes. He picked out a few items and put them into a small bowl to feed Susie. Xiaodeng grabbed a pair of chopsticks. Her fragile gaze was not fixed on the chopsticks or the bowl, but on nothing.

"Whatever the problem, he's still your father. He raised you all those years," Yang Yang said.

Snap! Xiaodeng slapped the chopsticks on the table and ran into the bedroom.

"Keep your mouth shut if you don't know what you're talking about!"

In the middle of the night, Yang Yang was awakened by a need to pee. He was about to get up when he saw two lights at the head of the bed, glowing green, like ghastly flames. On closer look, he saw that it was Xiaodeng, sitting at the head of the bed, hair disheveled and staring straight ahead in a daze.

Yang Yang was shocked. His voice ragged, he said, "What . . . what's the matter with you?"

"Yang Yang, I want to go overseas to study." Xiaodeng sighed faintly.

Yang Yang pulled his dangling heart back into his chest. Patting his wife on the shoulder, he said, "Let me get a good night's sleep and we'll discuss it in the morning, when I'm more awake."

They did not discuss the matter the following morning. In the days that followed, the topic did not come up in a conversation again. To tell the truth, Yang Yang forgot all about it. After four years of marriage, he was used to his wife's whims and impulses, and he didn't always take her words seriously.

But this time, he was wrong. Six months later, he learned that his wife had quietly secured a visa to study in Canada.

June 19, 1999
Toronto

Eaton Centre was in the most central part of Toronto's tangled downtown district. It was Saturday, so the crowds came later than usual. When the sun started to cast the sparse shadows of the trees onto the sidewalk, the colors and sounds on the street gradually grew richer.

Yang Yang put down his luggage beside a painter's booth. The painter had not yet started working. He had just gotten immersed in sorting out his tools. He wore a wide-brimmed straw hat. His face was hardly visible, aside from his blue T-shirt with the logo of a clothing brand associated with a famous Chinese gymnast. *He's also Chinese,* Yang Yang thought.

> Rat (*zishu*), Ox (*chouniu*), Tiger (*yinhu*), Rabbit (*maotu*), Dragon (*chenlong*), Snake (*sishe*), Horse (*wuma*), Goat (*weiyang*), Monkey (*shenhou*), Rooster (*youji*), Dog (*xugou*), Pig (*haizhu*)

Yang Yang spread the large piece of paper with the colored images of the Chinese zodiac on the side of the pavement and put his collection of stones and carving knives on each of the four corners. He had brought it all from home. Of course, when he had carefully packed them in his suitcase, he had not expected that they would be the means by which he would make a living in Toronto while his wife studied.

He intended to give everyone who stopped by his stall a beautiful Chinese name. For instance, after turning over the name of a British tourist, Mary Smith, in his mouth several times, he would name her 史美兰, Shi Meilan, a given name meaning "beautiful orchid," and the surname,

Shi, adding the air of antiquity. After chatting for five minutes with a Scottish man named William Burns, he would select the name 伯伟力, Bo Weili, suggesting strength and greatness. He would carve the person's new Chinese name onto a small seal. When done, he would casually ask their birth date, then point out their zodiac sign and explain the personality traits and fortunes of that sign. If he could manage to stir up their interest, they might even buy a carved image of their sign from him. He estimated that the complete process would take him about half an hour to forty-five minutes. If he was lucky, he could earn about twenty-five dollars from such an interaction.

This was what Yang Yang envisioned for himself. He didn't know how likely it might be for such an idea to become a reality, but he knew that he and Xiaodeng needed the money. Xiaodeng had come to the University of Toronto to study two years earlier. She was now pursuing a doctoral degree after completing her master's degree in English literature. Yang Yang and their daughter, Susie, had just come to Toronto on a family visit visa.

Although Xiaodeng had come on a scholarship, they had just moved into a more spacious apartment, and the rent was much higher. Xiaodeng had also bought a secondhand car because they were coming. The cost of gas, insurance, and occasional repairs, along with Susie's piano lessons, were all extra expenses that would need to be covered by Yang Yang's income.

The sound of footsteps, stopping heavily right in front of his stall. Customers! His heart beat so loudly he was sure it could be heard all over the street. But there was nothing to be afraid of. He had learned and perfected his skills carving seals and fortune-telling using zodiac signs while he was studying at Fudan and lived with international students. He had just never imagined that he would actually need to rely on such tricks to earn a living.

The first time. Just get through the first time, Yang Yang thought, trying to calm himself.

He slowly raised his head. He first saw two thick legs in blue uniform pants, then saw that they belonged to a big, tall police officer.

The officer smiled kindly at him, then rattled off a string of unintelligible words. The English Yang Yang had learned in the classrooms of Fudan University was put to the most brutal test on the indiscriminately jumbled streets of Toronto. He didn't understand a word. Flushed crimson, he waved his hands frantically and said over and over, "I'm sorry. Sorry."

The officer slowed down and repeated what he had just said. This time, Yang Yang picked up one phrase, a key phrase: *business license.*

His head was muddled. He rubbed the legs of his trousers with both hands, his tongue waggling uselessly in his mouth. He couldn't say a word.

Just then, the painter next to him stood up and uttered a string of words to the officer. The painter's English was far less fluent than the officer's, but the accent was familiar, and Yang Yang caught every word. She said, "This is my husband. We use the same license. He engraves seals for me to use on my paintings."

A bright smile spread across the officer's face. "Oh, my apologies!" he said. "These are such beautiful seals." And then he left.

It was only then that Yang Yang realized that the face under the wide-brimmed hat was that of a woman. She had a broad face and tanned skin, and there were freckles all over her cheeks. Every pore seemed to ooze sunlight.

I haven't seen such a healthy woman in a very long time, Yang Yang thought.

"Thank you—really," Yang Yang said. He felt these words were used too often by too many people, making them empty, but he couldn't think of anything else. He just looked at the woman and grinned like an idiot.

"It's nothing. We're all just begging for a few scraps," the woman said.

The casual remark made Yang Yang's heart sink. He remembered seeing a Chinese painting when he was a child. It depicted a beggar, and the inscription read: *Who doesn't eat? Who doesn't beg for a scrap? All you need is a few cheap tricks.* Though he was very young then, he was suddenly struck by what a burden it was to make a living. He never imagined that so many years later, after traveling thousands of miles across the ocean to Canada, he would be reduced to the status of a street beggar, no different from the one in the painting.

"It'll be better when your skin has grown thick. This money is actually pretty easy to earn. At least you don't have to keep office hours from nine to five. You can earn a year's wages in summer, then for the rest of the year, you can still pursue your dreams, if you have any left."

He was amused by the woman's words, and his face brightened. He said he just wanted to support his family; he had no ideals. Then he asked the woman's name.

"I'm Xiangqian," she said.

Inwardly, he thought, *Of course she would have a name like that—advance, progress, forward ho!*

"What school did you go to?"

She replied, "The Zhejiang Academy of Fine Arts, Department of Oil Painting."

"It's a famous school," he said. "Wasn't Pan Tianshou the head of the school?"

"You knew the former head?" The woman was pleasantly surprised.

"The things I know are far more than what I say. Look, I've got an excellent piece of bloodstone here. It's a real treasure, not like these fake ones. I'll take it out later and carve you a really nice seal."

She didn't refuse. Rather, a look of joy came over her face.

"Yeah, okay. I peeked at your seals. They really are beautiful. I was just about to ask you to teach me some seal-carving techniques."

The pair sat down and waited for customers. Yang Yang took out a thin whetstone and started honing his carving knife, while Xiangqian took an old book from her painting bag and started reading. Yang Yang glanced at the book and saw that the title was *Ruins*. Seeing the nervous frown on Xiangqian's face, he couldn't help but chuckle.

"What are you laughing at?"

Yang Yang said, "Nothing. I just didn't realize there were still people who read novels."

Xiangqian said, "I don't actually like novels much, but this isn't just any novel."

Yang Yang asked what was different about it.

Xiangqian said, "It really grabs the heart. Anyway, I can't really explain it. You can borrow it when I'm done and see for yourself."

With a slight smile, Yang Yang said, "No need. I know every chapter by heart. I wrote it."

Xiangqian was stunned, momentarily speechless.

He had written the book in his third year of postgraduate studies, the second year he had known Xiaodeng. It became an overnight sensation, even winning a national literature award that year. If his previous novels were only bricks stacked under his feet, this novel had raised him to luminous heights all at once. From there, he could faintly see the entire world. When he graduated, the Publicity Department of the Municipal Party Committee and several well-known newspapers and journals all came offering an olive branch after all that had happened to the writers of his generation and invited him to work with them, but he was unmoved. Instead of accepting their solicitations, he acted willfully and chose to remain a teacher at the school. He was afraid his peculiar sensitivity to words would be worn away by bureaucratic office routines over the years. But ultimately, it was not the workplace that left his talents bald.

After that book, he suddenly found himself no longer able to write a word, because the book had raised his standards and ushered him into a new world where anything remotely mediocre had no foothold.

Success and failure both came from the same source. The book had been his lucky star, and his curse too.

The flow of customers at Eaton Centre gradually picked up, and some people came to sit in front of Xiangqian's booth to have their portrait painted. Some walked over to Yang Yang's booth as well, watching him carve seals. After a while, Yang Yang finally had his first customer. Later, a few more came, one after another, some to have a seal engraved, some to have their fortune read, and some just to chat. Yang Yang tried his hardest, with his broken English, not to offend anyone in the latter group: Who knew whether they might eventually become customers?

Traffic was not too high, but because Yang Yang was inexperienced, he was so busy he didn't have time for lunch. It was not until dusk that he got a little breathing room and took the sticky, dirty roll of notes from his pocket. He counted them: one hundred and sixty dollars. At first, he thought he had made a mistake, so he counted again. When he came to the same figure, a wide grin spread across his face.

After packing up for the day, he said to Xiangqian, "I'll see you tomorrow," then stood on the corner, waiting for Xiaodeng. Xiaodeng would first pick up Susie from piano lessons in the afternoon and then pick up Yang Yang on the way home.

When Yang Yang got into the car, he saw that Susie's eyes were red and puffy, as if she had been crying. He asked Xiaodeng what was wrong.

She snorted. "Ask your precious little princess."

Susie said nothing, but her nose twitched, and the teardrops started falling, stinging Yang Yang's heart.

Seeing Xiaodeng's angry face, he didn't dare comfort Susie but merely asked, "What happened?"

Xiaodeng said that the piano teacher taught in English, and Susie had trouble understanding. Instead of trying, she gave up and sat on the floor reading children's books.

Yang Yang said, "She just arrived in a new place. She hasn't gotten her bearings yet."

Xiaodeng sneered, "I knew you'd take her side. I'll go to class with her next week. We'll see if she still dares to misbehave then. We've already paid for the lessons, you know. Did you even think of that?"

Yang Yang quickly took the thick stack of banknotes from his pocket. "Here are the fees," he said. "I didn't expect it to be so easy."

Xiaodeng glanced at the stack, and she was surprised too. Sensing the shift in mood, Yang Yang reached out and squeezed her shoulder. After a moment's pause, he said to Xiaodeng, "Relax. Don't be so high strung. Once the string breaks, that's it."

Xiaodeng said, "Bah! What do you mean, 'that's it'? If it breaks, you'll take care of me for the rest of my life." Her expression gradually softened. "Yang Yang, my short story, the one about Chinese New Year, it's going to be published in the *New Yorker*. I just got the letter. They sent it to the department."

"Oh" was all Yang Yang managed to say. Something welled up inside him—surprise, but it was not entirely pleasant. Xiaodeng had told him she wanted to write in English, but he had never taken her seriously. He had never dreamed that her first piece would be published in a magazine like the *New Yorker*.

And what about him? He hadn't published a single word in ten years.

November 2, 2002
Toronto

Xiaodeng and Yang Yang had started sleeping in separate rooms early on. The habit initially developed because of her insomnia, but eventually there were other reasons too.

At first, Xiaodeng urged Yang Yang to sleep in another room because she was afraid that her tossing and turning would wake him at night. Yang Yang was reluctant, and he always looked for excuses to stay in Xiaodeng's bed for a while longer. When it was time for him to leave, there were always many protests, big and small. Eventually, these protests subsided, becoming white noise. In the end, when it was time to sleep each night, Yang Yang took the initiative to move to his own room without Xiaodeng's urging.

By the time Xiaodeng noticed this shift, inertia had taken over. If she had wanted to reach out to him at that point, she could have stopped the situation from spiraling, but she didn't. Reaching out was not a gesture in Xiaodeng's repertoire. It never had been.

In the end, they settled into a routine of living separately under the same roof.

Each night around dinnertime, Xiaodeng's nerves tensed. Twilight inched her closer to sleep. Of course, it was only her body that was pulled toward sleep. Her mind always had the alertness of a leopard, prowling and observing the dark land of sleep from a distance. Her body swooped toward sleep again and again, but it was always caught by her mind and brought back at a safe distance from it. The exhaustive battles between mind and body raged, and dawn gradually licked the curtains until they turned white, and she began to wait for the same cycle again, another alternation between day and night. The worsening insomnia made the heavy load of coursework unbearable for her, and she finally decided to drop out of school, just a year before she was to complete her PhD.

One day, in the early hours of the morning, Xiaodeng was in a state of sleep thinner than a layer of oil floating on the surface of water. Even the slight movement of a blade of grass might disperse the oil, exposing the vast riverbed of consciousness beneath. She vaguely heard footsteps and the sound of running water. These sounds were wrapped tightly and suppressed, as slight as dust being swept across the floor. Later, Xiaodeng heard humming creeping through the wall, vibrating on her eardrums, soft, warm, and almost hypnotizing. The oily patch of drowsiness began to gather on the surface of her mind again.

Bees. It's bees' wings, Xiaodeng thought.

Rapeseed flowers, a whole yellow expanse of them, reaching to the horizon. A young woman, riding a polished bicycle along such a country road. Bees brushed past her hair, and the air was full of the hum of their wings. A thin girl sat on the back seat of the woman's bike, leaning sideways, with a bamboo basket on her knees.

Follow them. Follow them. Get a good look at the girl's face, Xiaodeng said to herself over and over. But just as she was about to catch up with the girl, she woke suddenly. The rapeseed flowers withered, the bees fell to the ground, and the woman and child disappeared into the darkness.

No, it wasn't the sound of bees. It was Yang Yang blow-drying his hair, Xiaodeng suddenly realized.

The opening ceremony of the Xiangyang Chinese Art School was to be held that day. The school name sounded a bit like a legacy of the Cultural Revolution, but it was actually just a combination of Xiangqian and Yang Yang's names.

In fact, Yang Yang had already opened his own Chinese school two years earlier. It was only recently that his school had merged with Xiangqian's painting classes to form a Chinese art school. Yang Yang and Xiangqian had been running their combined school for three months. The reason they had postponed the opening ceremony was that Yang Yang wanted to test the water for a period of time before officially announcing it to the public.

"We're getting along pretty well," Yang Yang said to Xiaodeng. *Getting along* was a complex idea with layers of meaning, but the implications Xiaodeng took away were not necessarily those intended by Yang Yang.

We can save money if we split rent and utilities. We can share student lists. If one of us needs time off, the other can at least keep the school running at a basic level.

That was how Yang Yang explained the proposal to Xiaodeng. She half believed him. But only half.

There was a dull rumbling sound, as if shells were being shot from an old rusted barrel and exploding in the corner of her room. The house shook, and the windowpanes hummed and trembled. Xiaodeng knew that it was Yang Yang starting his car. He carefully suppressed all his own sounds, but he couldn't control those of the old Ford. It was nearly ten years old now. The muffler had broken the previous week, and he had not had time to have it repaired. She listened to the rumbling as it gradually faded into the noise of the street. Xiaodeng could almost see a tail of light smoke dragging behind the car as it crushed the colorful leaves on the street and drove away. Xiaodeng even faintly saw the eagerness on Yang Yang's face.

Perhaps by now he had already arrived. Xiangqian had definitely gotten there before him. She would stand in the doorway, waiting for him to put his car keys in his pocket. She would take his coat and hang it on the hook by the door, then grab a cup of hot coffee and ask, *Just milk, no sugar, right?*

Then, when everyone had arrived, she would push him into the media spotlight and introduce him. *This is Yang Yang, a renowned China scholar and novelist, and the head of the Xiangyang Chinese Art School.*

The table facing the door must be filled with a display of his various writings. When she introduced him to the crowd, her tone would be exaggerated, eager, with an unconcealed desire to please. And her radiant smile would be enough to shatter all barriers and doubts. Even the greenest person could see that he had become her foundation, her substance; she was but a ray of light refracted through him.

Then there would be the speech. All sorts of prominent figures, people from the consulate, members of the overseas Chinese community, principals, teachers, parents, and students. Then would come the reading of congratulatory messages. Then the pair of them would stand in the hall filled with greeting cards and flowers, taking photos with various guests. Tomorrow—ah! tomorrow!—their smiles, his and hers, would fill the community pages of all the Chinese language newspapers.

When all the guests were gone, the pair would breathe a sigh of relief and say, *Whew! Finally over.* Then she would ask, *Are you hungry? I'll take you to lunch in Chinatown. There's a new Vietnamese restaurant.*

As Xiaodeng imagined it all, she felt a caterpillar with its many legs and crest of tiny spikes crawling through her heart. Every pore was itchy and irritable. She could not lie there any longer.

Susie woke late that day. She was in third grade now. Most Saturdays, she went with her father to his school to study Chinese. This week, classes were suspended because of the opening ceremony, so she took the opportunity to sleep in. Even when she woke, she wasn't fully awake. Eyes still half-closed, she opened the bedroom door to go to the bathroom. She tripped on something soft and nearly fell. It was her mother.

Her mother sat in the hallway, the hem of her nightgown raised, revealing her thin thighs. Her mother's legs were very pale, so pale that they had a bluish tint, with blood vessels running underneath the skin like feeble cobwebs. It was a paleness of someone who had been long deprived of sun and fresh air. She leaned against the wall, her hair in thick clumps from a night of tossing and turning. Her eyes were wide open, motionless, like two misty glass beads staring at the ceiling, bright, but cloudy.

"Ma, what's wrong?" Susie was totally awake, and her voice was shattered.

"Susie, that teacher Xiangqian, is her painting any good?" Xiaodeng asked with a vague smile.

"Sure, it's not bad," Susie said a little hesitantly.

"Does your father think so too?"

"I guess."

"Which is it? Yes or no?" Xiaodeng's face tightened, and Susie's body withered under her gaze.

"I don't know, Ma."

"When you go to the school for Chinese lessons, what does your father usually do for lunch?"

"He brings lunch from home and heats it up in the microwave."

"In which room? And who does he eat with?"

The further Xiaodeng pushed, the more Susie withdrew. Finally, Xiaodeng pushed her into a corner. Having nowhere left to retreat, Susie suddenly became desperate.

"Ma, if you want to know so much, why don't you ask Pa?"

Xiaodeng opened her mouth, but no sound came out.

Susie went into the bathroom and quickly cleaned up. When she came out, her face looked bright. Her mother had gone back into her own room. Susie went to knock on her door. Xiaodeng was changing clothes. She put on a sky-blue suit with a tight collar and cuffs, covering up everything that shouldn't be shown. She even put on light makeup. With makeup, her mother's face now had color, light, and shadow. Rarely seeing her mother paying such attention to her looks, Susie was a little bewildered.

"Ma, are you going out?"

Xiaodeng pulled a large, wide-toothed comb through her tangled hair, but she did not respond.

"Ma, there's a sleepover at Rebecca's house tonight. Linda and Chris are both going. Can I go?"

Susie was a cheerful child. There was a straight line from her heart to her mouth, and she could never hold back a word. She had long forgotten the earlier, unpleasant conversation, and her interest had now moved on to a new topic.

Xiaodeng squirted a ball of mousse the size of an egg onto her fingers and slowly rubbed it into her hair. Like grass after a rain, her hair started to show signs of life. But still, Xiaodeng said nothing.

Thinking her mother had not heard, Susie asked again as she followed Xiaodeng downstairs. This time, Xiaodeng gave a simple, direct answer.

"No, you can't."

"Why do you never let me go? All my friends can."

Susie stomped her feet on the floor and her face flushed crimson.

"No reason. You are not all your friends. You're you."

Xiaodeng glanced at her watch and walked toward the door. When she reached the door, she heard a sudden burst of music, like a tornado, from upstairs. The booming bass rolled like dull thunder, shaking the floor and the walls. She knew Susie had turned on the stereo. When she was angry, Susie always needed some channel through which to vent, and music was one of them.

Xiaodeng couldn't worry about it now. The thunder would always pass, no matter how urgent it seemed. She had to go her own way now. It was half past ten. It would take her forty-five minutes to get there by bus. By the time she rushed over, the opening ceremony would have probably just ended. If she was lucky, she would be able to block them squarely in the door as they went out for lunch.

I hope I'm not interrupting your plans, she would say.

Autumn 1989
Guangzhou

When they awoke that morning, good fortune was not waiting for them. Sitting quietly beside the door to eat breakfast, Sanzi felt the bowl in his hand suddenly crack, and the preserved egg porridge dribbled out, creating a map on his freshly laundered stonewashed jeans.

When he had changed, they went out the door. A gray pigeon circled Xiaoda's head, splattering a lump of warm droppings. Xiaoda wiped it with his hand, and the splat further blossomed across his face. Xiaoda exploded. "Fucking hell!"

"Bad omen. We better watch out today," Sanzi said.

The pair hurried to the market. It was still early, just in time to catch the residual flow of people from the food market. But before they could even open the zipper of the woven bag, the police came. Sanzi quickly slipped away, as if he had smeared oil on the soles of his shoes. Xiaoda was just a step too late, and he was caught. The woven bag was confiscated and an additional fine of two hundred yuan issued, effectively wiping out several months' worth of business.

Xiaoda stood empty handed in the street, looking listless, like a damp, wrinkled old shirt. With the sun gradually rising and sunlight licking the treetops, the noisy street market pushed him to and fro like the tide. There seemed to be thousands of roads in front of him, but he had nowhere to go.

It really was a good place, Guangzhou. When he and Sanzi had stepped out of the train station just a little more than a year earlier, they were dazzled by the magnificence of the city. The lights, the street scenes, the crowds—all the wonders he and Sanzi would have never seen in the course of an entire life in Tangshan, or even two lifetimes, for that matter. But no matter how good the city was, it was good in the way an iron plate was; no matter how sharp they made themselves, they would never be able to poke even the tiniest hole in it, not even one big enough for them to wriggle a toe through.

When they arrived in Guangzhou, they learned that Sanzi's uncle was not in the city at all, but in Zhuhai, a small town nearby. They also found out that he hadn't saved up ten thousand yuan, as he had boasted, but was simply looking after a grain warehouse, earning a slightly higher salary than he could have gotten in Tangshan.

Sanzi's uncle had recommended them to work as porters, but they were fired when Xiaoda, having only one hand, couldn't keep up. The pair went from one job to another—so many that they lost count—until they finally saved a little money, bought some cheap clothes and accessories, and set up a roadside stall.

There were all kinds of stalls, of various grades and ranks. The most elaborate was a cart with a plastic shed, which provided shelter from the wind and rain. The next was a topless flatbed cart, which was exposed to sun and rain. After that was a simple bike with a cargo box strapped to the rear of the frame. The simplest thing was to spread oiled paper on the ground and place a stone on each corner to hold it down. Xiaoda and Sanzi's stall was even lower than the lowest level, right down in the dust and mud. They didn't even have a sheet of oiled paper; their entire stall was stored in the woven bag. As soon as they unzipped it, they were open for business. Once they zipped it, they were closed, which saved them valuable time when they had to run. Heaven never gave those two boys anything more than a pair of legs each, legs as long as an egret's. No one could keep up with those legs, not the eagle-eyed street police patrols or the watchdogs from the business licensing bureau or local security teams.

Until today.

Xiaoda stood on the side of the road for a while. He really didn't want to go home, so he wandered aimlessly in the flow of people.

Xiaoda and Sanzi had been setting up their stall here for several months, and he thought he had become very familiar with this road. He could name every shop on the street with his eyes closed, and his soles recognized every stone along the way. However, in the past, he had always been too busy to really look: his feet had walked the street a thousand times, but he had never used his eyes. It was only today that so many of the things on the street leaped to life before him. For instance, on the red, white, and blue barber pole outside the hair salon called Golden Hair Boy, there was a plaster statue of Venus with half her face missing. And in the foyer of the newly opened hotel, there was a sign that said, *No entry to those in disheveled attire.* One of the characters in the line had been written wrongly as "angry," and then corrected over. And the price list in the window of the Chaoshan snack bar had been blown sideways by the wind, revealing a foreign movie poster underneath. The face of the blond woman in the poster seemed to be all mouth, and it was smeared in scarlet, but it was not unattractive.

Xiaoda walked a very long way. His legs and feet broke free of his mind and body and went their own direction. His mind looked on helplessly as his feet wore down the pavement. They grew weaker and heavier as he walked, but he couldn't rein them in. Later, his legs finally stopped moving. He slumped under a big tree. His backside had barely touched the ground when he tilted his head and dozed off.

When he woke, it was night, and he was hungry. As soon as he opened his eyes, he saw stars—not in the sky, but on the ground. It was a dense layer of stars, all in a row, touching each other, sleeping on deep black velvet. A gigantic shadow rushed into the stars' bed, panting heavily, awakening them all at once. The stars danced frantically for a while before quieting down again.

It was a ship. Xiaoda came to his senses then and saw that he had walked to the riverside.

His stomach rumbled. He propped himself up with his hand on the tree trunk behind him, feeling for a moment like the world was spinning.

"You're not going to jump into the river, are you?"

The voice came from the darkness, making Xiaoda's hair stand up. The Cantonese people were always superstitious, and he had heard too many sensational stories about ghosts and spirits since he came to Guangzhou. It was inevitable that shadows lingered in his mind.

The voice chuckled and said, "I've been watching you for a long time. I was afraid you'd do something crazy."

Xiaoda rubbed his eyes. In the dim light, he vaguely discerned the shape of a woman standing up from a tourist bench nearby. Her dress rustled as she moved toward him, swishing over the dew-covered grass. There were two gleaming spots on her face, eyes.

"You're the one who wants to jump into the river." The hair on Xiaoda's arms gradually settled, and there was courage in his voice.

The woman was not offended. She smiled. "You're right. I do want to jump into the river."

She was standing in front of Xiaoda now. She had fashionably cut straight hair, and she wore an equally fashionable denim skirt. She looked very young, but her voice was mature, as if she had lived much of her life already. Xiaoda felt that she looked a little familiar, but he couldn't say where he had seen her before. His heart skipped a beat, but he didn't know why.

"You're not really here to end your life, are you?" he stammered.

She snorted. "Can't you tell it's just a joke? Kill myself over a man? Do you think there's anything worth jumping into this river for? It'll just pollute the water!"

Xiaoda's stomach growled again. It was earth shattering, loud enough to be heard all through the street. He was so embarrassed he wanted to cut off his ears so he couldn't hear it anymore.

"Let's go for supper. My treat," she said casually as she led the way. He was a little hesitant. There was a scale inside him, and he was measuring to see which weighed more—his hunger, his curiosity, or his timidity. This time, his feet followed his heart.

The pair entered a small restaurant on the street. The woman ordered a bowl of steamed rice with salted sausage for Xiaoda and a bowl of river snails fried with peppers for herself. She slowly picked at the snails in her own bowl as she watched Xiaoda wipe out his rice like a whirlwind. She ordered another bowl for him, and he continued to gobble his food, though a little more slowly now.

"When was the last time you ate?" she asked, half jokingly.

"I left home early this morning. All I had was a bowl of porridge," Xiaoda said uneasily, and sweat appeared on his brow.

Once the hungry beast was contained, the shame began to revive. Before tonight, twenty-year-old Xiaoda had never eaten alone with a young woman. In the moment, he had not realized the significance of this meal. It opened a door for him to step through, and once he'd entered, he could not go back out. Now that he was through that door, he had left his boyhood behind. He was an adult now.

"Try some of this. It's delicious."

The woman pushed her bowl to Xiaoda, but he didn't move. The smell of peppers got into his nose, so strong it made him want to sneeze. He wanted to try the local delicacy, but he couldn't. He only had one hand, so when he held a snail, he could not hold a toothpick to dig out the meat.

"The hell with table manners." The woman laughed.

She tossed aside her toothpick and grabbed a snail between her fingers. She put the preclipped tail end to her mouth and sucked. Then she turned the snail around and sucked on the head end. A shiny piece of meat was now on her tongue. The sound of her slurping was coarse and loud, and Xiaoda knew she had done it to put him at ease.

"What rattled your world so much that you didn't even have time to eat?" the woman asked. Xiaoda couldn't tell whether there was curiosity or ridicule behind the question.

"Don't make fun of me. I'm just a street vendor. I ran into some shitty luck today. The police came and took everything."

"What do you sell?"

"I used to sell digital watches, dolls, and toys. Now, I sell clothes and women's pajamas."

The woman's eyes gradually focused on his empty sleeve. "Was it a fight?" she asked.

Xiaoda was startled, and it took him a moment to understand what she was asking. He was thrown off by this strange association. Blood instantly rushed to his face, and a blue vein popped out on his forehead. He opened his mouth, but the words dissolved in his throat.

Both fell silent. There was no sound but the slurping of snails.

After a while, the woman raised her head and asked, "Where are you from?"

"Tangshan."

This time, it was the woman who was surprised. When she spoke again, her lips quivered slowly.

"I'm sorry. I didn't realize . . . I heard that the earthquake was really awful."

"I'm alive, at least. A lot of people died," Xiaoda replied, swinging his empty sleeve, as if tossing out some old memory he never wanted to speak of again.

The pair finally finished the snails. Wiping their mouths, they walked out onto the street.

Xiaoda looked up at the sky and knew that it was after eleven. The night air was still close, and there was no sign that it would loosen. The neon lights went out, and the buildings along the street lost their outlines, the edges blurring into the shapeless darkness of the night. When the wind picked up, the leaves of the sycamores curled into angry fists and smashed down on the road. The sleeping neighborhoods were like people who had been stripped of their clothing. Naked, everything suddenly looked the same. The dim lamplight languidly cast the shadows of the two figures across the ground: hers tall and slender, and his solid and strong.

"Sis, where are you going? I'll walk you there."

"Forget it. I can't walk anymore. Take me to the bus stop, and I'll wait for the first bus to take me to school."

"School? You're still in school?"

"What do you mean 'still'? I just got into graduate school."

Xiaoda was stunned. His surprise registered clearly on his face.

"Do you feel that I don't look like the scholarly type?" The woman turned to gaze at Xiaoda, as if demanding an explanation.

"No, it's not that. I've just never met a woman in graduate school." Flustered, Xiaoda fumbled for words. "I think studying is really hard."

The woman laughed. "That's because you don't know how to just bumble along. For basic knowledge, it's a little bumbling, but for great learning, you need to bumble a lot more. Learning to bumble along is more difficult than any learning you do in school. I can teach you a few tricks, then you can even learn to solve the mysteries of sacred scriptures if they drop out of the sky."

Xiaoda was greatly amused. From the time he was a child until now, no one had ever taught him in this way.

"Sis, that man—" Xiaoda hesitated.

"Are you going to keep calling me Sis? Am I so old? I have a name. It's Aya," the woman interrupted.

"A-Aya, did that man really make you so sad?" This question had been weighing on Xiaoda for a while, leaving a sour taste in his mouth.

Aya looked at the inky river in the distance in silent fascination. After a long pause, she said, "He went to the US with a Taiwanese classmate for further studies."

Aya stopped, and the rest of the words remained on her lips, weighing down the corners of her mouth. Xiaoda wanted to reach out and break the downward curve, but he didn't dare. This impulse was bold, but the hand was shy. When emotion eventually found its way to his tongue, it came out in one coarse utterance.

"Fuck him, and his grandmother too."

Aya was startled, but then she suddenly burst out laughing. Their laughter rang through the air, shattering the serenity of the night.

"Silly boy, you came here from so far away. Do you want to make a little money?" Aya stopped laughing. Her eyebrows straightened and she spoke seriously now.

"Why not? I think of making money even in my dreams."

"What's the use of dreams? You're just running around like a mouse all day."

"What else can I do? Without money to invest and no connections, what choice do I have?"

"Stop whining. It can't be that you're entirely penniless. Tell me the truth. How much can you put together?"

Xiaoda made a quick mental calculation. "Sanzi and I still have around a thousand yuan. We planned to send it home, but we haven't yet."

"Then you need to get a little shop. Make sure it's in a good location. If you're in a good location, you can get rich selling shit in Guangzhou."

Xiaoda frowned. "How? I don't have a business license. Sanzi and I have been to the Industry and Commerce Bureau several times. You know them: no local contacts, so we can't get a license."

Aya took a piece of paper from her bag. She wrote a line of words on it and handed it to Xiaoda.

"This is the home address of Mr. Lu, the director of the Administration for Market Regulation at the Municipal Government. Go see him. It's probably best to go in the evening, between nine thirty and nine forty-five, when he has finished watching the news."

"Will it help?" Xiaoda took the note, but his face was full of doubt. "I can't afford any expensive gifts. People in Guangzhou have seen the world. You can't fool them with any cheap stuff."

Aya squinted at Xiaoda and said, "Did you know that, aside from money, there's something else called 'hitting on what one likes'? Mr. Lu is a retired soldier. His troops were stationed in Hebei. He was in Tangshan in 1976. Do you understand?"

It took Xiaoda a few moments. After some thought, his eyebrows started to twitch.

"Yes."

"Just don't tell him I sent you," Aya urged.

The pair stopped under a sign for the bus stop. They sat at the bus stop for hours, staring at the long street until its outlines gradually solidified in the faint dawn light.

"Aya, one day, there will be a building in Guangzhou with my name on it," Xiaoda murmured.

Xiaoda did not get home until early morning. Fumbling, he took out the key and opened the door. To his astonishment, he was greeted by a punch in the face from Sanzi.

"If you're going to kill yourself, at least let me know. I've been going crazy looking for you!"

Xiaoda got up from the ground, unperturbed. He sat on the edge of the bed with Sanzi and said with a raucous laugh, "Why would I want to kill myself? Maybe things are about to turn around. No one can be unlucky for his whole life."

Sanzi turned and looked at Xiaoda suspiciously. "What kind of drug are you on?"

Xiaoda stood up and scooped cold water from the basin to wash his face, splashing it all over the floor.

"Sanzi, educated women really are different," he said.

The next day, Sanzi accompanied Xiaoda to buy a light gray suit from a stall. It cost fifty-eight yuan. The texture was poor, but the style was trendy. Xiaoda took it home and mixed a bowl of starch. He sprayed the starch from his mouth onto the suit, then ran an iron over the fabric, and the wrinkles instantly disappeared. He had often watched his mother do this.

"It looks good, but whatever happens, you can't get caught in the rain and get it wet."

Xiaoda grabbed a handful of hair wax and slicked his naturally curly hair back into a big glossy pompadour. He put on his prosthesis, a clean shirt, his suit, and a tie, and he stood in front of the mirror. He hardly recognized himself.

Behind him, Sanzi grinned. "You really look the part of a gentleman. Better watch out, or Mr. Lu may decide to keep you as a son-in-law."

Xiaoda spat and said, "Ha! More like his daddy. You just stay here and wait for the good news."

Anxious, Sanzi grabbed Xiaoda's sleeve and said, "You want me to wait here, worrying to death? I'm going with you. I'll wait downstairs when you go up."

They walked out the door, laughing together.

It did not take them long to find the building. It was an old-fashioned dormitory in the old part of the city. The corridor was piled with junk, and the streetlights shining through the windows were dim, like kerosene lamps with shades that had not been cleaned for years. Xiaoda almost tripped over a cardboard box. He stumbled up the stairs. Looking at his watch, he saw that it was 9:37. He took a deep breath, calmed himself, and raised his hand to ring the doorbell.

The man who answered the door was in his fifties. He had a stubble beard, and he wore pajamas and had a toothbrush in his mouth. Xiaoda's sharp eye immediately noted that the hand on the door handle was missing two fingers.

"Who are you looking for?"

The old man's eyes ran up and down Xiaoda's body like a steel-bristled brush, shredding the deceptive suit to pulp. Under such scrutiny, Xiaoda felt naked.

"Lu, Mr. Lu, this is . . . for you."

On the way there, Xiaoda had planned a whole load of things to say as his opening remarks, but now that the moment had come, only this little trickle was left.

The old man glanced at the package Xiaoda handed him. With one look, he guessed what it was.

"I don't smoke. If you need something, come see me at my office."

He was about to close the door, but Xiaoda quickly grabbed his arm. He stuck his foot in the crack of the door before the old fellow realized what he was doing.

"Mr. Lu, it's urgent. Please."

Having seen plenty of presumptuous people before, the old man didn't even raise an eyebrow. He let Xiaoda into the apartment and left him in the room by himself, while he went to the bathroom to finish brushing his teeth. He gargled loudly, like nobody else was around.

Xiaoda walked around the room, looking at things. The home was not big, but it was neat and tidy. There was a sofa, a desk, and a dining table, all of which were old fashioned. On the opposite wall hung a large black-framed photo of a woman in her forties or fifties, dressed in old-fashioned clothes and with a dull expression. Xiaoda felt she was vaguely familiar, but he found that strange. He didn't know why he kept getting this funny feeling when he ran into people in recent days, as if he had seen them somewhere before but couldn't recall where.

A few photos were pressed under the plate glass on top of the desk. Most were of a man in various summer-style military uniforms or winter coats with Russian hats. It was obvious that this was the old man in his younger days. In the lower righthand corner, there was a two-inch black-and-white photo of a girl of seven or eight. She wore a white shirt and a floral skirt, and she had a red scarf tied around her neck. Xiaoda rubbed his eyes. He felt like a ladle had been shoved into his heart and was now stirring it, scattering the parts of it like soft tofu. His mind went blank.

"If you have something to say, say it. I go to bed early." The old man came out of the bathroom with a towel in his hand, wiping his mouth.

"Mr. Lu, who is this in the photo?" Xiaoda asked, pointing at the glass. His expression was very strange, and the muscles on his face quivered all the way from his cheekbones to the lower part of his jaw. He held his hand at his chest, like he was getting ready to catch his teeth, in case they suddenly fell out.

The old man was taken aback by his appearance.

"That's my daughter, Aya. Why?"

"Aya is your daughter?"

The surprises he had experienced in the past two days were like a series of bullets; before one shot had left the barrel, the next had already been fired. Xiaoda had read about being a soldier, but he had never been in battle. Overwhelmed by this rapid fire, he suddenly collapsed on the sofa.

"You know my Aya?" the old man asked.

Xiaoda shook his head. It began to dawn on him now. He recalled things Aya had said, putting them together like a puzzle, and suddenly the picture was laid out clearly before him. He became completely calm, and he knew what to say next.

"Mr. Lu, this photo looks like my sister when she was small. I thought it was her."

He stood up, undid his tie, took off his suit and shirt, and removed his prosthesis, laying each item on the desk in turn. It was like a slow motion shot in a Hollywood blockbuster, gentle, calm, and methodical.

The old man took two steps back. Though he had seen the world and met many people, he had never witnessed anything like this. He was in a bit of a panic. Out of habit, he reached for his waist, as if wanting to draw a gun that was no longer there.

Xiaoda told him his story. A mother's hard choice, a daughter's despair, and a son's guilt. A story he never told anyone who didn't already know. A story that had over the years become a nocturnal beast, sleeping unseen during the day in some unknown cave, only leaping to life in all its raw vividness at night, monopolizing his dreams. "My mother chose me," Xiaoda said. "But after she did, how could she go on living? How could I go on living?"

The man's mangled hand trembled.

"Give me a cigarette." He pointed to the package Xiaoda had placed on the desk.

Xiaoda opened the package and took out a cigarette. With the lighter that came with the package, he lit the cigarette for the old man. The way the old fellow smoked was strange. He held several puffs in him for as long as he could, then gradually released one puff through his nostrils. That puff had stayed in the belly for so long it had the smell of his singed innards, so hot and dry that it seemed to carry sparks with it.

"In 1976, our troops were stationed in Shijiazhuang. We rushed to Tangshan as quickly as we could." The old man spoke slowly. "My hand was injured then. So many people died that summer, and they were buried in haste. That winter, to prevent the spread of disease, my superior ordered us to move the buried bodies. One night, I was guarding the pit, and a boy and girl came, brother and sister, one nine, the other seven. They said they were looking for their mother. Their little feet stepped on the bags of bodies, walking back and forth several times. The remains were all icy filth by then. I said, 'Don't look for her, okay? There are thousands of them there. How will you ever find her? It's getting dark. Go home.' You know what they said? 'Ma's gone. Where's home?'"

The old man's three fingers trembled even more. The long line of ash fell to the floor and sizzled, raising the faint burnt scent of coke and pine.

"Have you rented the shop? I know you came for the license," the old man said, throwing the cigarette butt into the bathroom washbasin.

"Yes, on Zhongshan Sixth Road."

That was only partially true. The storefront was to be leased by an acquaintance of Sanzi, but they hadn't even spoken to the landlord. Before today, they had never dreamed they could get a business license.

"Do you have any retail experience? Don't lie to me."

Xiaoda paused for a while, then said, "Kind of."

The old man glared at Xiaoda. "What do you mean, 'kind of'? If you have experience, you do, and if you don't, you don't."

Averting his eyes, Xiaoda said, "We have done roadside stalls."

The old man let out a long sigh. Pursing his lips, he motioned for Xiaoda to get dressed.

"Bring your ID card to my office tomorrow."

As Xiaoda walked out the door, the old fellow came out after him and shoved the package at him.

"I'll keep the opened pack. You take the rest. They're Arrow brand, and hard shell. Those aren't cheap."

"Mr. Lu, I won't let you down." Xiaoda lowered his head and spoke softly, afraid the old man would hear the crack in his voice.

"That photo. I'll print a copy for you, later," the old man called from behind as he walked away.

February 14, 1991 (Chinese New Year's Eve)
Tangshan, Hebei

Over the past few years, Li Yuanni had learned not to keep track of the date. There was no calendar on her wall at home, nor was there a desk calendar. She even set the date on her alarm clock to still mode. When customers came to her house to have clothes tailored, she wrote, *Two-day pickup*, *Three-day pickup*, or *Urgent*, and pinned it to the cloth bag. Of course, she just wanted to erase the imprint of the dates on paper. She could do nothing about their imprint on the world. When new branches sprang up on the oleander in front of the door, she knew it was once again a new spring. When the geese flew southward in a line overhead, she knew summer was coming to an end. When the store windows in the street began displaying red-packaged goods and the sound of firecrackers rang out in the air, she knew another year was ending.

Yuanni wished that she were blind and couldn't see the changing of the seasons. She wished she were deaf too, so she couldn't hear the joyful bursting of firecrackers in the neighborhood. She wanted to bury her head and live a life without years, months, and days. But heaven refused to let her off, always reminding her that it was another Qingming, Dragon Boat Festival, Mid-Autumn Festival, or twelfth lunar month. As soon as she was reminded, she would think of him. He was like a knife she had inadvertently swallowed, welling straight up with her breath and blood. It stabbed her on its way up, poking her heart to shreds. The thought of him never came without pain. She was a mess, but she was too proud to talk about it.

He was her son, Xiaoda.

When Xiaoda told her he wanted to go to Guangzhou with Sanzi, the words he used were "to make a fortune," but the naked truth was, other than a vague attraction to that mysterious world, he had no idea what he was going to do there. "Having a look around" was more like it. Yuanni was resolute; she would not allow him to go. They fought endless battles, hot and cold, over this issue. In the end, she reluctantly yielded.

"One year. That's all. If you can make it, good. If you can't, pack up and come home at once."

Yuanni laid down this one condition before releasing him. Xiaoda nodded in agreement, but when the year was up, he did not keep his promise. He had been gone for nearly three years now. In the beginning, there were letters, but there were fewer and fewer as time went on, and the return address always seemed to change, arriving from Shenzhen, Foshan, Zhuhai, Guangzhou, and various other places. When Yuanni replied, the letters were often returned—at least sixty or seventy percent of them—because the recipient had already moved.

Over the past several years, Xiaoda had sent money home a total of three times: a hundred yuan the first time, a hundred eighty the second, and two hundred the third. Even the postman who delivered the remittance slip couldn't help but laugh. "Your son can't save up and send it all at once? This amount is hardly worth the remittance fee."

Yuanni also laughed. "He's afraid his mother is starving to death. If I were relying on him for money, I would be!"

She laughed, but she inwardly acknowledged that once she had allowed her son to go to the South, he had become a kite, and his string had broken. Whether he came back and when were not up to her, nor to him, but to the wind. It was useless for her to worry, so she let go in her heart.

Early on the morning of New Year's Eve, Mr. Qin came. He went into the kitchen and chopped meat for the filling to make dumplings. Yuanni was still leaning over the sewing machine, rushing to finish the last job she had in hand. She had put on her New Year's clothes, a newly knitted sweater with a dark green base and a big white plum blossom across the chest. She had stayed up all night to complete the sweater. She put it on as soon as she had bitten off the end of the thread. She did not want to wait until the first day of the new year to wear her new clothes, like everyone else did. The joy of a day was to be consumed within the same day. Since the earthquake, she had learned a hard lesson, and she was not about to leave today's mood to be enjoyed tomorrow.

The piece Yuanni held now was a navy-blue gabardine top to be worn outside a cotton-padded jacket. This sort of old-fashioned clothing couldn't be bought from any department store. A neighbor in the building had commissioned it as New Year's clothes for his elderly mother. The old woman had worn the same style for twenty years. In recent years, people had increasingly preferred to buy off the rack, and Yuanni's tailoring business had slowly declined. Most of the people who came to her now were looking for special styles that couldn't be found. Yuanni tried hard to keep these last few customers.

When she finally finished sewing the last cloth button onto the lapel, she cut off the end of the thread and folded the piece of clothing neatly. She put a piece of festive red paper on it and tied it off with thin hemp rope, then went into the kitchen to help Mr. Qin.

Mr. Qin quickly pushed her out of the kitchen. "Your clothes are too bright! It will be hard to wash them if they get stained."

Yuanni opened the drawer to find sleeves and an apron. "'Bright'? You actually meant to say 'vulgar,' right?"

Mr. Qin stopped what he was doing. Knife still in hand, he turned around and looked at Yuanni. After a moment's pause, he said, "It depends on who's wearing it. It might be vulgar if it was on someone else."

Yuanni couldn't help but purse her lips and smile, noticing how differently an educated man spoke. When Mr. Qin praised someone, he never used a word of praise, but somehow, the praise was still evident, and in this way, it always struck just the right chord.

Yuanni took the bowl of dough and started pulling out one dumpling skin after another.

"You'll need to go as soon as you've finished the filling. They'll be at your house soon," Yuanni said. She looked down at the lump of dough as she spoke, not at Mr. Qin.

They referred to Mr. Qin's daughter and son-in-law. He had had three children before, but two had died in the earthquake. The surviving daughter had married a man in Tianjin. She was going to be home for New Year's Eve dinner later that day.

"It's still early. The bus is at one thirty this afternoon," Mr. Qin said.

He worked quickly with his hands. The knife went up and down, like he was beating a drum, and big beads of sweat appeared on his forehead. Yuanni glanced at him and smiled. "Your mind is elsewhere. Are you in a hurry?"

He grew defensive. The beads of sweat soon formed a little stream on his eyebrows. "Why would you say that? I got up early this morning and bought the minced meat. Wasn't that so I could have New Year's Eve dinner with you?"

Yuanni snorted and said, "Is this what you call New Year's Eve dinner? A rushed lunch, maybe. Have I ever asked you to spend New Year's Eve with me? Do you dare to do it?"

Like a punctured balloon, Mr. Qin collapsed. There was nothing for him to say. All these years, he had hurried over to have lunch with Yuanni on New Year's Eve, then hurried back to have his family reunion dinner with the other side of town. It was one type of life here, and a totally different life there. The life over there was sickly, without color or light, but his feet were on solid ground. The days here were good days, the kind found only in movies or plays, but they seemed to be borrowed from someone else's life. He liked it here, but the ground beneath his feet was made of sand, unstable and unreal. When he was there, his mind was here. But when he was here, his mind was there. He could not let go of either. He had run from one to the other all these years, trying so hard to take care of both, but ending up not really taking care of either. It was enough to thin his hair and turn it gray.

"Did you get a New Year's letter from Xiaoda?" Mr. Qin asked cautiously. He knew talk of her son touched the thinnest part of Yuanni's heart, and a slightly heavy breath could blow a hole right through it.

Yuanni shook her head.

"Life must be difficult for him. He's not an uncaring child—"

Before he could finish, there was a thud. Yuanni had dropped the rolling pin, kicking up a cloud of flour from the table.

"I know how people on the street laugh at me. You don't need to put on a front. I gave birth to a heartless wolf."

Yuanni turned her back and lowered her head. Her shoulders quivered slightly. Mr. Qin put down the kitchen knife and walked over. He hesitated for a moment, then reached out and embraced her.

"Don't cry, Ni. It's New Year's Eve," he whispered in her ear.

She raised her head. There were no tears in her eyes, just a cold smile hanging about the corners of her mouth.

"Do you think I miss him? I can just pretend that I didn't save either one of them during the earthquake, can't I? There are plenty of people who were left all alone in Tangshan. I'm not the only one."

Her words were hard, like ice pellets. They scattered through Mr. Qin's heart and made him shiver.

"Ni, as long as we live, even if everyone else is gone, I'll be by your side. If I'm still breathing, you won't—"

He couldn't go on. He just held her tightly, pressing her face against his chest. She didn't reply, but he felt her body gradually soften in his arms. His chest grew hot and wet—her tears. They finally flowed. She grabbed his shirt, and they stood motionless in the gloomy room, listening to the north wind whipping the snow outside the house, slamming it onto the windowpanes. Their hearts suddenly surged with a sense of everlasting trust and dependence, even amid all the sorrow and desolation.

There was a sudden knock on the door, urgent and impatient. Yuanni pushed Mr. Qin away and said, "It's the neighbor, Mr. Jin. He's here to pick up clothes. Stay in the kitchen and don't come out."

Yuanni grabbed a towel and dried her face as she ran out of the kitchen, smoothing her hair. She picked up the clothing tied in red paper and hurried to open the door.

As soon as she opened the door, a big snowball rolled in. It stood shivering for a moment before coming to a standstill. It shook itself, and a sheet of little water droplets fell to the ground. It was a person, covered in snow. In a familiar manner, he took a large brush from the peg behind the door and wiped the snow from himself. He then wiped his face, revealing bloodshot eyes and a stubby beard. He grinned, baring teeth stained yellow from constant smoking.

"Don't you recognize me, Ma?"

The package fell from Yuanni's hands with a bang. The red paper cracked, and a cloud of navy blue flowed over the floor.

"I had to stand in line for two days and two nights, but I finally got a ticket. I almost missed the New Year!"

He walked straight into the house as he spoke. She wanted to stop him, but before she could, Xiaoda had walked into the kitchen.

"I'm thirsty, Ma. Is there any hot water in the pot? I—"

Xiaoda's words were cut off. He discovered a man in the kitchen—his former tutor. The fellow wore a floral apron and held a kitchen knife in his hand. There was a scrap of chive on the tip of his nose. Xiaoda ran his eyes over him, and the older man shriveled beneath the gaze.

"Xiaoda, you're home? Your mother was home alone. I was worried about her, so I came to make her some dumplings for the New Year," the man stuttered.

Xiaoda said nothing, still sizing the other man up. The man did the same. After nearly three years away, Xiaoda had grown taller and stronger, but no matter how tall or strong he became, there was no escaping his old form. The real change was not in his form, but in his eyes. Flustered, Mr. Qin still managed to search deep into them, and he drew something out. It was something he had not seen before: machismo.

"My mother has me," Xiaoda said, enunciating each word. "She's not alone."

"Xiaoda, Uncle Qin helps with everything around the house while you're gone," Yuanni interjected, but her words were like Mr. Qin's, spineless and soft.

"Ma!" Xiaoda glared at Yuanni. "It's time for lunch at his house. We shouldn't make our guest stay."

Mr. Qin searched for Yuanni's eyes, expecting her to say something, but he didn't find them, so he waited for her words. When he realized there would be none, he took off the apron and removed his coat from the rack and slowly put it on, then his boots, and finally, his hat, and he walked out the door. By this time, the snow had gone crazy, and backed by the force of the wind, it whipped across his body like dirty rags, bringing a crisp pain as it slapped his face. Yuanni wanted to walk him to the courtyard gate, but Xiaoda's eyes were like thick rope, binding her hands and feet, paralyzing her. She watched helplessly as Mr. Qin wobbled into the wind and snow. She noticed that his usually straight back was a little hunched. Something in her heart twitched, evoking a sudden burst of rage.

She slammed the door and walked straight to Xiaoda. "What does he owe to the Wan household? He works to help us year after year, and you begrudge him one meal?"

Xiaoda took out a cigarette and smoked it slowly. It was hard to watch him smoke. His face twisted in pain, as if he were inhaling a handful of chili powder, and a dark gray wrinkle appeared on his forehead. When his cigarette was still only half-smoked, he snuffed it out in the sink.

He turned around and spoke. What he said, he said softly, but it was as sharp as a knife, instantly cutting out the spine that had begun to grow in Yuanni's voice.

"Ma, if he didn't have a wife, I wouldn't begrudge him a single thing. Never mind a meal; I'd even kneel down and call him my father."

Yuanni searched her gut, but she found no answer to this. A flush of shame overcame her, and her forehead bulged and turned red. She suddenly grabbed Xiaoda's travel bag and threw it out the door.

"Go to hell! I'm not your mother. You've been gone for three years. Did you even care whether I was dead or alive in all that time? And the minute you come back, you want to be the master of my house?"

These words never passed through her brain. They went straight from her heart to her tongue, moving so fast that she couldn't keep up with them. If she really wanted to pull them back, there was still a way. She could have followed up with something else, some words that had passed through her brain. But her heart didn't want to lose to her brain, so she watched helplessly as her son zipped his down jacket, which he hadn't had time to take off, and walked toward the door. When he passed by her, she could have reached out, but her hand too fought her brain. Her brain fought battles on every front, and it lost every one of them.

The moment her son opened the door, the wind swirled, picked up a handful of snow, and hurled it at her with all the rage it could gather. Her face burned, as if she had been hit by iron pellets. The pain brought her to her senses. Where could her son go on such a day? She did not have time to put on her cotton shoes, so she ran out in her house slippers.

"Xiaoda!"

She began howling like her heart would break, but no sooner did her voice hit the wind than it was chewed to shreds and tossed here and there. The echoes of "da-da-da" reverberated, but her son had long since vanished.

Yuanni returned to her house in a daze and paced back and forth along the wall. When she saw the half-chopped meat on the cutting board, she realized she was in the kitchen. There was a mesh bag on the dining table, and inside it was a greasy paper parcel that Mr. Qin had brought over that morning. She opened the parcel and found a soy sauce duck dripping with fat, a string of sausages, and two cuts of bacon. When he had arrived that morning, Mr. Qin had hesitantly told her that this year his in-laws, his daughter, and his son-in-law would all come back to stay with him and celebrate the New Year together. There was more that he wanted to say, but he never said it, only barely muddling his way through this first part. But whether he said it or not, Yuanni had guessed: Mr. Qin would not be visiting for the first few days of the new year. These meats were for her to live on during that time. Yuanni tore off a piece of the duck meat, put it in her mouth, and chewed it slowly, thinking that this was how Mr. Qin had bought himself some peace of mind. The thought turned everything sour, and the meat was as flavorless as sawdust.

Her son was right; Mr. Qin had a home. The paralyzed woman over there, no matter how bad her situation, still shared a marriage license with Mr. Qin. As for herself, he could only take all the time he had and slice off small corners, like from a piece of malt sugar, for her. No matter how much Mr. Qin cared about her, he could only be scraps of cloth for her, never a whole piece of fabric.

Yuanni spat out the duck meat and walked into her room in a trance. Sitting on the edge of the bed, she stared blankly at the wall. Though it was daytime, the room was dark. The windows of the house across from hers were too close to her own, so she usually kept the curtains closed for privacy. She heard a bang outside the window, a huge firecracker exploding, followed by a string of smaller ones, which went dead after a few blasts, then silence. Those damned firecrackers should all be dead. Yuanni gritted her teeth. Turning her head, she suddenly saw two dots on the wall, glistening in the dim light like a ghost. Yuanni's hair stood up, as straight as needles, and goose bumps spread all over her body.

It was Xiaodeng's eyes, from the picture on the wall.

Yuanni's body slackened like a rice sack. She squatted on the ground and covered her face with her hands, and she started crying.

"Retribution! This is retribution. Deng, you've seen it all . . ."

There had never been a better time to cry than now. Up above, heaven was unleashing its last tantrum of the year, and down on earth, every family was preparing the last dinner of the year. Today, people were too busy merrymaking to notice a widow's tears, especially when the tears were no longer young and desirable. She could finally cry all she wanted, and for as long as she wanted.

There was another knock at the door.

Xiaoda! Oh! Xiaoda!

Yuanni stood up. She was momentarily dizzy. She leaned against the wall for a moment to steady herself, then stumbled toward the door.

The daughter-in-law of her neighbor Mr. Jin was at the door.

"Is something wrong?" Yuanni asked, her voice hoarse.

Mr. Jin's daughter-in-law looked at her, bewildered. "I'm here . . . for my husband's grandmother's clothes," she said.

That brought Yuanni back to her senses. She ran back into the house, picked up the package in torn red paper from the floor, brushed it off, and handed it to Mr. Jin's daughter-in-law.

Mr. Jin's daughter-in-law took the top, inspected it hastily, and packed it up again.

"Why don't you join us for our New Year's Eve dinner tonight?" She didn't look at Yuanni as she spoke, and her voice was hesitant.

Yuanni saw something she didn't recognize in the expression on the daughter-in-law's face. She came to herself after a moment and realized it was pity. There were all sorts of knives in the world, and no matter how sharp or blunt, she had endured every one that she had encountered. The only blade she had never felt before was pity. It was too soft, so soft she didn't know how to fend it off, so it went straight to her heart. A dull pain came on quite suddenly. As it was about to reach her eye, she thought, *Don't cry in front of this woman. Oh God, don't cry.*

Her mind, which had fought and lost several battles that morning, suddenly woke at that moment, growing a power that she didn't know was possible. Yuanni gritted her teeth and squeezed out a splendid smile.

"I was trying to finish up the clothes for your family. I'm running a little late. My brothers are on their way over now to take me home. We have a big family, you know. We fill up two tables. They're waiting for me to get there to start the dinner."

Mr. Jin's daughter-in-law said, "Oh. That's good."

She took a tightly folded banknote from her pocket and stuffed it into Yuanni's hand. With a slight twist of her fingers, Yuanni felt the weight, and she handed it back, saying, "That's too much. Wait, let me give you change."

Mr. Jin's daughter-in-law tossed the money on the table and started to run out. "We gave you a rush job. This isn't enough to thank you properly!" She ran a few steps, then turned back and whispered in Yuanni's ear, "I saw a beggar sleeping in the courtyard doorway just now. You're alone. Make sure you lock the door."

Yuanni's heart skipped a beat. It was like there was a flashlight in her heart, and it had suddenly lit up, but she remained calm. When she had seen Mr. Jin's daughter-in-law off, she put on her hooded cotton-padded coat and cotton shoes and walked slowly toward the corridor.

Someone was indeed sleeping in the courtyard doorway. The blue down jacket he wore was so dirty it shone with grease. He sat on a dusty travel bag, his arms wrapped around his knees and his head buried between them. He was curled up like a ball, and his snores were earth shattering.

Yuanni stretched out her toes and hooked them on the canvas bag. The man woke suddenly, rubbed his eyes, and looked blankly at Yuanni.

"Hey, Da, come home with your ma. Let's make dumplings for the New Year," Yuanni said.

She strode forward, and the swish of footsteps followed her. She knew Xiaoda was behind her.

"Ma, I met someone in Guangzhou," Xiaoda said in a low, muffled voice. "She's my lucky star. Good days are coming."

April 22, 2006
Port Hope, Ontario

Xiaodeng proposed that they all go to the town of Port Hope for the annual rock and hip-hop festival on Earth Day. Susie was a huge rock fan, and she had been clamoring to go to the festival the previous year, but Xiaodeng had not allowed it. This year, Susie hadn't mentioned it at all, but Xiaodeng suggested they go, surprising both Susie and Yang Yang.

When she called Yang Yang to make arrangements, she told him to bring a pair of earplugs. "We have to be ready for our nerves to be ground into powder. Your little princess has no mercy when it comes to music."

Yang Yang couldn't help but laugh when he heard that. The woman who might soon become his ex still spoke as luridly as ever.

This was the first time since the separation that they had traveled as a family. Susie seemed excited. She sat in the back seat, bobbing her head as she listened to earth-shattering music through her headphones. The lyrics and melody were swallowed by the headphones, so that what seeped through was only the rhythm of the bass, boom boom boom, like explosions opening a tunnel through a mountain, puncturing the eardrums with each beat.

"Turn it down a little. Don't give your mother a headache." Yang Yang turned and gestured from the driver's seat for Susie to lower the volume.

Susie pressed a button, and the sound of cannons exploding faded to that of distant rolling thunder.

"Who are you listening to, Susie?" Xiaodeng asked cheerfully.

She only saw Susie once a week, on Saturday mornings. After lunch, Susie would take a bus to Yang Yang's school for Chinese and calligraphy classes. Xiaodeng reminded herself over and over not to press her own emotional burrs into her daughter during their extremely limited time together.

"What did you say?" Susie asked, pulling off the headphones.

Xiaodeng waved it off. Relieved, Susie put her headphones back on and plunged back into the madness of the bass beat.

"Last year, she was crazy in love with the Spice Girls," Yang Yang said. "This year, it's the Backstreet Boys. There are two cousins, Kevin and Brian, in the band, both from Lexington, Kentucky. Susie even knows the name of the street they lived on when they were kids."

"How come you know all that?" Xiaodeng asked blankly.

Yang Yang turned and looked at her as if she were speaking a dialect he had never heard before.

"What's unusual about that? She's my daughter," he said.

"She's my daughter too."

Yes, Susie was her daughter, a piece of flesh ripped from her body. This bit of flesh and blood had left her body, and no matter how far apart in time or distance, there were ties between them that couldn't be severed. But Susie was in many ways unknown to her. Neither knew the other's love and passion. They were the most familiar strangers in the world. But this man who had never gone through labor pains knew Susie's idols, and her dreams.

"I'm sorry," Xiaodeng stammered.

Yang Yang was baffled. "Why?"

"All these years, you're the one who's been taking care of her," Xiaodeng said softly.

They both fell silent, because at the exact same moment, they both realized that the conversation was approaching a dangerous brink. If they moved further, they might find themselves on a field amid the smoke of battle. They had been fighting on that battlefield for ten years, and they were both bloodied and bruised. They were exhausted, and neither had the energy to carelessly provoke a quarrel that they could not end.

"You've tried your best, Xiaodeng." Yang Yang patted her shoulder lightly.

Something welled up in Xiaodeng, something soft and moist, lodging itself right up in her throat. Xiaodeng could not remember a time in recent years that Yang Yang had said such kind words to her. She understood that he was only willing to say it now because he no longer loved her. Love was a fog. When it was foggy, the road was not visible. But when the fog dissipated and there was no longer a barrier of love, the visibility returned, allowing them to clearly see the weakest, most helpless dead points in each other's hearts.

She looked at Yang Yang from the corner of her eye. He had cut his hair and blown the thick mass straight back, showing traces of the teeth of a comb. He was wearing a white sweater with a red-and-blue bar across the neckline and chest. It was a style she had never seen him wear before. She was surprised how good looking he was. When they had been together every day, she was used to everything about him. But distance now shattered the aesthetic inertia, and her vision reemerged with unexpected freshness.

On the steering wheel, Yang Yang's fingers pulsed gently to the beat coming from Susie's headphones. His eyes looked straight ahead, calm and steady. It was an expression Xiaodeng had never seen on him before, even before they were married. He was no longer tiptoeing around, no longer fearful. There was even a gentleness that came from understanding and empathy, all because he had broken free from the bonds of love. Getting used to being shackled, like a bonsai that was constantly bound to bend it into shape, had been a long process. But the process of getting used to freedom was much shorter, almost instant. Sometimes, separation papers were all that was needed. Years of shared life had blurred the details of their time together, and so Xiaodeng could only infer the cruelty of the process from the results. For the first time, she realized how unhappy Yang Yang had been in their marriage.

Only the free-spirited can truly give. Xiaodeng suddenly recalled this line from a book she had read.

"How have you been sleeping?" Yang Yang asked.

"The medicine Henry prescribed seems to work," Xiaodeng said.

Yang Yang laughed softly. "I've never heard you call a doctor by his first name before."

"Because this one seems a little more reasonable."

"You can't just rely on medicine. You need to exercise. I . . . heard it's good to do yoga when you have time. It can help you sleep."

The brief pause as he spoke aroused her vigilance. She wanted to ask, *Where did you hear that? From Xiangqian?* She almost blurted out the question, but swallowed it when it was on the tip of her tongue. She was trying to get rid of all her emotional burrs along the way, but there were so many. She had neither the eyesight nor the stamina for the impossible task of removing them all. She had to be very careful about how she allocated her limited energy. So she tried her best to squeeze out a smile and said, "I'll check with the community center and see if there are any yoga classes."

It was noon when they reached Port Hope and, from a distance, her eardrums started to reverberate: the sound of rumbling music. Susie looked like she would explode with excitement, like a dandelion releasing its seeds. She asked for Yang Yang's cell phone to make a call even before she got out of the car; she had made plans to meet two classmates in town.

The three of them got out. When they had taken a couple of steps, Susie asked hesitantly, "Is it okay if I don't have lunch with you?"

Yang Yang didn't say anything, just turned to Xiaodeng. She had already caught the meaning in his eyes. Two votes to one. Hers had always been the weakest voice of the three. It was better to go with the flow this time.

She took twenty dollars from her purse and handed it to Susie. "Take your dad's phone, and keep it on the whole time."

Susie was shocked. She had expected a fierce verbal skirmish. She had never imagined she would gain victory so easily. She took the money and stammered, "Thanks, Mom." Her expression even seemed a little respectful and humble.

Seeing Susie flit off, Xiaodeng couldn't help but sigh inwardly; her thirteen-year-old daughter was already fully developed physically. Though her mind remained that of a child, Susie looked like an adult who had filled out in all the right places.

Children always grew up, like flowers or grass. Even in the cracks between stones or tiles on rooftops, if there was a little space and soil an inch thick, a tree could find its footing. Susie, her Susie, had grown up just like that. She had wanted to give Susie fertile ground and a vast blue sky. This had been her earnest and eager desire when she gave birth to her daughter. It was only later she realized that she didn't have the things she wanted to give to Susie. How could she give what she didn't have? But Susie still grew up—in such a small gap, and in such barren soil.

"Am I too strict with her?" Xiaodeng asked Yang Yang hesitantly.

"You're even stricter with yourself," he said.

He took a pack of cigarettes from his pocket. Pinching his fingers together, he plucked one out. He had only recently learned to smoke, but from the looks of it now, it seemed he had been smoking all his life and was extremely skilled and comfortable in the art. He raised his head and took a few drags, then raised his hand and flicked, and a bit of ash made a beautiful arc in the air and fell slowly to the ground.

A man is really different when he has experience, Xiaodeng thought.

"Children are like grass; they'll grow up no matter what. It doesn't matter what the adults do. It never helps," Yang Yang said between puffs.

Xiaodeng's heart thumped. Yang Yang said exactly what she'd been thinking. He had lived with her for more than ten years. It seemed he did know her, after all.

"Is it time for me to let go?" Xiaodeng asked.

Yang Yang didn't answer; he just squinted in the sunlight. The fierce noon sun washed his face into the marble of a statue, erasing all the detail.

"We're two old folks abandoned by our child. How are we to spend this boring afternoon, then? I'm sorry. You could've spent a more interesting weekend with someone more interesting," Xiaodeng sighed, half jokingly.

Yang Yang was silent for a moment. He tossed his cigarette away, and a playful, boyish smile she hadn't seen in a very long time touched the corners of his mouth.

"Come on. Let's go to the fairgrounds and see how fragile your nerves are."

Along the way, Yang Yang bought cotton candy for Xiaodeng, a tall cone of vulgar pink. She reached out her tongue and licked it lightly, and a corner of the plump pink cloud immediately deflated. Her mouth was full of oily sweetness, but she liked the feeling of holding it in her hand. It was only the second time she had ever eaten cotton candy. The first time was when she was seven, and it had been bought by a woman named Li Yuanni. Her life was still like a piece of porcelain then, its bright glaze free of cracks.

Yang Yang and Xiaodeng rode a roller coaster together. Xiaodeng had never been very coordinated, and she had a strange phobia about all moving objects, making her feel that time and space had spun out of control. A sharp whistle sounded, and the car began to spin, throwing her into the air. She screamed and instantly lost all her senses; all she could feel was wind. There was wind in front of her, behind her, to the left, to the right—wind everywhere, carrying her away, leaving behind the world of worries and troubles that clung to life like fine dust. She had landed on another planet. She was tall, and the ground was small. The people had become ants. It was good, it was good—losing her balance was a good thing, after all. She closed her eyes and muttered to herself.

Suddenly, a window appeared before her, the window she had described to Dr. Wilson many times. The window frame was rusty, and the glass was covered with thick dust like old cotton wool. A thin slit opened in the window. As soon as she reached out, her hand pushed it open, and she saw a woman behind the glass. The woman was young, too young to quite be called a woman. She wore a white shirt with green flowers and had a pea-green plastic hairpin clasped in her short hair. The woman waved and said, "Deng, come here." Then, Xiaodeng turned into a breeze, flew through the crack in the window, and sat beside the woman. She sat firmly, only to realize that the woman was also sitting in a rotating bucket. When the car flew up, she was afraid, and so was the woman. She screamed, but the woman's scream was even louder than her own. The woman held her tight, as if trying to wring all the moisture out of her. She leaned against the woman's body and got a whiff of the fragrance of freshly mowed grass in the woman's hair. *Don't stop, don't stop,* Xiaodeng reminded herself. But she found that she had stopped and was now on firm ground. When she opened her eyes, the woman and the window were gone; only Yang Yang was there. From the way Yang Yang's mouth twisted at the corners, she guessed that her own face must be quite a sight too.

"I shouldn't have pulled you onto this ride," Yang Yang said apologetically as he helped her out of the car.

"It's all right. I've been on a ride like that before." Xiaodeng gradually regulated her breathing.

"You have? When?" Yang Yang was shocked. Xiaodeng was afraid of heights. Even when she was learning to ride a bike, it had taken several tries for her to take a solo trip.

"When I was little. Seven years old," she said.

"Seven?" A suspicious expression came over Yang Yang's face. "That was during the Cultural Revolution. How could you have visited a carnival?"

"Henry said that a flawed memory is better than no memory. Many, many times better." A pale smile gradually blossomed across Xiaodeng's face.

The pair walked slowly, looking for a place for lunch. As soon as they turned a corner, they again came to a lively crowd. Someone was performing a street dance. Yang Yang was interested, so he shoved his way through, parting the crowd of onlookers as he dragged Xiaodeng along to watch. There were three adolescent dancers, two boys and a girl. One boy stood on his head, with his arms and legs performing some dazzling moves. At intervals, there were loud cheers from the crowd. Another boy had a basketball in hand. His body twisted and turned around the ball, but the ball never moved, as if it were suspended and his palm was glued to it. The girl's dance style was different, very wild, but a bit like ballet. She moved around frantically on her tiptoes, turning faster and faster, making a whirlwind of her body. A whirlwind of black mixed with purple, black hair, purple T-shirt, black, purple, black purple. She finally stopped, winning a burst of mad applause from the crowd. She bowed and stood straight.

It was Susie.

It was not a small shock. Yang Yang and Xiaodeng had the wind knocked out of them. Xiaodeng was about to step forward and call her daughter, but Yang Yang stopped her firmly.

"Don't say anything to her in front of so many people. She would die of embarrassment."

They found a KFC and sat down for lunch, but they still had not recovered from the shock. Xiaodeng could not help but sigh. "Yang Yang, how much do we know our child? We knew she liked to watch street dance, but I had no idea she could dance at that level. Maybe we can think in that direction. Do you think it's a little too late for her to start learning ballet now?"

Yang Yang smiled and said, "Piano, calligraphy, oil painting—what didn't you let her try? Dancing is just a hobby for now. If you ask her to *really* learn, she'll rebel. Let her be herself. She doesn't take things too seriously. Isn't it strange? I have two left feet, and you're as clumsy as a donkey, and our sense of balance is poor. How did we produce a child like that? Is it some genetic mutation?"

Xiaodeng's hand holding the fried chicken drumstick suddenly stopped in midair. Her expression became remote and vague, like she had flown to a planet far away.

"Maybe not a mutation. She may have inherited it from my mother," Xiaodeng muttered, more to herself than to Yang Yang.

Yang Yang was puzzled. "Wasn't your mother a middle school teacher? I've never heard you talk about her dancing."

Xiaodeng rolled her eyes at him. "Not that one. My birth mother."

Yang Yang shook his head. "Didn't you say you don't remember anything before the earthquake? What magic potion did you take to make you remember it now?"

Xiaodeng laughed. "Yang Yang, Henry says selective amnesia is also a type of memory."

Henry, Henry again. It seems that this doctor's special kung fu is brainwashing, Yang Yang thought.

They stopped talking and finished the rest of their meal in silence.

When they were clearing the food boxes from the table, Yang Yang suddenly asked Xiaodeng, "Do you remember that book, *Northern Rivers?* The one Zhang Chengzhi wrote."

Surprised, Xiaodeng glanced at Yang Yang. He was becoming nostalgic in his old age.

"Of course I remember it. We read it in Fudan. 'The Yellow River was coppery red at sunset.' I have a thick notebook full of notes on it."

"Do you remember the young man who was determined to take the postgraduate entrance exam in human geography, and the woman he met on the beach?"

"Yes. 'I am who I am. I can't be you. Even if you struggle alone, I can only watch silently,'" Xiaodeng recited softly.

"They loved each other so much, but they still had to separate. They could only watch each other suffer from a distance. She couldn't help him, and he couldn't help her, and they couldn't fight this world."

Xiaodeng's eyebrows ticked up gently. "Are you talking about you and me?"

Yang Yang sighed. "Xiaodeng, I can't get inside your heart. I've been trying for eighteen years, but it's no use. You've wrapped your heart too tightly."

Another soft lump surged up, blocking Xiaodeng's throat. She coughed and swallowed the mass with some difficulty. After hesitating for a moment, she finally reached out and squeezed Yang Yang's hand.

"If I told you my heart was wrapped too tightly even for me to get in, would you feel better?"

Yang Yang did not speak, but there was a thin layer of tears in his eyes.

It was evening when they made their way home. It had been a sunny day, and the ending was as exciting as the beginning. The sun dropped below the skyline, and the clouds piled up like a thick blob of spilled ketchup on the horizon. A flock of birds flew by in neat formation, scratching the sky with their wings.

"Mom, why are there geese now? Didn't you say they only fly south in autumn?" Susie asked.

Xiaodeng pulled a tissue from her bag and handed it to Susie to wipe away the sweat. She had sat in the back seat on the way home so she could talk with Susie more easily.

"Silly girl, those are returning geese. It's getting warmer, so they're returning home now." Xiaodeng's tone was extraordinarily gentle. It felt unfamiliar even to her own ears.

"Susie, when did you learn to dance?" Xiaodeng asked. The question had been gathering in her heart for a while. She couldn't let it come out sooner because she hoped to first smooth over every burr. When it finally came out, it was very smooth.

"I didn't learn anywhere, Mom. I just watched other people, then practiced on my own."

"If you told us, we could have found a good teacher for you."

Susie hesitated, then mumbled, "I didn't dare tell you. I was afraid you'd be mad."

Xiaodeng could tell that the accusation was aimed at her, not her and Yang Yang.

"I'm sorry, Susie," Xiaodeng said. "I've always been too strict with you."

Susie's eyelashes fluttered. Everyone had a lot of surprises to absorb that day, including Susie.

"It's not your fault, Mom. Dad said you're sick and need help," Susie finally said, after a moment's hesitation.

Xiaodeng turned to look out the window. This was the closest she had come in her entire life—or, no, just since she was seven—the closest she had come to crying. But her eyes still remained dry.

After a while, Xiaodeng turned back and asked Susie breezily, "What have you been reading in literature class?"

Susie felt a little guilty. She had agreed that the three of them would go to the festival together. It seemed that she had treated her parents as a driver and a banker all day, so she decided to make a full effort to take part in any topic Xiaodeng introduced.

"We read *Roots* this semester."

"Did you like it?"

"It's okay. It's hard to remember all the names, but the homework is more interesting than the novel itself. The teacher told us to dig out our own ancestral records. Dad helped me trace my family tree back five generations. My classmates could only do four, at most."

Yang Yang turned his head and said to Xiaodeng from the driver's seat, "Your daughter got the only A+ in the class. It seems that she not only has the potential to become the next Isadora Duncan, but also to be the next Virginia Woolf."

"It's too bad I didn't have the family tree for your side," Susie said.

Xiaodeng went over countless answers in her mind, but finally settled on silence.

"Mom, how come all my classmates have grandparents on their mother's side, but I don't?" Susie wasn't willing to drop the subject.

"Because yours died early on, when I was seven," Xiaodeng said. The words were covered with thorns. By the time they passed through her throat and over her tongue, they had pricked her until her mouth was covered in blood.

"But you never even mention them. Anyway, most of the people in the family tree are dead," Susie said.

Fortunately, Susie was tired, and she soon fell asleep. Xiaodeng put her face close and smelled the damp, sour smell of sweat in her daughter's hair.

What a soft, resilient character this girl was. If she was crushed, she bounced back quickly. When she was wronged, she never held a grudge. Xiaodeng took off her jacket and gently covered Susie with it.

When Xiaodeng got out of the car, Susie took the initiative to come over and hug her tightly.

"Mom, you seem happier since you and Dad separated. If you want a divorce, don't worry about me. I'm fine," she whispered in Xiaodeng's ear.

Watching Yang Yang's car lightly cut through the flow of traffic and gradually melt into the thick night, Xiaodeng felt that a heavy weight on her was disintegrating.

Free from my shackles, they're all happier than before, Xiaodeng thought.

When she went inside, Xiaodeng sat down beside the lamp and wrote a letter to the Tangshan Civil Affairs Bureau, inquiring about the whereabouts of someone named Li Yuanni. When she had finished the letter, she collapsed onto the bed and fell asleep almost immediately, and she slept until dawn. It was the longest, deepest sleep she had had in twenty years, and it was completely dreamless.

Summer 1994
Sun Yat-sen University, Guangzhou

Lu Aya was absent-minded throughout the whole class. Fortunately, it was the day of the final exam, and she only needed her eyes to rove over the class as she proctored; she did not need her mouth or brain to be active.

As soon as the bell rang to signal the end of the period, she took the students' exam papers and hurried back to the office. She closed the door and leaned her head back in a daze. Her colleagues had all finished their classes. Hers was the last in the department, so she was left alone in the office. She did not want to see anyone right now. She just wanted to be alone so she could think things through properly.

A few days earlier, she had received a letter from her former boyfriend. He had completed his PhD at the University of Pittsburgh and was now staying on with his adviser to work on his postdoc. He had secured a scholarship from his mentor, sufficient to cover the cost for a "suitable candidate" to study abroad. As for the girlfriend who had taken Aya's place, he explained that in four words: *She's returned to Taiwan.*

After finishing her master's degree, Aya had remained at the school as a lecturer, teaching while doing her doctoral studies. The department looked out for her, only requiring her to teach one class per semester. Her studies were not too strenuous, her teaching duties quite relaxed, and her relationship with her colleagues harmonious. Aya's career was like a pair of old cloth shoes that had been well worn in. It couldn't be called fresh or exciting, but it was comfortable and fit well. The thought of studying abroad had been burning in her own mind for a few years. The flame had not been extinguished, but there was no strength in it. The letter in her pocket, though—that had added new kindling, and a new flame had burst with a crackle. Her mind was torn.

She and her ex had been college classmates. From the beginning, she had felt they were meant to be together for life, and she had never thought twice about that. They had applied to study abroad together, but because her TOEFL scores were on the poor side, he left while she stayed. She was very secure, always feeling that they would eventually reunite, whether in the US or China. She didn't expect him to change his mind so quickly and so ruthlessly. He had severed himself so cleanly from her life with the sharpest knife, leaving little trace of skin or blood. Although the pain had been so unexpected and heartbreaking at the time, looking back now, she was grateful for his decisiveness; at least he hadn't led her on. She would rather die instantly with her eyes open than succumb slowly to a dull knife while blindfolded.

Over the years, she thought of him from time to time. After all, he was her first love. But no matter how strong the memory was, it couldn't withstand the rough millstone of time. She was surprised to find that his face gradually grew pale and foggy in her memory, like an old photo. First, the details were lost, and then the outline blurred. In the end, she couldn't even remember what he looked like, until she saw the photo he sent with the letter.

That photo instantly brought back memories lost to the sands of time. The process of loss had been long and gradual, first partial, then complete. But the recovery process was achieved overnight. All the lost details seemed to respond to the same command, and they fell into place in an instant, filling in the blanks. When Aya looked at the photo of him in the graduation cap, holding flowers, the memories of a distant past welled up in her heart with an irresistible force, catching her totally off guard. She thought that remembering him would instantly dredge up her pain, just like thinking of a fire called up a feeling of heat. She was surprised, then, to find that it actually reminded her of many warm moments they shared when they were together. Of course, the warmth in the memory was at best a copy that had long lost the brilliance and clarity of the original. She realized that she no longer hated him, which was another way of saying she no longer loved him. The feelings had all just faded. There was such a thin line between love and hate, so that if you got one, you got the other too. But once you got yourself out of the love/hate game, there was space for feelings such as warmth.

But that full scholarship was still very tempting. Over the past few years, she had applied to many universities in the US. The application fees alone had cost thousands of yuan. She had been through the hassle of going from one place to another, pleading for acceptance, and she definitely didn't want to repeat the same dreary process. But he had already traveled down this thorny path and made it safe and ready for her. All she had to do was move her lips and say yes. She had passed the GRE, and her level of English had improved drastically, so the TOEFL should not be a problem. The problem was the word *yes*. It was heavy, sitting like a rock on her tongue. It wasn't that she didn't have the strength to move the weight; what had really deterred her was the realization that once the word was uttered, she would simultaneously embark on two paths of no return. One was a path to a committed academic career, and the other, a path to an equally committed life. If she accepted his money, she was accepting him. This was common sense that even a woman raised in the sticks could understand. Though he made no mention of the future, Aya was not naïve; she knew there was no such thing as a free lunch.

It was almost noon, and the sun was in the middle of the sky. No matter how well the cicadas hid themselves in the shade of the trees, they were not able to escape the omnipresent midday sun. They screamed wildly, beating her temples like drums. She had a splitting headache.

It was not only the letter that had been giving her headaches, but also the number of blind dates she had gone on this summer, seemingly one after another. Her mother had died long ago, and like any girl without a mother, she was the center of her father's life. She was twenty-nine and still to be married, and she had become a heavy burden on her father's heart. He introduced her to one prospect after another, through all his social relations. Aya had seen several of these men, but she had not kept in touch with any of them. Each time she rejected someone, she felt she lost a little stature in her father's eyes. After several attempts, she was practically in the dust, so low that she could no longer look into her father's disappointed, pitying eyes. She chose to stay in the school dorm now, rarely going home, even during school vacation.

Perhaps going abroad really was a way out, a way that addressed two major issues at the same time, career and marriage. Though she no longer loved her ex, in the marriage of a woman who was about to turn thirty, perhaps love was a luxury that could be dispensed with. She didn't hate him. That should be enough for them to live a normal life.

Thinking of this, Aya was relieved. She took out a stack of stationery, placed it on the table, and started writing the letter she had been putting off for several days.

Someone knocked at the door. A student, she thought. She turned the letter over, put her pen on top of it, and went to open the door.

She was surprised to see Wan Xiaoda there. It had been a while since she'd seen him.

"Aya, I'm here to take you out for an ice dessert."

Xiaoda raised his empty sleeve. He always held up this flag of his handicap, swaggering about without the slightest hint of uneasiness or embarrassment, a free, gallant, dashing swagger.

Xiaoda was like a gust of wind in Aya's life. He came and went without warning. When he showed up, he would hang around for several days, and when he left, he would disappear into thin air for months in a row. Aya never took the initiative to contact him. She knew he had his own timetable. Each time they reunited, he raised his empty sleeve and called, "Aya," in a familiar manner that easily welded together the gap of several months, as if they had not spent a single day apart.

"How did you know I'd be in the office?" she asked. She only came to the department when she had class, and she rarely had classes on weekdays.

Xiaoda put on a slick smile and said, "Don't you know I'm a psychic?"

Aya put the half-written letter in a drawer, closed the door, and left with Xiaoda. When they walked to the side of the road, Xiaoda pointed to a brand-new Santana sedan and said, "Have a seat, ma'am."

Taken aback, Aya said, "This is your car? Did you buy it or borrow it?"

Xiaoda said, "If you think I bought it, then I bought it. If you think I borrowed it, then I borrowed it."

Xiaoda's words were always like that—both true and false. Aya had long ago learned not to take him seriously.

They sat, and Xiaoda started the car and whizzed into the heat of the street. The air conditioner hissed and sighed, and the body of the car gradually cooled down, while the tires felt the softness of the sun-scorched asphalt road.

Aya tilted her head to look at Xiaoda. "When did you learn to drive? It's even more showy than someone driving with two hands."

Xiaoda didn't say anything, but just grinned broadly, baring his teeth. Aya's eyes were dazzled, and she suddenly realized Xiaoda's smoke-stained teeth had turned very white.

"Wow! Look at those teeth. Tell the truth. Did you get hooked by some woman?" Aya asked.

Xiaoda stopped smiling and said mysteriously, "Something like that. But first, tell me, do you like my teeth? I had them all fixed. It cost me a bundle."

Aya said, "Do you want the truth? You're pretending to be something you're not. That's what I think."

Xiaoda wasn't offended. He smiled and said, "Well, you just have to get used to it. I have to meet some foreign devils from time to time, for business, you know. A little touch-up always helps. I couldn't even get past the receptionist, the way I looked before, so yeah, I have to pretend a little."

Aya snorted and said, "Go on faking it. You'll be exposed one day."

Xiaoda said, "So what? I've got you. You can always take me in."

They hardly paid attention to where they were going as they bantered, and before they knew it, they had come to a very busy street.

"These are all office buildings. Where are we going to get ice desserts here?" Aya grunted.

Xiaoda parked on the side of the street and said, "I want to show you something first."

He rolled down the window and pointed to a tall building with blue glass. "See that?"

Aya looked at it for a few moments, then said, "It's a building. What's to see?"

Xiaoda shook his head and said, "You've been in school for too long. The more books you read, the stupider you become. Count from the bottom to the eighteenth floor. Look carefully and tell me what you see there."

Aya squinted, counting the floors, until she saw a neon sign. Though it was daytime and the sign had not been turned on, she could vaguely make out the words. *Wanda International Trade Corporation.*

She gasped and said, "You moved your company here? How much is the rent? An inch of land is an inch of gold in this part of town."

Xiaoda patted Aya on the shoulder and said, "Does it scare you? Do you know the old saying 'You can't entrap a wolf if you're not willing to sacrifice your child'?"

Aya suddenly fell silent.

Xiaoda asked again, "What's wrong? Did I say something wrong again? You look troubled."

Aya sighed and said, "Xiaoda, you've got some ambition. And your heart is really big."

Xiaoda said, "If my heart wasn't big, how could it hold a goddess like you?"

Aya saw that Xiaoda said that with a half-serious expression, and she didn't know how to respond.

They went to an ice dessert stall and ordered two large glasses of red bean ice. They ate slowly.

"Aya, do you like teaching?" Xiaoda asked.

"It's okay. The salary is kind of . . . well, it's pitiful. I have to think twice before I buy a flower to pin in my hair," she said.

Xiaoda couldn't help but grin again. He had been wandering around in the business world for several years, meeting all sorts of people along the way, but there was no one like Aya.

"How about finding you a job, a new job? Then you can buy all the flowers in the world. Would you quit this job then?" Xiaoda asked.

She tossed the long-handled spoon that came with her ice dessert aside and said, "Don't! Someone like me—I'm too young to be running a brothel and too old to sell my looks. Forget it. There's no use even thinking about it."

Xiaoda laughed loudly. A red bean lodged in his throat, and he started coughing so hard tears came to his eyes. When he finally stopped laughing, he grew serious and said, "Aya, I'm not kidding. I want you to come work in my company. You've studied finance and accounting, so you can manage the money. You can also speak English, so you can deal with the foreign devils. The fixed salary is a thousand yuan a month, but there's no upper limit on bonuses. You'll own a third of the company's shares. I can't estimate the dividends, I have no idea how far it'll go."

Aya was so startled she was speechless. She didn't need to think too much; she could guess how her future earnings would compare with her current salary.

"Why?" she asked.

He looked at her and said slowly, "The position requires someone I trust. I don't trust anyone else, so I can only give it to my woman."

She was caught off guard again, and her response came in a string of flustered stutters. "Si . . . Since when am I your—"

Before she could finish, Xiaoda cut her off, saying, "Back when you pointed me to my first pot of gold, I told you that one day there would be a building in Guangzhou with my name on it. There was one other thing I wanted to say then, but I didn't say it out loud. It was that when my name was finally on a building, I would take you home as my woman."

Aya blushed. The blush was like a drop of vermilion, falling accidentally on rice paper and slowly spreading out, all the way to the base of her ears. Xiaoda had never seen her like this. It wasn't that she was shy—*shy* wasn't a word in her dictionary. But this woman who appeared to have seen so much of the world was confused at the moment.

"I'm four years older than you," Aya said.

"If you weren't older than me, I wouldn't marry you. I like older women," he said.

Autumn 1995
Tangshan, Hebei

In the fall, Li Yuanni moved to a new house. Or, to be more precise, she moved into her old house, newly renovated.

The lease to the old house had been purchased, then it was remodeled inside and out. The outer wall was covered with clean white tiles, and a balcony with railings was added. The railings were also clean white, and the balusters were carved with a delicate pattern. From a distance, they looked like a row of fine porcelain vases. The door was replaced with a shiny steel door with a fan motif carved above it and a poster of carps playing in water pasted in the middle.

This was just a facade for outsiders to see. The real fashion began inside. The floor was purplish-red hardwood, and the walls had been fitted with white embossed cornices and baseboards. The furniture was all creamy white, including a creamy-white sofa. There were home appliances of all sizes, including a microwave oven, an appliance rarely seen in Tangshan at that time. A few years later, this sort of decor would be in every home in town, but now, it was a marvel on her street.

Yuanni had stayed with her parents for more than a month while she waited for the renovations to be completed. The day she moved into the new place, firecrackers popped for half an hour, sending the birds scattering in fright, and the air was full of shreds of paper falling like red rain. Having never seen such a commotion, the dogs on the street were so frightened they forgot to bark. A circle of neighbors gathered at the house, commenting on how well equipped it was; it had everything.

Everyone on the street knew the house had been bought and renovated by Yuanni's son, Xiaoda. It had not been his original plan to spend money on a house in Tangshan; he had wanted to take his mother to settle down in the South. Xiaoda and his mother spent two years haggling over the matter. There were several versions of the excuses Yuanni gave for not going to the South: it was difficult to leave home, she couldn't get used to the heat in Guangzhou, and she didn't want to be in his way. None of these excuses made Xiaoda give up. In the end, it was something else. Yuanni said, "If we're both gone, then when your father's and sister's souls come back, they won't find a home." Xiaoda fell silent when he heard that.

There was much speculation in the neighborhood about Yuanni's son. Some said that Xiaoda must have made money trading stocks in Shenzhen, some said he found a rich woman who was backing him, and some said he made a big fortune running a clothing trading company in Guangzhou. Yuanni smiled at the speculation and kept silent, but her mysterious expression was really just a way to hide her ignorance of his whereabouts and doings.

The street had been rebuilt long ago, and not at its former location. Of course, the neighbors were not the same people as before, but even now, so many years after the earthquake, Yuanni was still a subject of gossip for everyone on the street.

Of course she had lost a husband and a daughter to the quake, and of course she was left with a son who had only one arm. These were just facts, hardly reasons for her to be pitied or hated. Everywhere you looked, there were families who had lost loved ones in the earthquake.

The earthquake had rubbed every heart raw, forming thick scars and leaving no place for tenderness or nuance. Humans were powerless before natural disasters, and since they could not settle accounts with God, their only choice was to accept fate. It was like a peasant hurrying on his way on a dark night. If he stepped on a rock, fell, broke his head, and bled, the scar would remain forever. He couldn't even bear a grudge against the stone; he could only wrap the wound and continue on the road.

When disasters struck, people were more tolerant toward each other, because disasters didn't pick and choose. They knocked everyone down equally. The way people fell was basically the same. But once the disaster passed, the ways people got up varied a great deal. When the state of equality and equilibrium was broken, there would be gaps between people, a convenient space for the barnyard weed of jealousy to sprout and grow.

Yuanni was disliked because she was the first to get up and start walking again. A few years after the earthquake, Yuanni had tossed aside the iron rice bowl—her work unit—and returned home to open a small tailor's shop. No one had expected this little shop to gain a reputation beyond the immediate neighborhood. Yuanni knew instinctively that the first thing a customer saw when they walked into her shop was her own clothing, just as a customer walking into a hair salon would first notice the hairdresser's hairstyle. Whatever advertising she did, she herself was the most effective, most direct ad, so she paid more attention to the clothes she made for herself than she did for others. In everything—fabric, color, and style—her attire was always on the cutting edge of fashion.

Yuanni chose not only her clothing carefully, but also her hairstyle. Sometimes she wore her hair long and rolled it into a bun in a style common in the Republican era, tied at the back of her head, like a noble lady. Sometimes she wore it shoulder length and straight, like a pretty, innocent college student. Her hair, which had turned gray suddenly in the year of the earthquake, slowly grew dark again. Though she was no longer young, Yuanni was always clean, tidy, and trendy, a beautiful sight when she led her son, Xiaoda, through the streets. She was used to walking around with eyes all over her, even though the earthquake had left her with a slight limp in one leg. The folks on the street just wanted to find a comforting trace of panic yet to be calmed from the disaster—perhaps the lowered eyebrows a widow should have—but they never found even the slightest hint in Yuanni. Naturally, no one knew what she looked like behind closed doors, but in public, she held her head high, walked with a slight limp reminiscent of the dance steps of a Peking opera singer, and lived every day like it was Lunar New Year.

At various times, different men showed up at Yuanni's home. Many rumors about her love life circulated on the street, the most elaborate one involving a man who wore glasses. It was said that he was her husband's former colleague who had a disabled wife at home. Someone saw him carrying a mesh bag of meat into Yuanni's house once, and when he came out, he was wearing a new set of clothes that Yuanni had made. A few nasty gossips said it was an exchange of "flesh for flesh," but the rumors ultimately remained in the realm of speculation, and Yuanni never remarried.

When Yuanni had dared to toss aside her iron rice bowl, it had not been out of courage or vision, but merely to look after her only son, Xiaoda. But even though she finally managed to prepare three hot meals a day for him, he did not grow up according to her wishes. Xiaoda walked a path she had never dreamed of, and he did it right under her nose. For the simple, honest folk of Tangshan, Guangzhou was a name that often showed up in radio and newspaper reports. The people of Tangshan knew there were many wonderful things there, but once their ears and eyes had had their fill of these wonderful things, they kept them in the radio and newspaper, never bringing them into their own lives. But not Xiaoda. He had planted his own feet squarely in the midst of that brilliance.

Over the past seven or eight years, Xiaoda had returned home a total of three times. The first time he came back, he had been away for almost three years. He had stayed for six days, arriving on New Year's Eve and leaving on the sixth day of the first lunar month. Xiaoda bought a new refrigerator to put at home and replaced the old nine-inch black-and-white TV. He also left Yuanni with a bank passbook with two thousand yuan. She asked over and over how he earned the money, but he just laughed it off and said, "Don't worry, Ma. I'm doing things the right way. I know how to earn money, just like Pa."

The second time Xiaoda came home was two years later. He only stayed for half a month that time, and he bought cemetery plots for his father and sister, though, of course, the graves were cenotaphs. When he left, he took his mother with him. He wanted her to stay in Guangzhou for a year or so, but Yuanni returned home after just a month.

The third time Xiaoda came home was after Yuanni moved into the renovated house. He arrived in a Toyota Crown. The driver honked all the way along the narrow street, passing through a gauntlet of food stalls of various sizes, and he had attracted a number of onlookers when he finally stopped at the gate of the Wan household. Xiaoda wore a nicely fitting dark blue wool suit, and his hair was combed straight back, dark and shiny, displaying his wide forehead and neat hairline. His clothes had filled out substantially, and he wore a thin leather glove on his right hand, exposed at the cuff. Having been accustomed to Xiaoda looking like a one-armed praying mantis, no one recognized him at first.

He did not come back alone. There was a woman with him. She looked a few years older than Xiaoda, and she had very long, straight hair, pulled into a thick ponytail and clipped with a red hairpin. She wore a thin orangish-red leather jacket and whitewashed jeans with a pair of high dark brown leather boots. The colors and style of her clothing instantly illuminated the drab street.

Xiaoda stood a few steps away from the door and looked carefully at the new balcony before pulling the woman up the steps.

"This house was built after the earthquake," Xiaoda explained to the woman softly. "It's getting kind of old. It was really difficult to renovate a house like that. This was our only option for the layout."

The door was not closed. Xiaoda pushed it lightly. Stepping into the house from the bright sunlight, he needed a moment to adjust to the dim light inside. Then he saw a woman in the room who was just beginning to grow plump. She was leaning over a table with her back to them, cutting a length of fabric. She was so absorbed in what she was doing that her whole upper body looked like it was stuck to the table like soft dough.

Xiaoda called, "Ma."

The woman was so startled her scissors fell to the ground with a clatter.

"Ma, this is Aya. I told you about her," Xiaoda said.

Yuanni raised her body and saw a red cloud slowly drift toward her from the door. She took off her reading glasses, and her eyes slowly measured the slender outline. Eyes as dark as lacquer flashed back at her.

"Isn't she a teacher?" Yuanni asked.

"Ma, Aya isn't teaching anymore. She's helping in my company now," Xiaoda said.

The red cloud flowed over and stopped beside the table. There was a suit of black satin on the table, Chinese style with a collar that stood up, and double-breasted, with pairs of plaited cloth buttons down the front.

"The workmanship is very detailed. Is this style fashionable here now?" Aya asked.

Her voice was thin, and the end of the sentence raised slightly, as if there was a hint of surprise that was suddenly cut off. Now that Yuanni got a good look at the woman her son had brought home, she felt that the woman seemed like anything but a former teacher. The woman reminded her of her own youth, which had frozen on the branch before it had time to bloom completely. She didn't know what to think of this woman.

She hesitated, then said coldly, "A living person would not like this style. It can only be a shroud."

Aya was a little embarrassed.

Xiaoda pushed Aya in front of Yuanni and pointed at his mother, saying, "This is my ma. She's your ma too. You can do what you like to me, but you've got to be nice to my ma. My ma dug me out of the rubble with her own fingers after the earthquake."

Aya took Yuanni's hand and spread it out, examining it carefully. Her palm was very thin, and there was a layer of sticky chalk on it. The lines on her palm were like fine cracks in porcelain, crisscrossing in a delicate but messy way. Half the nails of the index and middle fingers were missing, and the exposed flesh was a solid black mass, as if covered with mud. Aya tried to dig with her own fingers, but she couldn't get anything out.

"Now I understand where Xiaoda learned to endure hardship," Aya said.

Yuanni felt the wall in her heart being dismantled brick by brick. A trail of water wound its way through the ruins, flowing over the dry, parched ground with a lively hiss. She turned her head and ferociously swallowed the soft lump building in her throat.

"Have you two eaten yet?" she asked, coughing slightly.

That night, the three of them went to the most expensive restaurant in town for dinner. Aya looked languid, and she ate very little. She ran to the restroom many times.

"How far along? Boy or girl?" Yuanni asked Xiaoda in a low voice when Aya next went to the restroom.

Xiaoda couldn't help but laugh. "Ma, your eyes really are sharp. It's twins. Three and a half months."

Yuanni's eyes lit up like lanterns, illuminating the room. "Isn't that something? The Wan women know how to make twins."

"Yes, a dragon and a phoenix too," Xiaoda exclaimed, beaming with pride.

Yuanni's eyes lit up again. This time, it was the kind of bursting light as when the wick popped in a candle. "Do you think it's your sister coming back to life? She couldn't be my daughter, so she's returning as my granddaughter."

Xiaoda was momentarily stunned, then he said, "Ma, don't say such things in front of Aya. She's an educated woman. I don't want her to laugh at us for being so backward."

Yuanni snorted and her face tightened. "What's an educated woman? Even if she were a queen, she couldn't tell me how to feel. You can forget your sister, but I can't forget my daughter."

Xiaoda quickly put on a cheeky smile. "Ma, do you know why I went after her? Don't you see who she looks like? You should see the pictures of her as a child. It's amazing. She looked just like my sister."

It suddenly hit Yuanni. "You know, when I first saw her, I wondered why she looked so familiar. The corners of her mouth twitched when she smiled, and she really looked like Xiaodeng."

"Is it possible that my sister couldn't be your daughter, so she came to you as your daughter-in-law?" Xiaoda said, with the same shameless expression on his face.

"Don't talk shit! Your sister is younger than her. How could she be Xiaodeng reborn?"

"It doesn't matter who she was in her last life. We're one family in this life. That's all that matters."

"You'd better hurry up and settle things. We're not one family yet. She's pregnant, but you are not yet married. Don't shame her family."

"I know. Her pa is always pressuring me too. As soon as I go back to Guangzhou, I'll get that piece of paper, then we'll have a banquet in Tangshan and one in Guangzhou. Will that do?"

When they got home, Aya was tired, so she went to her room early to rest. Xiaoda stayed up with his mother in the living room, chattering away.

"Ma, why don't you find someone too? It's quite lonely to live alone," Xiaoda said haltingly.

Yuanni laughed. Her laughter sounded like clucking, like a hen laying eggs. "Search all over this street. Can you find anyone who looks like a man? You can bring the closest thing you find back to put on a leash and keep him in the pen. Is that what you want for a stepfather?"

Xiaoda laughed and thought, *After all these years, Ma's tongue is still sharp. It hasn't dulled a bit.*

"Does Mr. Qin still come around?" Xiaoda asked.

"It's been a while. His wife is seriously ill." Yuanni pointed at the half-sewn burial garment on the table. "That was made for her. I'm afraid she won't make it through the winter."

They both fell silent, each thinking their own thoughts. Something rolled back and forth in Xiaoda's mind before it finally rolled off his tongue with some effort.

"Ma, could you be with Uncle Qin? You know, afterward."

Yuanni snorted and said, "Did you forget how you abused him? You may have forgotten, but not everyone has."

Xiaoda grew anxious, and his face flushed. "That was then. He still had a wife back then. If he bears a grudge, would it make it right if I apologize?"

Yuanni chuckled softly. "Da, do you think Mr. Qin is the sort of person to bear a grudge? It's me, not him. I know very well what the neighbors said about me over the years. If I end up with him, wouldn't it mean that what they said was true after all?"

Xiaoda searched inside himself for something to refute Yuanni's words, but he found nothing. His face gradually grew solemn.

Yuanni patted his leg and said, "If you really worry about me, then put your little ones here for me to look after when they come. They will keep me company. And anyway, you're busy."

The moon was big that night. Moonlight licked the curtains and climbed into the room, creating glistening snags on every item. Aya drifted in and out, but she never really sank into deep sleep. In the middle of the night, she woke completely. Her eyes were wide open, staring at the two enlarged black-framed photos on the wall. The figures in the photos stared at her from twenty years away. She could faintly hear the sound of the midair collision between her eyes and theirs.

"Your sister looks so much like I did as a child." She couldn't help but push Xiaoda as he lay beside her.

"I know." His voice was calm and sober. He had not slept either. "Aya, I want to talk to you about something. When our kids are born, let's call the boy Jideng and the girl Niandeng, okay?"

"Which Deng?" Aya asked. She shook her head disapprovingly when Xiaoda clarified. "You mean, Deng as in 'climber'? It sounds kind of tacky."

"Deng was my sister's name, and *jinian* means 'commemorating,' so we can use those two characters with her name. After all, her life was exchanged for mine during the earthquake."

Aya sighed and said no more.

April 29, 2006
St. Michael's Hospital, Toronto

"Xiaodeng, why is the woman in *Dream of Shenzhou* so reluctant to return to the place where she was born and raised?" Dr. Wilson asked.

"Because there are some things you'd rather forget for good."

"But no matter how much a person runs, she can't escape her shadow. It's better to turn around and face the shadow. Maybe you'll find out it really is only a shadow, and it isn't as insurmountable as you think."

"Maybe. Could be. Henry, how can someone without shadows understand shadows, and how can they help others who are plagued with shadows?"

"Are you questioning my professional qualifications as a psychiatrist?" Dr. Wilson raised his eyebrows, playfully fighting back.

"No, I'm just questioning your life experience."

Xiaodeng lowered her head, digging at the dead skin on her finger. After an Ontario winter, her hands were overgrown with tiny cracks and crevices. Any time her hands touched her clothes, they hooked onto a thread.

Dr. Wilson was silent. The conversation was moving into somewhat dangerous territory. The boundary between professional and personal life had suddenly become blurred. It was a new experience that he had never faced in his twenty years of medical practice. Perhaps with this woman, he needed to tighten his defenses, like an eagle. He decided to change the subject.

"What about your childhood? You never talk about anything that happened before the age of seven."

Xiaodeng's hand trembled. The skin broke, and a bead of dark blood oozed out. It rolled down the cuticle like a well-fed beetle, a thin black line creeping downward.

"Xiaodeng, remember our agreement. You can choose to be silent, but you can't lie to me."

Xiaodeng held the bleeding finger tightly. After a long pause, she said, "I'm going to China next week."

Dr. Wilson's eyes lit up. "Are you going back to the place where you were born?"

Xiaodeng shook her head. "Maybe, but I'm not sure. I haven't made up my mind yet. I still have a thirteen-hour flight to think it over. I'm mainly going back to settle some paperwork. Marriage documents. Or, more precisely, divorce documents. We registered our marriage in Shanghai, so we need notarized documentation verifying the original marriage certificate before we can get a divorce here."

"So soon? It's already decided?"

"Yes. I saw that everyone was doing so well after they left me, especially Susie." She looked a little tired as she spoke, but there was also something else in her expression that Dr. Wilson couldn't pinpoint. She carried a determination in her that he hadn't seen before.

"You seem to be in a good mood, Xiaodeng. Is it because you're sleeping better?"

"Yes. Thank you for the new medicine. Of course, you have to consider the freedom I've just gained too. Now I know that what I gave Yang Yang was just a little bit of freedom, and what I gave myself was a good deal more. At least I don't have to worry about who he eats with during the day or who he sleeps with at night."

Dr. Wilson laughed loudly, the fat on his neck vibrating like rippling water.

"The umbilical cord. You finally cut it."

"Henry, can you give me a little more of the new medicine? I need to take it with me when I travel."

"How long will you be in China?"

"I really don't know. I'll just see where the road takes me."

Dr. Wilson said, "Wait here a moment," then walked out of the room.

Xiaodeng stood up and paced back and forth. She had been to the clinic several times, but she had never observed Dr. Wilson's office so carefully. As in all clinics, the walls were lined with a display of degrees and licenses. When Xiaodeng drew nearer to one, she read the words *Harvard Medical School* in Old English script. On the desk, there were several thank-you cards from patients. In the middle of the cards was a silver frame. It faced the doctor's seat. Xiaodeng walked around the desk and saw a photo of a woman with blond hair. Half her face lay against a violin, and she held a violin bow in her slender hand. The sun of a season had gathered in her eyes, and her expression was focused and intense.

"These are the samples provided by the pharmaceutical company. That should help save you a bit of money, since you don't have insurance now." Dr. Wilson handed her a pile of medicine boxes. "It's the same medicine, just with a different name. There's enough for three months."

It would be some time before Xiaodeng found out that all the medication Dr. Wilson had given her over the past few months had been placebos.

"Is your daughter a musician?" Xiaodeng asked.

Dr. Wilson was baffled. "My daughter?"

She pointed at the frame on the table, and Dr. Wilson understood. "Oh! Too bad I look so old to you. That's my wife, Vicky, one of the best ophthalmologists in Toronto. She used to play the violin as a hobby, but she was as good as a professional—I mean, almost."

"She used to? Do you mean she's not playing anymore?"

He hesitated for a long moment, then said, "Nine months ago, she went with the Mobile Eye Hospital to Africa. She was in a plane crash."

The last sentence was thick and rough, and he struggled to say it. His face remained as calm as ever.

"I'm sorry. Oh, Henry, I'm so sorry," Xiaodeng murmured, clutching the hem of her blouse with both hands.

Dr. Wilson looked up at the sunlight, sliced into patches by the half-opened blinds. Silver dust particles flickered in the white strips of light. "It's okay," he said. "Don't be sorry. We all have shadows, sometimes more than one. Now you know mine. Feeling better?"

Xiaodeng clutched the hem of her blouse tighter. "Henry," she asked haltingly, "can I . . . have your cell phone number? I mean, for an emergency?"

Dr. Wilson was silent, his temples tense as he thought. The room was quiet, but the silence was loud. After a while, he smiled gently and said, "You have the number of the clinic. If you need me, call and Casey will forward the message."

When Xiaodeng walked out of the consultation room, Casey was waiting at the door. She handed Xiaodeng a small box wrapped in colored paper. "This is a small gift Dr. Wilson and I got for you, with our best wishes for your special day."

It was only then that Xiaodeng recalled that it was her birthday. She opened the box. Inside was a metal paperweight in the shape of a thick book. A few lines were engraved on it:

Shirley Xiaodeng Wang

Near-perfect writer

Less cooperative patient

Struggling between falling and getting up

Xiaodeng hugged Casey, saying nothing.

When she walked onto the street, the paperweight bumped against her with each step, as if it had much to say to her. *Maybe that will be a suitable epitaph for me,* she thought. *Maybe, somewhere in China, there's already a tombstone with my name on it. Maybe it reads*

Wan Xiaodeng (1969–1976)

Died along with 240,000 people

in the Tangshan earthquake

Maybe I should go back and take a look at that headstone, since it's held me down my whole life.

Xiaodeng raised her head to look at the sky. Thick clouds rose, and the sky became gloomy again. The sun was just an association of light and shadow now. The branches along the street suddenly became much thicker. On closer inspection, she saw that they were sprouting.

Winter was very long in Ontario. But it had eventually come to an end.

May 15, 2006
Starbucks, Shanghai Hongqiao Airport

Aya's fingers quickly brushed the keyboard of the laptop, continuously clicking, like silkworms munching on mulberry leaves. It was still an hour before the flight to Guangzhou was scheduled to take off. She wanted to take advantage of the time to modify a contract with an American company, but she kept making mistakes. By the time her thoughts reached her fingertips, they were all jumbled, and she knew why.

There was a slight trace of warmth on her cheek, the gaze of the person sitting at the table across from her and to her right. She had bumped into this woman in the restroom. The woman had followed her out and past the gift shop in the departure lounge, then into the coffee shop. The woman's eyes were like a frightened, restless rabbit's, dodging, yet still curious. Aya could virtually hear the sound of those eyes scurrying away in embarrassment under the pursuit of her own peripheral glance.

She couldn't tell the woman's age, but she wore a well-made, though old-fashioned, black dress with gray flowers and a high neckline, so high that it covered the whole neck and half her lower jaw. The woman was very thin, her shoulder blades almost poking holes in her clothes, and her chest was as flat as a prepubescent girl's. The woman carried simple luggage, just a small trolley case with a metal exterior. It was also well made. She pulled a book from the luggage and casually flipped the pages as she sipped her coffee. Aya knew she was just pretending to read.

Aya could see the woman's body clearly, but she couldn't see her features because she wore a white sun hat with the brim pulled so low it covered almost half her face. From the corner of her eye, Aya saw the woman's eyes flit from beneath the brim of the hat, then quickly retreat. The probing and retreating were obvious.

Such eyes were not unusual to Aya. They could appear anywhere, so why not in a coffee shop at the airport?

But could the woman's belly, so like an empty sack, bear the pregnancy of two children like Aya's had done? Could the breasts like date pits feed two small mouths that were always hungry? Aya sneered softly. Since giving birth to twins, she had grown much plumper. Almost every season, she needed to replace the previous year's clothes, but she never tried to lose weight.

"Life force. Do you know what life force is? When there is a catastrophe or serious illness, anyone who has fat in their belly will survive to the end," she always told Xiaoda fiercely when his complicated gaze fell on her belly.

But who could keep up with this man's aesthetics, when they were so mutable? Over the past few years, every few months, a woman like this would find her through various channels. Sometimes it was on the doorstep, sometimes in one of her favorite shops, sometimes in a massage parlor she frequented, sometimes in the restroom at a theater, and sometimes even in the face of the little secretary in the office. She knew that these women had put in serious work to find her when Xiaoda was not around, which was not an easy task.

Without exception, they all came to negotiate with Aya, and of course, it was always about Xiaoda. In some ways, these negotiations were no different from ordinary negotiations, but in other ways, they were quite different. The similarity was there were two parties, A and B, but the difference was they were not evenly matched. One side usually spoke vociferously, while the other hardly said a word. The one who spoke fiercely always quickly came to realize that silence was an extremely high, hopeless mountain, and there were no words that could scale it.

These women were of different ages and backgrounds, and they had a variety of occupations: they were flight attendants, white-collar office workers, shopping mall salesgirls, young actresses still making a name for themselves, and even online shop owners. Aya soon noticed a common thread, though. They were all skinny, looking like innocent college girls. They reminded Aya of how she had looked on campus ten years earlier.

Now that she thought about it, Aya had to admit that men's tastes were so stubborn. To say they liked the new and despised the old was to do them an injustice. The new they liked was actually their old; it was just that they wanted it constantly refurbished. Aya couldn't help but sigh.

At first, it was hard for her not to take these women seriously, and she brought them into her pillow talk. Xiaoda never defended himself. He just chuckled and said, "The company is in your hands. What are you afraid of?"

She had known Xiaoda for nearly twenty years, and she knew him well. His heart was always wherever his money was. It was just that his heart had so many doors. Some were wide open, some ajar, some closed but not locked, and some not just closed, but securely locked. His affections fell in this last category. She and Xiaoda hadn't gone through the dating threshold, but had walked directly into marriage. He was extremely stingy in his use of any language that had to do with attachment or feelings. Extracting the word *love* from his mouth was more difficult than pulling one of his teeth. She knew that Xiaoda had married her for many reasons, and it was possible that none of them had to do with love. But she also knew that all these reasons bound together, even if they were not love, were strong enough to last a lifetime. As a result, she eventually calmed down and stopped mentioning these women to Xiaoda.

But this woman seemed a little different from the others. To start with, she was the first one to block her on her journey. In addition, she used the same weapon Aya herself did: she did not make any attempt to talk to Aya at all. With both sides in this war employing the same weapon, the only test was skill. It was the first time Aya had felt threatened.

The woman's eyes continued advancing and retreating, dodging here and there, scanning Aya's cheeks. Aya's brain turned into a broken egg yolk and could no longer be gathered into a ball. Eventually, she could not bear it anymore. Closing her computer with a snap, she walked over to the woman.

"How long are you going to follow me? Stop pretending. If you have something to say, say it—to me or to Xiaoda, no difference." She stretched out a finger and gently closed the woman's book.

"Xiaoda?" The woman raised her head in surprise. The barrier formed by the brim of her hat was finally broken, exposing her face to Aya.

Aya was taken aback. The face was a replica of her own, though one size smaller.

"I'm sorry. I didn't mean to follow you," the woman said, somewhat flustered. "I just noticed that you and I look a bit alike. I mean, quite a bit. I've never met someone who looks so much like me."

Aya couldn't help but laugh softly. "You do look a bit like me—ten years ago. Back then, I wasn't so fleshy."

"Can you teach me some tricks to gain a few pounds?" the woman said.

Aya knew the woman meant it as praise. Her tone didn't have the pretentious feeling common to skinny beauties these days, and it sounded somewhat sincere. Aya was flattered, so she turned around, picked up her bag and her coffee, and moved to the woman's table.

"Husband, children, mother-in-law, company. If you're brave enough to carry all four things together, it's not hard to get fat," Aya said.

The woman covered her face with her palms and laughed, quivering. Her laughter was thin and weak, as if it were about to break at any time. It sounded more like a cough that she was trying to hold in. Aya was suddenly aware of her own strength and health.

"You've come from overseas?" Aya asked.

The woman was again caught off guard. "How did you know?"

Aya pointed to her clothes. "This style hasn't been worn in years."

The woman straightened her collar and mumbled, "I rarely go out. I keep the same outfit for many years."

The woman's answer made Aya feel a bit sorry for having said anything. She felt as if she were playing a game with this woman, a fishing game. Every word she said was casual, and what she reeled in was the woman's serious reaction. She patted the back of the woman's hand and said, "I'm sorry. That's the way folks chat nowadays. We're probably too casual. You're not used to it. Have you been away long? Abroad, I mean?"

"Ten years. Does that count as long?" the woman asked.

Ten years—what is that? In some countries, it's several changes of government. In others, it might be an entire dynasty, Aya thought.

"Do you come back often?"

The woman paused for a moment, then said, "This is the first time."

"Didn't you miss home?" Aya asked.

"There was no one worth coming home for," the woman said softly.

"But there's always something worth coming back for, right?"

The woman held her coffee mug and turned it around in her hands, as if to chase away the cold. "There's really only one thing: divorce."

Aya was startled. This woman, who seemed to have crossed thousands of miles to share this table with her, must have brought her story with her. At this age, who didn't have a story? It was just that this woman's story was too distant and too dense for Aya to get into. Both women remained silent.

Eventually the woman put down her coffee mug and looked up at Aya. There were faint smile lines in the corners of her eyes.

"Since I was a child, I thought that when I grew up, I would be somebody like you—strong, an able worker, and a good fighter if needed. I didn't expect myself to grow up into such a scrawny weakling," the woman said.

Aya's heart grew warm, then immediately cooled, thinking of her husband.

"But what men like is not someone like me," Aya said, sighing.

The woman shook her head violently, as if shaking all the worries out of it.

"Not all men are like that. My man, I mean the man I am about to divorce, likes women like you."

Aya snorted. "Men all over the world have the same taste. They love the one they don't have."

They both laughed at the same moment. Their laughter bounced on the glass surface of the table like little beads, clanging and clattering, filling the whole room with their crisp ringing. Aya suddenly decided she liked this strange woman who could laugh at the precise same point as her.

When they finally stopped laughing, the woman suddenly recalled something. She asked Aya, "Did you mention someone named Xiaoda just now?"

"My husband. Why? Do you know him?"

The woman smiled again. "It seemed you were a little nervous. Were you afraid I was some woman who's after your husband? The Xiaoda I knew was a child. But of course, if he were still alive today, he would be an adult."

"You mean, he died?"

Dark clouds crossed the woman's face, instantly shading the trace of vividness that had bloomed only a moment earlier.

"I don't know if he's still alive."

The woman put a finger to her mouth and bit the nail. She bit hard, as if she had been feuding with that nail for generations. The crackling sound was a little alarming.

"At least half the men in China have the character 'da' in their names, because their parents all had the same dream of rising to the top," Aya said resentfully.

"Tell me about your Xiaoda. How did he offend you?"

When the woman had finally bitten the nail to her satisfaction, she settled down and picked up the coffee cup again. Aya noticed that the woman's hands could not sit still; she always had to hold a coffee cup or a book, or bite her nails. When her hands were not busy, she looked a little lost.

"There are so many stories about my Xiaoda. You'll never get to the end, once you start on them. You wouldn't have the patience for it." Aya shook her head.

The woman raised her wrist and looked at her watch, then smiled faintly.

"I've got an hour and a half before my flight. Is that long enough?" she asked.

The First Lunar Month 2003
Tangshan, Hebei

Aya ran frantically in the street. The wind against her face was like needles, making her skin burn. The moisture in her nostrils had turned to frost, and every breath carried weight. The tears on her cheeks had not yet dried; the old ones became ice, and the new ones flowed down, melting the old and forming new ice. The first lunar month in Tangshan was gloating and bullying this outsider who was used to warm southern winters.

Finally, she could not bear the cold anymore. She went into a restaurant on the corner, a place her mother-in-law, Li Yuanni, frequented. When she had found a seat in a quiet corner, she suddenly noticed that she was wearing a suede shoe on the left foot and a leather boot on the right. When she had rushed out of the house in a fit of rage earlier, she had not noticed that she was wearing two different shoes.

The argument had broken out today, but the grievances had been building for a long time. Like a pustule, it had festered under the skin for days before the pustule could emerge. The head finally broke this morning.

The break came because of something Niandeng said. Xiaoda's company had wrapped up its work early this year, allowing him and Aya to fly back to Tangshan to see Yuanni and their two children on the twenty-sixth day of the twelfth lunar month. They would stay in Tangshan until the tenth day of the first lunar month and then return to Guangzhou.

When they got up that morning, their daughter, Niandeng, saw a plastic hairpin that Aya had placed on the tea table and asked how much it cost in Guangzhou. Aya answered breezily that it was ten or fifteen yuan.

Niandeng shook her head and said, "Ma, you've paid your old nose for it. Nainai took me to the big market, and the same pin cost just one or two yuan."

"Paying your old nose" meant overpaying. The northern colloquialism pricked Aya's ears. She grabbed Niandeng. "What do you mean, my 'old nose'? Can't you speak Mandarin? Didn't your teacher teach you anything?"

"My teacher says the same thing." Niandeng was startled by Aya's sudden change of expression. Her mouth twitched, as if she were about to cry.

Seeing this, Xiaoda came over and hugged his daughter, glaring at Aya. "So what if she said 'your old nose'? Which place doesn't have a local dialect? Your Guangzhou has ten thousand of them. For God's sake, it's New Year's Eve. Do you have to pick today to scare the children?"

Aya's temper flared. "Where you live decides what school you go to. Bad schools have bad teachers, don't you know?"

Jideng and Niandeng had been sent to Tangshan just after they were born. Xiaoda's business was constantly expanding, and the couple often made business trips. It was better to let the children stay with their grandmother than to hire a nanny to take care of them at home. That was how Xiaoda persuaded Aya. The children were being raised by Yuanni, and Xiaoda and Aya went to Tangshan whenever they could, visiting Xiaoda's mother when they saw the children.

As the children grew, the couple began to feel the house in Tangshan was too small; each time they visited, their family of five was a little more cramped. Aya suggested they buy a new house in the new section of the city, where the homes were bigger and the environment was better. More importantly, there was a good school there, a key provincial school that had better teachers.

Aya mentioned it to Xiaoda several times. At first, he just brushed her off with "We'll talk about it later." When Aya backed him into a corner, he told the truth: it was Yuanni who disagreed with the idea. She was familiar with the old neighbors and the neighborhood, and she didn't want to move to an unfamiliar place. But this was just one reason. The real reason came out when Xiaoda backed his mother into a corner. It was the same reason she had earlier refused to move to Guangzhou: *If we all leave, how can your father and sister find our home if their souls come back?*

"What age are we living in? She's still so ignorant," Aya couldn't help shouting when Xiaoda finally told her the real reason.

Xiaoda covered her mouth, afraid Yuanni would hear. "You haven't gone through an earthquake; you don't understand."

Aya lowered her voice and grumbled, "This isn't the original plot your house was on. Your father's and sister's souls can't find it, even if they come back. I know your mother is ignorant. Are you really that ignorant too?"

Xiaoda's face darkened. "Say whatever you want about me, but don't say such things about my mother."

They had reached a dead end. The topic of relocating was often discussed over the next several years, but it always got stuck at this hurdle.

Their argument on this particular morning was just one of the many in recent years. Just when it seemed they were reaching the same dead end they had run into so many times before, it took a sudden sharp turn. At the time, neither of them realized that the infection that had been festering under the surface for so long had already gnawed at the skin until it was tissue thin.

"I'm ignorant. The smart one is in America. Too bad he didn't want you," Xiaoda said coldly.

The pustule broke, and the pus finally flowed freely.

"You didn't need to marry a wife. You should have married your sister. Too bad she's dead, and she won't come back even if you have a hundred kids and name every one of them after her."

Even Aya hardly recognized the vicious words coming out of her own mouth. But she was completely out of her mind by that time. Her tongue was seized by a burst of rage, and she would suffocate if she did not let it loose. At that moment, all her tongue cared about was escape.

"You bitch!" Xiaoda grabbed a teacup and threw it violently against the wall, shattering it with a crash. The leftover tea leaves blossomed into a sinister flower across the floor. "If someone like you had lived in the time of the earthquake, you would have been beaten to a pulp."

"Don't just keep going on about the earthquake. That was nearly thirty years ago. The dead are dead, but the living have to move on. Your mother saved you, not your sister. That's a fact. Even if you pay her back with your kids' lives, will it really buy you peace of mind?" Aya's vocal cords were torn, and she could taste blood in her mouth.

Hot air churned in Xiaoda's belly. The anger raced with its full force to his face, but it changed its mind halfway and took a shortcut, gushing to his arm. He raised his hand and slapped Aya hard.

There was a click. Time stopped. Everything fell silent, holding its breath.

Jideng and Niandeng were the first to wake. They clung to each of Aya's legs and burst into tears.

The children's tears woke Aya's. She pried herself free from their grip and ran from the house like a mad wind.

Xiaoda was the last to come to his senses. He clenched his fist and felt the warmth of Aya's body lingering on his fingertips, making him realize that he had hit someone, the woman who had given birth to his two children. His head split in two. One half told him to go after her, while the other said no, he couldn't give in. The two halves fought an earth-rending battle. By this time, Aya was nowhere to be found.

"What a drama."

Xiaoda turned and saw Yuanni standing at the bedroom door. She wore pajamas, and she looked disheveled. Her mouth drooped at the corners.

"Ma, I thought you were shopping," Xiaoda said, surprised.

Yuanni stared at him, her eyes looking straight through him, as if he were a glass wall. Ever since he was a child, he had not been afraid of Yuanni's scoldings—or even her whippings, for that matter. What he did fear was her silence. Her silence was a mountain, and it instantly reduced his courage to powder.

"Ma, it's not what you think. We are just worried about the children," Xiaoda stammered.

Yuanni said nothing as she stared at Xiaoda, pinning him in his panic.

"I had a dream last night. About your pa," she finally muttered.

Aya had been sitting in the restaurant for hours, and she still had no intention of leaving. It got dark early; it was not yet five, and twilight already covered the northern sky like dirty cotton wool. The wind from the northwest sounded like a mountain wolf who had lost its cubs, a shrill, terrifying howl that made its hearers feel their days were coming to an end.

Aya sat, blank, yearning for winter in the South. There was wind in the South too, but the wind there had very fine teeth. It didn't feel like it was gnawing at you when it blew, but more like soft, wet licking. Beneath the southern sky, huge kapok branches spread. Ah, kapok! Looking at it on a sunny day, it was all bright red and blue.

Blue and bright red. Those were her colors, her sky.

Certain plants grew in certain types of soil, and certain people lived under certain kinds of sky. Perhaps the dispute between her and Xiaoda was simply a matter of acclimatization. But what about her children? Which soil and sky suited them?

Perhaps it all had nothing to do with north or south. Perhaps it was just because of the earthquake.

The earthquake took not only the lives of those who died, but also the hearts of those who had survived. Before her death, Aya's mother had said that her father was a changed person when he returned home from earthquake relief work in 1976. Her father was often awakened by nightmares and sat in a daze on the bed in a cold sweat. He suddenly spent money lavishly, but stopped talking. In Aya's childhood memories, there was always a family of three at the dinner table. With a tired smile, her mother had constantly teased her father to try to make him talk. Her father worked hard too, but the only result of his hard work seemed to be that it carved deeper wrinkles into his forehead. "The earthquake ate your father's heart," her mother had once said.

She had not expected that she would eventually marry someone whose heart had been eaten by the earthquake too. Xiaoda's heart was missing a piece, and he was no longer capable of giving her, or anyone, his whole heart. She could fight against every woman around him, but she couldn't fight the earthquake that had happened twenty-seven years before.

The waitress brought her a new cup of tea, but this time, her voice was different.

"Daughter, drink this cup of tea, then let's go home."

Aya looked up and saw Yuanni.

"Ma, how did you—?" Aya asked in surprise.

"The waitress called me. She knows me. Xiaoda is going crazy looking for you. He's still on the road."

Aya told herself, *Don't cry. Don't cry.* But it was no use. The tears flowed uncontrollably. She had shed many tears that day, and the salty water had turned her cheeks into two pieces of preserved vegetable, bloated and numb.

"Daughter, what you said this morning was harsh, but it woke me up." Yuanni took off her hooded, cotton-padded jacket, then her big, thick scarf and sat down across from Aya.

"Ma, I'm not—" She suddenly stopped. She found she did not have the strength to offer even the palest explanation.

"Aya, I came here today to tell you something I've never told anyone before."

Aya turned the teacup in her hand, not knowing what to say. She had had a smooth relationship with her mother-in-law during her eight years of marriage, but never a heart-to-heart talk. Neither of them had a need to do so, because the communication between them had always been through Xiaoda. Xiaoda was an all-purpose rasp, smoothing all sorts of splinters in their feelings. What might come out as a snarky comment was made smooth as it passed through Xiaoda's mouth. The two women looked at each other from afar in a castle that Xiaoda guarded, each going her own way, feeling safe and secure. But now, the gates had suddenly fallen, and the distance was completely eliminated. With Yuanni presenting herself naked like this, Aya was flustered.

"During the earthquake, Xiaoda and Xiaodeng were both buried. When their uncle asked me which one to save, I wanted to save Xiaodeng."

Aya's heart thumped. This was a truth she was completely unprepared for.

"Wh-why?"

"Since I was small, my mother had told me that a daughter was like a mother's snug-fitting padded jacket. As a mother, I thought that when I was old, it would be best to have a daughter. But for the sake of my elderly in-laws, I saved Xiaoda. Xiaodeng was killed by me, and I didn't even find the corpse. This has ripped my heart out for more than twenty years.

"The day Xiaoda brought you home, I saw that your eyes and eyebrows were like hers. She had a birthmark on her left arm, and you have one on your hand. Later, I asked your mother's name, and you said Liu Yunni, which sounds like my name. It nearly knocked my breath away. I thought God must have known my suffering and sent my daughter back to me. This morning, you were harsh, and only then did I understand that I had harbored this dream for so many years, all in vain."

"Ma, I—"

Aya wanted to explain, but Yuanni cut her off with a glance.

"When you said those harsh things, I realized that you are not my daughter, and you can't be of the same mind as me. My daughter has been gone for twenty-seven years, and no matter how much I miss her, she's not coming back. All I can do is get a handle on my own feelings and start thinking about those who are still living."

Yuanni stood up, put on her padded coat, and wrapped the scarf around her neck.

"Come home, Aya. When the New Year holiday is over, you and Xiaoda can go choose a house."

By the time Aya followed Yuanni home, it was already dark, and the streetlights cut big yellow holes with blurred edges in the thick night. An occasional firecracker sounded but found no response. This Spring Festival was like a flower that withered before it had fully bloomed.

"Ma, maybe you don't have to move right away. Wait until the children reach middle school," Aya said.

I have no mother, and she has no daughter, Aya thought. *I can't be her daughter, and she can't be my mother, but there's a man connecting us, Xiaoda—so full of flaws, but overall, not a bad man. We have to find a way to all live together. No matter how big the world is, there will always be a small place to shelter three ordinary people like us, where we can hold each other, take our time to explore, and find a way through.*

May 20, 2006
Tangshan, Hebei

By the time Xiaodeng turned into the street, it was evening. The rain stopped abruptly, and the wind ripped the clouds apart, revealing a sun like a runny yolk whose light fell heavily on the treetops, dyeing the trees and clouds a shocking orange. Fetid water flowed in a zigzagging line to the low-lying ground, washing the street clean. Having slept for a season, the oleander was awakened by the rain, and in an instant, the tree was full of flowers.

Xiaodeng scrunched up her pants and walked on tiptoe toward a building, avoiding puddles on the roadside. When she reached a spot opposite the building, she stopped. The building was old, a mosaic of gray and yellow mud stains marking the passing seasons, like nicotine marring the teeth of an old smoker. The original color had long since become indiscernible. The window frames had been repainted white, but they were now cracked to reveal taupe underneath. The balcony's design—a railing connected by small potbellied balusters—hinted at the care and thought put into the house's renovation, but even this had been heavily eroded by wind and rain.

There was a woman in her fifties on the balcony, arranging flowerpots that had been knocked down by the elements. She wore a long-sleeved shirt with a blue floral print on a bluish-white fabric, and she had a sky-blue silk scarf tied around her neck. The shirt was a little tight, and there were long, thin wrinkles at her waist and elbows. When she bent over, her movements were a bit labored. Her hand slipped, and the pot clattered to the ground and shattered. The woman cursed, then stood up and called into the house, "Niandeng, bring me a broom."

Though the woman's voice was a little hoarse, it was still loud and clear, ringing through the whole street.

Two children, a boy and a girl, walked onto the balcony. They were around ten, and they looked very similar. The boy came out first, followed by the girl. He carried a dustpan, and she carried a broom. When the girl stopped, she handed the boy the broom and said, "Jideng, sweep the floor."

The boy took the broom, but reluctantly. He grumbled, "Nainai told you to sweep."

The girl leaned against the door, raised her eyebrows, pointed at a spot between the boy's eyebrows, and said, "Are you gonna sweep or not? Tell me."

The boy immediately fell silent.

The woman took the broom, slapped the girl lightly, and scolded, "Don't be so bossy."

The woman was about to bend over and sweep the floor when a gray-haired man in black-rimmed glasses ran out onto the balcony. Frowning, he grabbed the broom and said, "Your back! Why don't you listen? If you fall, who's going to take care of you?"

The woman let go of the broom and leaned against the door. She glared at the man and said, "How is it that the older you get, the more naggy you become?"

The man swept up the broken pottery, found a plastic bag to put it in, then stood up and wiped the sweat from his brow.

"They look just like Xiaodeng and Xiaoda when they were young. Sometimes when I glance at these two, I get confused, as if I've gone back in time." The woman sighed as she watched the boy and girl go back into the house.

"It's been thirty years. How can you go back? I don't have a single photo left from that time, and for the life of me, I can't recall what my two kids looked like back then." A trace of guilt flashed in the man's eyes.

At just that moment, they both noticed Xiaodeng standing across the street. The woman was momentarily stunned. She leaned over the railing, her eyes wandering back and forth over Xiaodeng, probing deeper with each pass. There was something in her eyes that scraped the dust from Xiaodeng's face, as if there were some earth-shattering mystery hidden underneath.

"Qin, come here." The woman waved to the man. "Do you recognize her? Why does she look so familiar?"

The man she had called Qin laughed. "I think it's your eyes. Everyone looks familiar to you. It's like you're friends with every person in the world."

The woman wanted to laugh too, but her smile sprouted, then pulled back.

"Girl, who are you looking for?" the woman asked.

Xiaodeng's lips trembled, but for a long time, she could not say a word. Her face started to itch, so she scratched it with her hand. It took her a moment to realize what the itch was. Tears. The first tears in thirty years.

"I'm looking for, looking for—"

She never finished the sentence.

May 29, 2006
Intensive Care Unit, First Hospital of Shijiazhuang, Hebei

Clouds. Big clouds. Softer than any silk quilt. He lay on it; every muscle and every inch of flesh on his body was so cozy, so relaxed. There was light before his eyes. Boundless light. He couldn't see where it started or where it ended. He wanted to find a color for the light, but after racking his brain, he couldn't find a word to describe such a color. Perhaps it was not a color at all, but a feeling, an invisible, ubiquitous warmth.

So, all the world's legends about death were ultimately unreliable, and the road to death was actually easier and more pleasant than any path in life. Unfortunately, he couldn't go back to tell the truth. The mystery of death belonged to the dead; the living could never comprehend it.

He was floating in the clouds, looking at the ward from a distance. A man lay there, covered in tubes. Around him was a group of people in white coats.

"He was sent here three days ago with a cerebral hemorrhage," a young white coat said, explaining his case to a senior doctor. "He's been in a coma the whole time."

"Blood pressure! Blood pressure!" A woman in a nurse's cap tugged the sleeve of an older white coat, alerting him to the graphs on the monitor.

"Call the family of Wang Deqing," someone shouted in the corridor.

"He has no family. He's alone," said another.

Although these sounds were far away, they carried a harsh edge. He knew that as soon as he let go of the hook in his heart, he would shut out these sounds forever. But the time had not yet come; he had to keep waiting, a while longer. The hook had two ends: at one end was his tender heart; on the other, a face. The face was obscured by fog and indistinct, a trace of a smile here, and a strand of hair there. He couldn't bring the parts into a whole.

He heard a beeping sound. The ripples on the screen flattened, eventually becoming a straight line.

He couldn't wait any longer. He was too tired. He had no choice but to let go of the hook and walk out of this door and into another, one through which he would never return.

But he was not totally ready to accept the inevitable. Not just yet. He had waited for so many years.

"Extubate?" a white coat asked.

"Yes."

"They say he has an adoptive daughter, somewhere," a nurse whispered as she proceeded to remove the tubes.

"What's the point of having children these days, a heartless bunch," one of the white coats said, shaking his head sadly.

"Wait!" A woman burst into the room, grabbing a white sleeve.

Before Xiaodeng entered the ward, she slipped into the bathroom to wash her face. She had been on the road for the last two weeks. Jet lag, road dust, fatigue—signs of travel showed on her face. Gravity had been working on her for the last two decades, persistent, unflinching, and ruthless, leaving a cobweb of fine wrinkles. Thirty-seven. She was thirty-seven—although half of the time she didn't even remember her own age. Birthdays were something she dreaded, not because she was afraid of growing old, but because every year was inevitably associated with particular memories, mostly unwanted ones. She'd rather not go there, forfeiting the luxuries of flowers, cards, and gifts, often given to her as a peace offering after an argument.

As she was wiping her face dry with a paper towel, she saw her own chilling eyes staring back at her from the mirror, half pitying, half mocking. *What's all this? You still want to look your best before seeing him?* She had no best to give to anyone, and even if she did, he was not the one she should give it to. She threw her comb back into her purse, took a deep breath, and walked into the ward.

He lay in a small hospital bed sectioned off with a curtain, tubes all over his body, an octopus with a thousand legs. She sat by his bed, surrounded by a few white coats, their stares full of blame. He had been sick for years. This cerebral hemorrhage was sudden, though not unexpected, a neighbor had told her. She knew he was sick, but she didn't know he was on the verge of dying.

She couldn't see his face well with the ventilator, but what was the point? Dying men all looked the same. A soulless body was just a bag of bones thinly covered with a layer of skin, and this bag was not much different from any other. It was the soul that made the difference. But did he even have a soul?

Veins—that was something she noticed right away. She couldn't believe a body could have so many veins, purplish, bulging, crawling all over his bare arms and down to the backs of his hands, interrupted only by tubes, bandages, and bruises from the numerous injections he had received.

His hands. Memories rushed back like a flood in typhoon season. What should she remember about these hands? The hands that had warmed her milk early in the morning on his only day off, so that she could stay in bed for an extra fifteen minutes? The hands that took her to the cinema, the park, and the local market on national holidays? Or the hands that had put a letter containing a remittance slip into the mailbox on the first day of each month, never failing, for the entire four years she attended college? He was a good accountant, and he knew how to split his income, right in the middle, half for her and half for himself, down to the last fen.

No, not those hands. What she remembered was another pair of hands. That pair of hands had ripped a hole in her youth that could not be patched up with all the milk, all the movies, and all the remittance slips in the world. A hole that nothing in the universe could ever repair.

Maybe death could. Death wiped everything clean, resetting all the clocks and calendars, and perhaps minds too. Death did not always forgive, but it sometimes forgot.

"Is he gone?" Xiaodeng asked a white coat.

"He has no vital signs," he replied coldly.

"You mean, he's gone?" she pressed.

"He's gone, but he hasn't gone far yet."

"Can he still hear me?"

Silence. But she heard their answer, loud and clear, vibrating in the air. *Where have you been?*

They started to remove his tubes. She didn't know how long it had taken them to create the maze of tubes, but clearing them away was easy. A fresh sheet quickly replaced the soiled one, and it was pulled up to his chin. He looked clean and pale, with a faint hint of surprise on his brows. Death was so new, and he was still acquainting himself with it.

"You'd better make arrangements for the funeral," the head nurse said flatly. She had said the same thing many times before, to different people. Repetition wore off any edge of emotion.

Xiaodeng heard her, but it took her a moment to register the meaning. *Funeral.* A strange word. She had seen enough deaths when she was seven, probably more than most people, but she didn't remember a single funeral. After the earthquake, she saw people buried with a headstone—a haphazard marker—and others thrown into mass graves. There had been no funerals. The only funeral she had ever attended in her life was her adoptive mother's, but it was all arranged for her. All she had to do was show up.

"Hearing is the last sense to go," said another white coat quietly as he passed her on his way out. He was younger and more sympathetic.

Everybody left. The room fell quiet. She was alone with him, or what remained of him. A private moment of farewell. They meant well.

She bent down and put her face near the ear of the body covered with a clean sheet.

"Our accounts are settled," she whispered. "You can go in peace."

Long after she left the hospital, she still wouldn't be sure whether she had actually said those words. It might just have been her imagination. She had often been told by different people that she *imagined* things.

She held on to the wall as she slowly stood up, staggering as if she were about to fall. She steadied herself, searching her brain for a number to call to "*make arrangements.*"

When she looked back at the body, she noticed a cloudy tear rolling down from the corner of an eye.

July 28, 2006
A Suburban Cemetery in Tangshan, Hebei

The cemetery was just a few years old. It had been more than three months since the Qingming Festival. The flowers and fruits left by the tomb sweepers who had come to observe the festival's traditions had long since been removed by the groundskeepers. Glimpsed briefly, the cemetery appeared very clean. The sun had just risen halfway, but the sky was already fully ripe, and the neat rows and columns of tombstones reflected a naked white light in the scorching sun. Each tombstone had once been a living soul, and each line of inscription reflected a story, whether extraordinary or mundane. If the people buried there could stand up from beneath the tombstones, it would be a vast, majestic army. There were so many stories there that all the ears in the world were not enough to hear them all. Fortunately, there were the tombstones, and they were tight lipped.

By the time she had climbed just halfway up the hill, Xiaodeng was exhausted, so she sat on the steps to rest. When she had set out in the morning, the whole family had planned to accompany her. Xiaoda and Aya had made a special trip back to Tangshan the day before just to do so. But in the end, Xiaodeng insisted on going by herself. This was a major turning point in her life, and she needed to face it alone. She had traveled halfway around the world and burned up thirty whole years before she was ready to confront the huge black shadow. Some things in life were too private, or too cruel—like relieving oneself or looking at a naked wound—and it was difficult to bear the intrusion of a second pair of eyes on those moments. The courage to face them required absolute solitude.

She finally climbed close to the top of the mountain and found the two tombs with the aid of the map. The name on the tombstone on the left was Wan Chunan, and there was a photo embedded in the upper part of the grave marker. The photo depicted a man in his thirties, almost clean shaven, with a faint shade of stubble on the chin. He was probably not used to facing a camera, and his smile was restrained. The photo evoked a mass of memories in Xiaodeng. She felt a sting on her cheek—her father's rough beard poking her. Her father had always liked to tickle her with his beard when she was a little girl. That old prickly sensation suddenly revived in her, sending a thrill through her.

She had asked her mother what objects were in her father's tomb. Her mother said it was some old clothes dug out from the rubble of the earthquake and an electric fan whose core had burned out. Oh, that electric fan! Standing in front of the tomb in a daze, Xiaodeng felt its breeze on her cheek. It was once the glory of the street when she was small. It had been such a source of pride for her among her childhood playmates. It had cooled one scorching summer night after another, sending her into countless sweet dreams. Then, she woke: the nights of incurable insomnia in her later life were a result of the loss of this fan and the sort of breeze it produced.

"And your schoolbag," her mother had said. Her mother had found the schoolbag on the remaining half of the locust tree in the front yard after the earthquake. She had resewn the broken strap and kept it for many years until they bought this plot in the cemetery.

The schoolbag! Army-green canvas, with an image of Tiananmen Square. Her father had bought the bags specially from the Wangfujing Street Market in Beijing for her and Xiaoda. When her mother saw them, she scolded him, calling him stupid for buying two identical schoolbags—how would they tell them apart? Her father chuckled and said, "It will be easy." Then he cut a small aluminum star at his work unit and glued it to the strap of her schoolbag with all-purpose glue. "Hers has a star. I'm picking stars for my little girl," her father said proudly as he lifted her to his shoulders.

The schoolbag was supposed to open a new door for growth as she started school, but a natural disaster turned it into the last sacrificial offering of her childhood. Her father should have remained in her post-disaster memory, but the memory of him was entangled, like blood vessels, with other memories leading to the black shadow that had haunted her. She couldn't separate her father from the shadow and just hold on to him alone. The only way she could get rid of the shadow was to get rid of him too.

"Pa, I'm back." Xiaodeng put her face to the photo, and tears welled up in her eyes.

She had cried often in recent days. Once the tears started, it was like a floodgate had been opened. The tears had accumulated for thirty years, forming a sea, an ocean, but her eyes were just two small springs. Now, maybe they would never dry up.

Xiaodeng cried for a long time before she finally turned her attention to the tombstone beside her father's. She had envisioned this tombstone numerous times, both waking and sleeping, but now that all the mists of illusion were wiped away and it truly stood before her, she was stunned by how sharp, how rough it was.

Wan Xiaodeng

April 29, 1969–July 28, 1976

Remembered by her mother, Li Yuanni,

and her younger brother, Wan Xiaoda

The real tombstone was so simple. Whether one was seven years old or seventy, no matter how many entanglements and hardships there were in life, in the end, it was all filtered through a tombstone with just a name and a series of numbers. Death needed no explanations, and it entertained no emotion. Death cut off all stories in the same style, leaving behind no hints.

How many people could experience a thorough understanding of death in advance? Xiaodeng leaned on her own tombstone in a daze. It was so heavy. Its weight had been pressing on her for thirty years, and it had left a raw wound on her heart. Over time, she had become attached to the wounds. Saying goodbye to those wounds was painful too.

Going down the mountain from here, perhaps she would have to gradually adapt to another kind of life, to days without weight and wounds. She did not know if there would ever come a day when they would be all gone. If that day came, perhaps she would be too light-footed. Perhaps even lost.

July 30, 2006
St. Michael's Hospital, Toronto

Dr. Wilson was ten minutes late for work. As he stepped into the office, his secretary, Casey, handed him a stack of telephone messages. Dr. Wilson had just been named Doctor of the Year by the Ontario Medical Science Association, and he was in a good mood. He could not keep from joking with his secretary. "Anything worth noting? An earthquake? A war?"

Casey shook her head, half-amused. "Of course, every hour, but it will be a while before they send people your way."

When there were no patients around, they could afford to be cruel. She started to go through his patient list for the day. A usual day, a normal caseload, nothing that stood out. As he moved to put on his white coat, she suddenly added, "Wang Xiaodeng, that writer, called from China."

Dr. Wilson raised his eyebrows. "Any message?"

"Something about a window. She opened it. She said you would understand. What is that all about?"

A smile touched the corners of his mouth. It seemed Wang Xiaodeng had finally found a way through.

ABOUT THE AUTHOR

Zhang Ling is the award-winning author of ten novels and numerous collections of novellas and short stories, including *A Single Swallow*, translated by Shelly Bryant; *Where Waters Meet*, her first novel written in English; *Gold Mountain Blues*; and *Aftershock*, which was adapted into China's first IMAX movie with unprecedented box office success. Born in China, she moved to Canada in 1986 and, in the mid-1990s, began to write and publish fiction in Chinese while working as a clinical audiologist. Since then, she has won the Chinese Media Literature Award for Author of the Year, the Grand Prize of Overseas Chinese Literary Award, and *Chinese Times*'s Open Book Award.

ABOUT THE TRANSLATOR

Photo © 2016 Susie Gordon

Shelly Bryant is a poet, writer, and translator who divides her time between Shanghai and Singapore. She is the author of twelve volumes of poetry, a pair of travel guides, a book on classical Chinese gardens, and a short story collection. She has translated more than thirty books from the Chinese and edited two poetry anthologies. Her translation of Sheng Keyi's *Northern Girls* was long-listed for the Man Asian Literary Prize, and her translation of You Jin's *In Time, Out of Place* was short-listed for the Singapore Literature Prize. Shelly received a Distinguished Alumna Award from Oklahoma Christian University of Science and Arts in 2017, and her company, Tender Leaves Translation (Singapore), was short-listed for the Literary Translation Initiative Award by the London Book Fair in 2021